# Holliday Drama
## By: Jessica Terry

HOLLIDAY DRAMA

**First edition. July 9, 2025.**

Copyright © 2025 Jessica Terry.

ISBN: 979-8999506900

Written by Jessica Terry.

I'm so thankful to God, my family, other loved ones, my coworkers, and any and all readers who take a chance on me and my books. I'm also appreciative of my fellow authors, whether we've actually met in person or not, for the inspiration, advice, and encouragement.

Y'all are awesome.

Chapter 1

ENYA HOLLIDAY SAT THERE watching the phone ring, hoping her man-of-the-moment would finally get the hint. After three straight calls, she heaved a huge sigh and snatched up the phone.

"*Yes*, Vaughn?"

"Baby, what's up? I've been trying to get at you all day."

"Yeah, I know. I've been a little busy."

"What's going on? You all right?"

Enya plunked more sugar into her black tea and mindlessly swirled it with a spoon, leaning a hip against her marbled quartz kitchen counter. "I'm fine."

"Well, I wanted to see what was up for tonight. You know we have to do it up together for New Year's Eve."

"I told you I'm going to my sister Emberly's for our annual family New Year's Eve party. And I can't miss that."

"Oh damn, that's right." There was a pause and Enya waited for what she knew was coming, already preparing her response. "What time does that kick off?"

"Officially eight o'clock. Realistically more like nine or ten."

"You want me to pick you up? It'd be cool to see your family again."

"Not necessary. I might go by early to see if Emberly needs help, since she usually fusses about us not showing up until everything is done."

"Well, that's cool. I don't mind helping out."

Enya took her time responding with a long sip of her tea. Vaughn had no idea that the countdown of his time with her was on its last ticks. He was a cool guy and she liked him just fine, but she had officially grown bored of their relationship. She didn't get 'that' feeling with him. There was no future for them and Enya didn't need him thinking there was.

Hopefully she'd be able to be done with him as easily as she wished, though. She just hadn't been able to make herself find out.

"Actually, Vaughn, I'm going alone," she finally informed him. "I'll call you sometime tomorrow, though."

"Why can't I go with you tonight? I wanted to bring in the new year together. Some say the midnight kiss is good luck."

If only she could get the good luck without the New Year's kiss, because she would surely need it.

"Yeah, but still," she replied, putting down her cup. "Don't take it personally or anything but I'm gonna need to just hang with the family tonight."

Vaughn was quiet for a few moments and she wondered if he was going to keep putting up a fuss. She hoped not, because she wasn't in the mood. And the last thing she felt like doing was going back and forth with him.

"Fine," he thankfully resigned with a sigh. "Guess I don't have much of a choice, if you wanna go alone. Can you at least *call* me at midnight, let me see you on video chat, or something?"

"Sure." Enya just wanted to get off the phone. "I have to go, Vaughn; there are some more things I need to do before I head over to Emberly's later."

"All right. I guess."

Enya could hear the slight attitude in his voice but she didn't care. He'd be all right. "I'll talk to you later."

She barely gave him a chance to respond before hanging up the phone. She ran her hands down her face wearily before grabbing her cup of tea and heading over to the living room, tucking her bare feet underneath her on the soft white couch. Her brow furrowed as she took another long sip and set the cup on a coaster on the glass coffee table. If she had her way, she'd spend her evening in that very spot, watching old music videos under her huge fuzzy blanket and eating loaded nachos. But she knew her family would raise a major fuss if she did, especially her fellow triplet sisters, Emberly and Evelyn. Her brother Noah might cut her some slack, but he'd still pepper her with enough questions to where she didn't want to bother.

It was New Year's Eve and the last thing Enya felt like doing was partying or being around a lot of people; she had too much on her mind. Usually, she lived for going out and enjoying herself, painting her city of Terston red. But not this year. And she didn't want to spend the evening with Vaughn because he was part of the reason for the mood she was in, though he didn't know it.

Glancing at her silver watch, she was thankful that she had a few hours before she'd be expected at Emberly's. Sliding down and wiggling into a comfortable position, she closed her eyes and hoped to oversleep.

LATER THAT EVENING, Enya grudgingly slipped into a silver top and some skinny jeans, ran a flat iron through her short hair, donned her signature huge silver hoop earrings, and headed over to Emberly's loft. She'd hoped the anxiousness she'd been carrying around for the past few days would have eased some, but no such luck.

"This is for the birds," she muttered, pulling up to her sister's building. Briefly resting her head on the headrest, she made herself open the door, knowing it would only be a matter of time before one of her sisters started calling or texting her, asking where she was. Usually, she'd already be up there, sneaking some of Emberly's desserts and grilling whoever Noah's girlfriend-of-the-moment was.

"It's about time!" Emberly exclaimed when Enya finally made it upstairs. 90's R&B played through the hidden speakers. "I was just about to call you."

"Hmph." Enya's eyes scanned the room. "Where's Noah?"

"He's on the way. He had to pick up Kimmy."

"Kimmy?"

"Yeah, that's his 'boo'," Emberly clarified with a wiggle of her fingers. "For now, anyway. Evelyn and I already have a bet going on how long it'll be before he finds something wrong with her."

"I give it a month," Evelyn called out from where she was lounging on the blue velvet sectional. Her phone was in its usual spot in front of her face. "You want in?"

"Nah, I'll try to think positively this time," Enya droned, even though she really didn't. They all knew about their brother's tendency to dump a woman once he found a seemingly-dire flaw. "Plus, y'all remember what happened the last time we bet on him like that."

"Ehh, he got over it," Emberly dismissed with a wave of her hand. She headed back over to the kitchen.

"Yeah, it's not like he doesn't know that he changes women like I change socks." Evelyn finally looked up from her phone, adjusting her glasses as she glanced at her younger sister by three minutes. "Oh, you look cute."

"Thanks." Enya started to join her on the couch but the aromas wafting throughout the room had her detouring to the kitchen area. Emberly was an in-demand pastry chef and owner of an increasingly popular dessert company called Oh My Decadence. She always had a spread of sweets prepared for when they all got together, and this time was no different. Enya snagged a mini apple pie taco from the tray on the counter, earning a brief glare from Emberly. She took a bite, licking the cinnamon sugar from her lips. "Damn, girl, this is good!"

"Why are you sounding surprised?" Emberly asked with a smile. "This is what I do."

"I know, I know." Enya surveyed the spread in front of her. "What else you got? Actually, it doesn't even matter; I plan on eating some of everything."

"Whaaaat?" Evelyn marveled, turning around. "Usually your skinny behind only wants to nibble on stuff. What's going on? And how come you didn't bring Vaughn with you?"

"Ugh. You know I told you I was starting to cool off on him."

"Oh, so you're really gonna end it, huh? I thought you were just PMSing when you said that."

"Wait, you're dumping Vaughn already?" Emberly asked, her eyebrows shooting up. "Why didn't I know that?"

"Oh, Ev and I talked about it when we went to lunch the other day, that's all," Enya explained.

Emberly's expression melted into a slight frown. "You two went to lunch?"

"Yeah. You were busy catering some event," Evelyn chimed in. "And it was kind of spur of the moment, anyway."

"Hmm. Okay." Emberly went about wiping down the already-clean counter, the frown still on her face.

"Ev, you haven't put that phone down since I got here. You're not stalking Travis's social media page, are you?" Enya asked, taking another apple pie taco.

"*No*. I am not *stalking* anything," Evelyn refuted. "I'm simply trying to see what he's up to. There's nothing wrong with that."

"He's your ex-husband for a reason."

"So? I'm still Mrs. Holliday-Sears. And we're still friends."

"Does *he* know that?"

Before Evelyn could retort, the doorbell rang. Since Emberly was still busying herself with needless cleaning and made no move towards the door, Enya went to answer it, stuffing the rest of her treat into her mouth.

"E3, what up?" Noah, the triplets' older brother, greeted Enya when she swung the door open. Enya just shook her head.

"E3?" the woman on his arm inquired curiously, looking back and forth between Noah and Enya. Her black hair was smoothed into an intricate bun on top of her head. Her curvy body was poured into a tight white scoop-neck top and high-waisted skinny jeans, and she wore strappy stilettos that showed off her pedicured toes. "What in the world is that about?"

Noah glanced at her as they entered the loft. "They're triplets. All of their names start with E. She was born third of the three of them. So I call her E3."

"Oh, how cute!"

"Yeah." Noah closed the door behind him before wrapping an arm around Enya's shoulders and pulling her in for a hug. "Her name is Enya, though. The one with her face practically in her phone is Evelyn, and that's Emberly over there in the kitchen."

"Is she the one responsible for all the yumminess I smell?"

"Yeah. She's a pastry chef. Hope you like apples 'cause they're in damn near everything she makes."

"I *love* apples!"

"Good. Oh, little sisters, this is Kimmy," Noah introduced half-heartedly.

"Hi!" Kimmy waved enthusiastically. "So if you're E3, Enya, which one is E2?"

"That'd be me," Evelyn raised her hand, eyes still on her phone.

"It's so good to meet you all. I've never met actual triplets before." She peered at Enya, actually squinting. "Are you all identical?"

"Nope."

"Aww. Well, it's still fascinating."

Enya glanced up at Noah amusingly before sliding from underneath his arm and joining Evelyn on the couch. Kimmy excitedly scurried over to the kitchen, her hands clasped together in front of her chest as she surveyed the desserts Emberly had laid out.

Noah looked relieved for the brief reprieve as he removed his coat and flopped onto the end of the sectional. "Why am I the only one here with a date?"

"Mine is running late," Emberly called out. "He should be here in a little bit."

"Nice. Who is this dude? I didn't know you were dating anybody."

"We've only met for coffee once. Well, technically it was over webcam, but it still counts, I say. His name is Dallas and I'm really feeling him."

"That's great, E1; I'm happy for you," Noah said with a sincere smile. "Is Camilla coming?"

"My assistant? Why would she be coming? We're cool and everything but we don't hang out on holidays."

"Just wondering." Noah cleared his throat and glanced over at Enya. "Where's Vaughn?"

Enya huffed as her hand dropped to her lap. "Y'all sure are worried about Vaughn considering you only met the man once."

"That's because of *you*. You didn't ever want to bring him around, remember? You've been dating him, what, four months? Six months?"

"Six. But it doesn't matter 'cause I'm thinking about ending it."

"Hmph. And y'all talk about *me*," Noah muttered.

"No, don't even try it, Noah!" Enya sat forward, pointing a finger at him. "You know you're *way* worse than I am about that. I wouldn't be surprised if homegirl over there is gone by MLK day."

They paused, listening to Kimmy incessantly chatting to Emberly in the kitchen, not seeming to notice or mind that she wasn't getting much response.

"But I thought you really liked this one, though," Noah persisted, attempting to snatch Evelyn's phone from her hand but she dodged it. "I know you're not itching to get married or anything like our apple-obsessed sister over there, but you seemed into the guy. And when we *did* meet him, you two were all over each other. Just wondering what could've changed so fast, that's all."

Enya slumped in her seat, her head falling against the back cushion. "I don't wanna talk about it."

"Why not?" Evelyn glanced at her.

"Just don't."

Just then, Kimmy came over holding two fresh apple chestnut cheesecake turnovers, handing one to Noah before taking a seat on his lap. "What are we talking about?"

"Nothing," Enya spoke up before her siblings could. It wasn't any of this stranger's business and she wanted to change the subject, anyway. "So, how long have you known Noah?"

"About a month. We met at the museum."

"Yeah? Noah has always been a bit of a nerd. He used to always try to drag us there with him. He practically lives at the art history museum. Is that where you met?"

"No, it was at the selfie museum. I work at the information desk."

Enya and Evelyn turned slow and curious eyes to Noah. Even Emberly stopped glazing the rest of the turnovers to whip her head around.

"You mean to tell me *you* actually went to a selfie museum?" Evelyn asked Noah. "What the hell is a *selfie* museum, anyway?"

Noah sucked his teeth. "Stop sounding so judgmental. It's more like an art studio; you can go and take pictures and videos in all kinds of different settings. Y'all know I love photography."

"So why don't they just call it an art studio?"

"That's a question for the owners. Send 'em an email and ask."

"Ehh. I don't care that much." Evelyn turned her attention back to her phone.

"Hey, Emberly, can you bring me some more of those apple pie tacos?" Enya called out over her shoulder.

Back to her turnover-glazing, Emberly didn't even look up when she responded, "I bake all this; doesn't mean I serve it, too. Come get it yourself."

"Damn, what's wrong with you?"

"What's wrong with *you*?"

"Nothing!"

"You *have* seemed a little edgy since you got here," Evelyn noted, her thumbs scrolling the screen on her phone.

"Ooh, Travis went to a club last weekend?? He never used to do that!"

Enya snatched the phone from her hands, immediately hiding it behind her back when Evelyn tried to retrieve it. "You're looking real thirsty, studying that man's timelines like that. You didn't pay *this* much attention to what he did when you two were married."

"Give me my phone back, Enya!"

"No."

"Do you think I can't get it from you? You know you don't weigh anything. If I cough on you, you'll blow away."

"You cough on me and I'll knock you into Valentine's Day."

"She'd probably like that if you knocked Travis there, too," Emberly muttered from the kitchen.

"Shut up, Emberly!" Evelyn tried to get her phone back from Enya, but was thwarted. "Give it!"

"I *said* no!" Enya tucked the phone under her shirt and into her bra. "Now, what?"

"Don't think I won't go in there!"

"Please. You're not gonna-"

She screamed when Evelyn practically tackled her, diving on her and trying to yank down the collar of her shirt. Enya tried to fight her off, screaming warnings about snapping Evelyn's glasses in half if she ruined her shirt, not to mention making her pay for it.

"Well, this isn't embarrassing at all," Noah mumbled sarcastically, shaking his head as he stuffed half his turnover into his mouth.

"This is so much fun! It's like having a front row seat to one of those reality shows!" Kimmy exclaimed, actually clapping her hands excitedly. "Noah, I'm so jealous of you for getting to grow up with triplets as sisters!"

"Yeah, it was a blast."

"I *bet*!" Kimmy replied, clearly not catching the sarcasm. "You have no idea how much I wished my parents had some more kids. I *hated* being an only child. I didn't have anybody to talk to. I had cousins but they were all older so they didn't want to spend a lot of time with me. They only did it when our parents forced them to, which of course wasn't any fun for me because I pretty much got ignored when our parents weren't looking, or they played pranks on me. One time they actually taped my mouth shut; can you believe that??"

"No kidding," Emberly droned, coming over with a tray of champagne and glasses. "Did it actually work? What kind of tape did they use?"

Noah shot her a warning glare but she just widened her eyes innocently.

"Duct tape! And that hurts when you take it off!" Kimmy shook her head. "They always tried to say I talk too much and wouldn't shut up. But that's silly, isn't it, Noah Love?"

"Noah Love?"

"Shut up, Emberly," Noah admonished. "Shouldn't your date be here by now?"

Emberly glanced at her watch, a worried look flitting over her face before she quickly erased it. "He's probably just stuck in traffic; you know how crazy it gets on New Year's Eve. I'm sure he's probably left a message; I've been trying to get everything together and haven't checked my phone in a while." She looked at her tussling sisters. "Y'all both have my Venmo if you break anything."

"Stop playing, Enya!" Evelyn screamed, she and Enya now hanging off the couch. "Or else I'm gonna eat the rest of those damn apple pie taco things!" She pushed Enya to the floor before pouncing on top of her, causing her sister to release a startled yelp.

"Ouch! Damn, Ev, watch my stomach!"

Frowning, Evelyn paused, brushing her long bangs from her face. Her shoulder-length brown hair was in its usual slightly-haphazard high ponytail. "Why should I watch your stomach?"

"Yeah, that's a specific thing to say," Emberly added, narrowing her eyes. "What's up with that?"

"Ooh, are you bloated?" Kimmy exclaimed. "I know I feel like I've swallowed a hot air balloon when my time of the month hits. Of course, since I don't have any siblings, I didn't have anybody to-"

"We get it; you had a lonely childhood," Noah interrupted, unwilling to hear any more of her only-child regrets.

"And it is not my time of the month," Enya grunted, nudging Evelyn off of her and sliding away a little. She ran her hands down the back of her head. "It's supposed to be but it's not."

Her sisters gasped, and Noah's head fell against the back of the couch with a groan. Kimmy applauded.

"Congratulations!"

"You're pregnant??" Emberly exclaimed.

Adjusting her earrings, Enya sighed. "I don't know. Might be. I haven't taken a test yet."

"What are you waiting for?"

"Because it might be positive. And I'm not sure I wanna know if it is."

"You need to find out. The sooner you know, the better," Noah spoke up. "Make an appointment with your doctor. In the meantime, I'll run out and get a test for you. That oughta be fun to be seen buying on New Year's Eve."

"No need. I already bought one on the way here."

"Thank God. Now get up and take it."

"I'm not ready, Noah."

"Come on, Enya," Evelyn encouraged, sliding an arm around her shoulders. "I get that it's a big deal but you don't have anything to worry about."

"Yes, I do. Y'all know I've never been gung-ho about having kids. I'm totally fine being the fun sexy cool auntie when *y'all* have 'em but I don't really want any of my own."

"Wait, is that why you're talking about ending it with Vaughn?" Noah asked. "Is that whose it is, if you *are* pregnant?"

"Yeah," Enya grunted.

"Does he know?"

"No."

"Enya."

"There's no need in telling him anything until I know what the deal is," Enya quickly defended. "He'd probably propose to me if he thought he'd knocked me up."

"Yeah, we don't want *that*," Emberly commented, drawing curious looks from everyone. Her eyes widened, as if she hadn't realized she said that out loud. "I just meant that you've always said you didn't really want to get married, either."

"I'm not against marriage but I'm not pressed about it. And I wouldn't want to marry Vaughn, anyway, baby or not. He's a good guy but he's not it for me."

"Regardless, he deserves to know what's up," Noah told her. "Just take the test, find out for sure, and go from there. Because either way, you don't need to be stressing and he shouldn't be left hanging when he hasn't done anything wrong."

Enya glared at him but her expression eventually softened in resignation. "I guess you're right," she finally conceded. "I know he doesn't deserve to be shut out like that. He's sent me like ten texts since this afternoon."

"Go on and take the test," Evelyn instructed, standing before helping her glum sister off the floor. "Just get it over with. You know we've got your back, whatever comes of it."

"All right." Enya grabbed her purse and with a deep breath, headed for the bathroom.

"Well, how 'bout that, huh?" Noah whistled with a shake of his head.

"I think it's wonderful," Kimmy commented. "There's nothing like a fresh little juicy baby. I know I want to have a whole bunch."

"Oooh, you hear that, Noah?" Evelyn teased, grinning pointedly. "A *whole bunch*."

"Yes, Evelyn, I heard her. She's sitting right here." Noah cut his eyes at his sister before patting Kimmy's hip, signaling for her to get up. "I'm gonna go stuff my face with some more pastries."

"Did I tell y'all about how Travis and I actually started getting a bunch of stuff for the baby we planned to have?" Ignoring her siblings' subtle groans and eye rolls, Evelyn fondly continued. "We had a whole trunk full of stuff; onesies, those cute little baby socks, blankets, diapers-"

"I think I hear my phone," Emberly cut in, scurrying back to the kitchen.

"Did you want a lot of kids, too?" Kimmy asked, intrigued. She popped the last of her turnover into her mouth and turned fully towards Evelyn.

"Oh yeah! Travis and I always talked about having a house full. Ever since we were in high school."

"You were high school sweethearts? That's so romantic!"

"Yeah." Evelyn looked off, a smile playing on her lips. "We got married right out of college. He's definitely my soul mate."

"I love that! That's too bad to hear about him divorcing you, though. Hang in there, girl. Maybe he just needs some time apart and will come back. Sometimes men need to experience different women to appreciate the one that's best for them. That happened to my cousin. Come to think of it, it happened to my mama, too; my dad left her for a while but came back a couple of years later. I think he said he felt suffocated. Mama tried to act like she wasn't going to take him back but everybody knew she would. She was too sprung over him. But I was glad they got back together because she was really moody when they were apart. And now they're totally happy and in love so keep hope alive, girl!"

Evelyn smiled, actually looking encouraged. "Thanks, Kimmy. I needed to hear that."

In the kitchen, Noah shook his head as he cut into a spiced apple pear tart. "Great. As if she needs any more encouragement to keep pining over the man who left her."

"I know, right," Emberly muttered absently, staring at her phone with a frown.

"What's the matter?"

"Hmm?" She glanced up at him briefly. "Oh...nothing. I just thought I'd have heard from Dallas by now. I hope nothing's wrong."

"So that wasn't him texting you a minute ago?"

"No. That was something to do with work."

"Did you try to call? Maybe he got lost trying to find the place. You know they're doing all that road construction and there's a bunch of detours."

"Yeah, good point." She called the number Dallas had given her and her face flushed when it went straight to voicemail. "Maybe he's somewhere with bad reception..."

Noah pursed his lips. He sensed that his sister was getting stood up and figured she probably did, too, but didn't want to admit it. He watched her brush her waist-length locs that were held back with a scarf off of her shoulder as she chewed her bottom lip. Noah didn't know who this Dallas guy was but he wanted to twist his neck for doing his sister like this.

"Hey, don't sweat that," he advised, putting down the knife and going over to give her a reassuring hug. "Let's hope there's an actual good reason for him not being here. *And* for not taking your call. But if it's just him being a punk-ass, then *he's* the one missing out, not you."

Emberly smiled up at him before resting her cheek against his chest, hugging him around the waist. She appreciated his words, even though they didn't totally soothe the sting of being stood up. Noah always had her back, even when they were kids. He was her protector when she'd get teased for being overweight, especially since her sisters were always thinner and people would wonder if they were actually related.

Her mind briefly flashed to when she and her sisters were thirteen and there was a sleepover that all the eighth grade girls wanted to be invited to, Emberly included. Evelyn and Enya got an invitation; Emberly didn't. Noah, who was seventeen at the time, cancelled his date so he could stay home with her and keep her company. They had a cookie baking contest, ordered pizza, played cards, watched movies; they even made a couple of prank phone calls to some girls at the party. Emberly ended up having a blast that night, all thanks to Noah. It was just one of many times he'd stepped up for her, and it hadn't stopped once they became adults.

She and Noah were sharing the tart and Evelyn and Kimmy were sharing love stories when Enya finally emerged from the bathroom. Everyone looked at her expectantly.

"I couldn't do it," she announced, shame-faced. "I think the anxiety of it locked up my bladder. Maybe if I stop thinking about it for a little bit, I can try it again. Emberly, you have any juice? And please don't say apple."

"No, I have other kinds," Emberly replied, nodding towards her stainless steel refrigerator. "Knock yourself out."

"It would help if we all just continue on and have a good time and not focus on this," Enya announced, strutting to the kitchen. "Let's talk, let's laugh, let's dance, let's pig out and drink-"

"Maybe you should hold off on that until you know what's up," Noah suggested.

"Whatever. I just don't need to be reminded about my possible...you know. I'm still gonna take the test, though, I promise, 'cause now I wanna know just as much as y'all do."

Everyone mumbled their agreements and continued to enjoy the evening. After the siblings completed their Holliday tradition of each naming the top five things that had happened to them that year (which Kimmy insisted on joining), Evelyn poured the champagne and Kimmy proceeded to dance around the living room, eventually getting Noah to grudgingly join her. Emberly tried to stop checking her phone and get into the spirit, chugging the champagne and popping caramel apple puffs like candy. Enya finally acknowledged Vaughn's texts, letting him know she'd call him soon and apologizing for being so standoffish; she really did like him. But the novelty had worn off for her and she was ready to move on, which only made her more anxious about her possible pregnancy.

Finally, she couldn't take it anymore. As everyone else laughed and ate and danced, she skitted off to the bathroom in her stilettos a few minutes to midnight.

Chapter 2

"JUST BECAUSE THEY HAVE apples in them doesn't mean fritters are a good breakfast, Emberly."

Emberly glared at her sister. "Just because I let you crash on my couch doesn't mean I need nutrition advice, Evelyn."

"I'm just saying. You lost all the weight and the way you're eating, it's like you're trying to gain it all back."

Emberly slammed down her glass of mango-lime juice so hard she was surprised she didn't break it. "Go home."

"I'm sorry, I'm sorry," Evelyn quickly replied, rolling off the couch and scurrying to where Emberly was hunched over the kitchen island in the same clothes from the night before. She ran a hand through her disheveled hair. "I didn't mean to be insensitive."

"Well, you were. And for the record, I don't have those hangups about my weight anymore, thank you. I'm more than proud now to be the sister with the curves."

"I have curves, too."

"Where?"

"Enya is the super-thin one, not me."

"You're not far behind her."

"*Anyway*," Evelyn huffed. "I know you're upset about your date not showing. That's terrible, that he'd do that to you. He never even texted or anything?"

"No. And I see he read the ones I sent him but was apparently too busy to grace me with any responses. I just...I don't know what I did to deserve that."

"Girl, you didn't do anything. It's not on you that he didn't have enough courtesy to be honest. Don't start blaming yourself for this."

"It's just so embarrassing. Not to mention infuriating. This can't be good for my love luck for the year. I can't afford to lose that time."

"What does that mean?"

Emberly started, as if realizing what she just said. "Nothing. I'm just delirious right now."

Evelyn eyed her strangely for a moment before shrugging it off. "Whatever. I still say you have nothing to worry about with that. Davis obviously wasn't it."

"Dallas."

"Davis, Dallas, Doofus. What-the-hell-ever. Forget him. Now quit eating this stuff and get some *real* food." She took the rest of the apple fritter that Emberly was about to bite into out of her hand and stood.

Pouting, Emberly dropped her chin into her hand. "It's real funny that you're telling me to get over Dallas when you can't get over Travis."

"That is *not* the same thing," Evelyn quickly insisted, whirling around. "Travis and I were married. He was my high school sweetheart. We have *years* of history. All you and Dallas have is drinking coffee together on camera one time. You can't compare the two."

"It's essentially the same thing."

"It's not. And Travis and I are getting back together once he sows whatever oats he needs to sow. He'll realize he already had what he needs and come back home before we know it."

Emberly started to dispute that, but decided against it. Her sister was clearly still delusional about her divorce. Travis had left Evelyn because he felt their relationship had run its course and they were better off as friends. So he asked for a divorce after eleven years of marriage and eighteen years of being a couple, and Evelyn hadn't been able to let it go.

"Do you have something I can wear for today? I didn't plan on staying over here and I don't feel like driving back home," Evelyn asked, pulling some eggs from the fridge.

"Yeah. Though I wouldn't be mad if we skipped the hike today. I'm not really feeling up to it."

"You know that's not an option. Our New Year's Day hike is a family tradition and you're not gonna miss it just because you're in your feelings over some man." Evelyn glanced at her watch. "I guess Enya and Noah will be back pretty soon."

"Umph. Yeah." Emberly slid off the bar stool and pushed her tangled locs over her shoulder. "I'm gonna take a shower."

"Yeah, go do that. I'll have some breakfast fixed for you when you come out."

"Great."

Emberly did thankfully feel better by the time she took a long hot shower and changed into a hoodie and some leggings. She tried to make herself put Dallas out of her mind and trust that she would find someone else sooner rather than later.

The doorbell rang as she rejoined Evelyn, and Enya practically danced in as soon as the door was opened for her.

"Still riding high off that negative pregnancy test, huh?" Emberly surmised, closing the door behind her.

"You better believe it! I'm not knocked up, Vaughn is a fling of the past, I'm about to hang with my family for the day. Life is too good!"

"Did you tell Vaughn that you thought you might've been pregnant?"

"For what? I'm not, so there was no need to mention that."

Just then, Noah made his appearance, and everyone was surprised to see he was alone.

"Where's Kimmy?" Evelyn asked.

Noah went around hugging his sisters. "I left her at home. Needed a break from her."

"Come on, Noah, she's a nice woman."

"Yeah, she is. But she oftentimes doesn't know how to shut up. I can only take so much of that."

"So why are you with her, then?"

"I like her. In relatively small doses. It's not like I expect people to be flawless."

"But if you can't even spend two days in a row with her, maybe that's a hint," Emberly observed.

"Hmph. I guess we'll see."

The siblings congregated in the kitchen to eat Evelyn's breakfast of fried eggs, cinnamon toast, and smoked sausage before they moved into the living room to do their New Year wishes.

"Who's gonna go first?" Enya asked.

"You know we always go from oldest to youngest," Evelyn reminded. "You ask that every year. You just don't like going last."

"Hush."

"Well, my first wish for the year is to have more time for my painting," Noah commented. "Work has been so busy these past few months that I haven't been able to get to it. And I need that 'cause it calms me down."

"Understandable," Emberly replied. "Mine is simple: find the man I'm gonna marry. And I hope the good Lord doesn't wait all year to send him."

Evelyn shook her head. "I know y'all probably think my wish is gonna be something about me and Travis getting back together, but since I already *know* that's gonna happen, there's no need to waste a wish on that. What I wish is to get back to doing splits. I haven't been able to do those since I was a teenager."

"*That's* your wish?" Enya marveled.

"One of 'em. We get two more."

"Uh-huh. Well, anyway, my wish is to get a promotion at work before the second quarter hits. Then I'll be the only Black woman in management at my brokerage firm."

They all went through two more rounds of revealing their wishes, since their family tradition was that they each get three for the year. Once that was done, Noah said a prayer of thanks for them getting through the previous year and into the new one, and asked for protection and grace so that they each got what they wished for and more.

"Y'all ready to hike?" Evelyn asked, rubbing her hands together.

"Not really," Emberly droned. "But I already know y'all will trip if I try to stay home, so..."

"Hell yeah, we will. You know the deal," Noah told her. "We've been doing this since we were kids; it's one of the things Mama and Dad made me promise to keep going after they passed."

"I know," Emberly replied, her voice softening. Their parents had died within months of each other almost ten years earlier, and she missed them something terrible. Pneumonia had taken their mother while stomach cancer claimed their father's life. They were huge on family and being together, and had drilled it into her and her siblings since before they could talk. For them, it was family over everything.

"So let's get going!" Enya exclaimed with a clap of her hands. "It's a beautiful day and I have a lot of apple pie tacos and champagne to work off. By the way, Emberly, when are you gonna be making some more of those?"

"I don't know. That was just something I was trying out. They're not on any of my menus."

"They should be. I'll gladly pay you for those things."

"You know those are the magic words."

They headed out to Buttercup Mountain to do their annual New Year's Day two mile hike, some of them enjoying it more than others. Emberly had always been the least athletic of her siblings and never looked forward to this as much as they did, but at least she didn't have as hard a time of it as she did in her overweight years. She didn't see stars or feel like she was going to pass out by the time they got to the top.

Once they arrived, Noah handed them all bottles of water before they began their trek. Emberly, unable to let Dallas's brush-off go like she thought she could, tried to call him to see if she could get an explanation. She told herself that there *had* to be one; they had hit it off too well for him to just leave her hanging like that for no reason. While she waited on him to respond to her subsequent texts, she checked her dating profiles to see if there were any more viable inquiries. She was on a mission this year and was determined to achieve it, and having to start all over meeting someone new would only set her back.

Her siblings either didn't notice that she was preoccupied or didn't comment on it, because they just talked amongst themselves as they trekked along the trail. It was mostly Evelyn and Enya doing the talking, while Noah led the way as he usually did. When he looked up and noticed someone familiar a few yards ahead of them, he cursed under his breath.

Turning towards his sisters, he tried to appear cool when he asked, "Y'all ready to head back?"

"What? We're not even halfway to the end," Enya pointed out.

"Yeah, I'm actually enjoying this thigh burn I'm getting from all the walking. Let's keep going," Evelyn suggested, starting to walk past him.

Noah stopped her with a gentle grip of her arm. "I just figured we could hit up the pancake house, get our grub-on..."

"We just ate, Noah."

"So?"

"What's up with you?" Enya asked. "You're usually the one getting onto us about not being able to keep up and now you wanna stop in the middle of it?"

Emberly stayed quiet, since she wouldn't have minded cutting the hike short. She glanced at her phone for the hundredth time.

Noah moved in front of Evelyn, trying to turn her back in the other direction. "I just realized I don't have on the right shoes for this. And you really don't, either, E2."

"Since when has that mattered? We aren't training for the Olympics."

"Still-"

"Oh my god," Emberly muttered, having noticed who Noah was trying to avoid. She grabbed Evelyn's other arm. "Yeah, um, we should head on back now. My knees are hurting so it must be about to rain."

"What are you, sixty?" Enya joked. It wasn't until Emberly subtly jerked her head towards what they needed to get away from that she got the message. "Oh damn...uh, yeah, let's go, Ev. I think we've gotten enough steps in today. Ooh, let's go shopping!"

"What is wrong with y'all?" Evelyn exclaimed, looking back and forth between the three of them. "You're acting weird. That's usually *my* area."

Sighing, Noah finally turned her forward and stepped to the side. Evelyn's almond brown skin paled when she saw Travis up ahead with his arm around another woman.

"Oh..."

"Let's just go," Enya suggested. "We can walk another trail."

"Why should we change anything? This is the trail we always walk and Travis knows that; he's come with us plenty of times," Evelyn retorted. "He must've wanted me to see him so I'm gonna make sure he knows I did."

With that, she took off running uphill towards her ex-husband. Noah groaned before going after her, with their sisters close behind. Just as Evelyn got within a few feet of Travis, she slipped and fell, skewing her glasses and kicking dirt into her face.

Travis turned at the commotion and upon seeing Evelyn sprawled on the ground, immediately went to help her up. Noah and Enya caught up right as he was easing her to her feet, with Emberly just behind.

"Evelyn, what in the world..." Travis began curiously. "Are you all right?"

"I'm fine," Evelyn muttered, her face burning as she adjusted her glasses and brushed off her clothes. "I'm surprised to see you here. Today of all days."

Enya quickly moved over and took her sister's arm from Travis's grasp, giving him the evil eye. "Yeah, it *is* pretty curious timing, isn't it, Mr. Sears?"

Travis's eyes flitted to all of the Holliday siblings, seeing the displeasure in their expressions. He glanced at his date, who was looking around at all of them curiously. "It's an unseasonably warm day so Perla and I decided to take advantage of it."

Everyone's eyes turned to the afro puffed-woman standing next to Travis. The triplets' gazes narrowed, studying her. She was clearly older than Travis, which filled Evelyn with questions. Since when did he like older women?

"Aren't you gonna introduce us?" Enya demanded, folding her arms across her chest.

"Oh, yeah..." Travis adjusted his baseball cap and cleared his throat, forcing a smile. "Everyone, this is my date, Perla Fowler. Perla, these are my...my friends, Noah, Enya, Emberly, and Evelyn."

Evelyn felt her face flame hotter than the sun beaming down on them. Friend? Not only was he downplaying who she really was to him, he introduced her *last*?

"It's nice to meet you all," Perla greeted politely with a smile. "Have you known Travis very long?"

"Oh yeah, we all go *way* back," Evelyn replied before Travis could. "Maybe Travis will tell you all about it sometime."

"Okay..."

"We should get going; we have plans in a couple of hours," Travis hurriedly informed, taking Perla's hand. He looked at the siblings, deftly avoiding his ex-wife's glare. "It was good seeing y'all."

They continued on up the trail, Travis pulling Perla along swiftly. Evelyn stood and watched them, her face crumbling with every step they took.

"Girl, I'm so sorry," Emberly soothed, coming to stand next to her.

"Me, too," Enya concurred, flanking her other side. "It's so jacked up that he'd come here to rub his new fling in your face like that."

"Come on now, y'all...we don't know that's what he was doing," Noah countered. "Let's not assume anything."

"Noah, stop. Travis was around us long enough to know what we do every New Year's Day," Enya argued. "He absolutely brought his raggedy date here on purpose to show Ev up." She turned her eyes to Evelyn. "Which is another reason why you need to put him in your rearview mirror, sis."

"Yeah, you don't need to be crying over him like that, come on," Noah added, smoothing Evelyn's quiet tears with his thumbs before pulling her into his chest for a hug. "He's moving on. You need to move on, too. Don't let him have so much power over you."

"That's right. And I'm gonna help you get past that high-yellow chump. I can think of at least three guys off the top of my head I can hook you up with tuh-*day*."

"No thank you," Evelyn immediately dismissed, her face still buried in Noah's chest.

"What do you mean, no thank you?"

"I'm not interested."

"Hell, why not? You need to quit pining over Travis. He's clearly doing his own thing. I bet he hasn't even told that cougar that he used to be married to you. Why would you want to get back with somebody like that?"

"I don't expect y'all to understand; especially you, Enya," Evelyn replied, lifting her head and swiping a hand across her cheek. "You've never been with anyone longer than a year, if that. But Travis is my soul mate; regardless of what's happened, I still believe that. And I don't want to waste time with anybody else when my heart is still with him."

"I still say you're wasting your time. All you know is Travis; he was your first boyfriend and then y'all got married when you were barely adults. You need to experience someone new. Maybe if you did, you wouldn't be so glued to your ex-husband."

"She's got a point, E2," Noah agreed, rubbing her shoulder.

"I don't know," Emberly spoke up, rubbing the back of her neck. "Maybe Evelyn is doing the right thing, holding out like she is."

Enya's head snapped to her. "What?"

"I know what it's like to be with someone who isn't all in. If Evelyn is just gonna be going through the motions with whoever you set her up with, why bother?"

"Are you serious??"

"Totally. If you ask me, she should just stop worrying about Travis or any other man and just put her focus on something else. Take up a hobby, get a pet, take some night classes in something you're interested in. Everything doesn't always have to be about men."

"*You're* actually saying that, when two of your three wishes for the year were dick-focused?"

"Ugh..." Noah groaned.

"You didn't have to say it like that," Emberly muttered. "But Evelyn and I are in different places; *I'm* emotionally stable enough for a relationship."

Evelyn's jaw dropped. "Hey!"

"Girl...you know what I mean. And anyway, Enya, if you should be trying to hook anyone up, it's me. Of the three of us, I'm the most ready. Yet I notice you haven't even offered."

"Because I know you wouldn't like the men I'd suggest."

"Why wouldn't I?"

"They're not your type."

Emberly's eyes narrowed. "Are they not my type, or do you not think I'm *theirs*?"

"That is not what I meant!"

"I think it is. I think you don't believe I'd be good enough for any of the precious men in your arsenal."

Enya reeled. "Don't put words in my mouth, Emberly!"

"Let's not act like you're not quick to share everything with Evelyn but get all stingy when it comes to me. It's always been like that and is clearly still the case. But that's all right. Trust, I'll find my own man. I don't need your damn leftovers, anyway."

"What the hell is *wrong* with you??"

"Y'all, chill out!" Noah cut in before Emberly could respond, stepping between them. He gave them both admonishing looks before letting his frown rest on Emberly. "All that wasn't even necessary, E1."

Emberly rolled her eyes. "Sure, take her side. It's not like *that's* anything new, either."

"Emberly!"

"Look, can we all just take a few chill pills and calm down?" Evelyn spoke up, her hands raised. She grabbed an arm of each of her sisters, trying to pull them closer together. When they each resisted, still glaring at each other, Evelyn yanked harder, sending them crashing together. "We should not be fighting, especially not about men. This is our family time. I promise not to mention Travis for the rest of the day if you two kiss and make up right now."

"No," the stubborn sisters immediately chorused.

Noah cleared his throat, giving each of them stern looks with his arms crossed. Huffing and sucking their teeth in concession, Emberly and Enya mumbled apologies before letting Evelyn push them together in a half-hearted hug.

"That's more like it!" Evelyn grinned triumphantly.

"Yeah, whatever," Emberly muttered, turning her attention back to her phone as she stepped away from her sister.

Noah shook his head as he took a swig from his water bottle. "Y'all done acting like little girls now?"

"Shut up, Noah," Enya snapped. "And anyway, Emberly started it."

"Yeah, real mature."

"Just one last thing on the subject and then we can all forget about this for the day," Evelyn announced. "I know y'all think I'm delusional for being so attached to Tr-,um, to my ex-husband, but I'm not. I'm not putting my life on hold; I'm just being patient. There's a difference. And I look forward to all of your apologies when Tra-, *he* and I get re-married. We might even have the ceremony up on this mountain, at sunset. Romantic, huh?"

"Totally," Enya droned.

"You're mocking me."

"Yes, I am. 'Cause you still sound delusional. It's wild how you can't realize that."

"Just take the next few years and be by yourself," Emberly deadpanned, bored with the conversation. "That'll fix all of this."

"The next *few years*? There's no way," Enya shook her head.

"That's not a lot of time. Really, I think you just need to go celibate and close up shop indefinitely. You clearly have some issues, Evelyn."

Noah peered curiously at Emberly. "What's up with this advice, E1?"

Emberly tried to keep her face even, despite the nervousness that instantly coursed through her. "What?"

"I get the part about E2 shifting her focus, but basically telling her to become some kind of nun?"

"Nothing wrong with that. I bet she'd be a lot happier than she is now."

"Hell no," Enya grunted. "Ev, don't listen to that. Emberly has clearly been out in this sun too long."

Sucking her teeth, Emberly stepped around them and continued up the trail, even though she'd rather have headed back to the car. "Let's just keep going."

Her siblings wordlessly followed her, with Noah still wondering what was going on with his sister.

Chapter 3

ENYA AND EVELYN WAITED for their Aunt Miriam to reemerge from her bedroom, having scurried in there when her husband Tariq got home. They turned up the television to drown out the sounds of the afternoon quickie that was clearly happening.

"I've said it once and I'll say it again; I wish to high heaven I have it like Aunt Miriam when I get to be her age," Enya chuckled.

"What, you mean oversexed with little to no shame?"

"Hell, that's almost me now. I'm talking about having someone you're *that* on fire for all the time. It's like every time they look at each other, they're mentally tearing each other's clothes off."

"Maybe that's why she married someone damn near twenty years younger. Men her age probably can't keep up with her."

"I don't doubt it."

It was another ten minutes or so before Miriam finally strolled from her bedroom, flushed and smiling. She smoothed her burgundy bobbed hair from her face and plopped into the armchair, her short silk robe coming slightly untied and revealing the dark green lace bra and panties underneath.

"Didn't wanna throw on a nightgown or a hoodie or something, huh?" Evelyn asked, adjusting her glasses.

"My house." Miriam shrugged.

"And let's not act like she's modest even when she goes out," Enya chuckled. She'd always loved how uninhibited her aunt was.

"Hey, just because I'm in my fifties doesn't mean I need to be acting or dressing like some Sunday school teacher. I take damn good care of myself and I'm proud of it."

"Hey, no arguments here. You're my shero, Auntie."

"Thank you, baby." Miriam winked at Enya before crossing her legs and leaning back in her seat. "So what's been going on? Where's Emberly?"

"I'm not sure; I think she's working," Evelyn mused. "I haven't talked to her in a couple of days."

"Me, either," Enya added. "Though I did text her this morning. She's been acting kind of funny recently."

Miriam quirked a brow. "Funny how?"

"I can't really explain it but she's been a little distant. Probably sill bummed about getting stood up on New Year's Eve. She seems a little desperate about finding somebody. Maybe that's why she's been giving out such off-the-wall advice."

"Yeah, like when she told me I needed to just forget about Travis and be by myself for the next few years," Evelyn spoke up, sitting forward. "*Years*! How crazy is that?"

"Not crazy even a little bit," Miriam replied coolly. "You *do* need to get over Travis. It's ridiculous that you're still pining over that man after he made it more than clear that he only wants to be friends with you. Focus on something else, child."

"That's what *she* said! As if getting a hobby is going to keep me warm at night."

"It will if your hobby is making blankets."

"Aunt Miriam."

"What? Ever since you got here, you've been fussing about seeing him with that other woman at Buttercup Mountain. I didn't *just* go jump my husband because he came home looking like a Pinterest model. I got tired of hearing your yammering."

Evelyn's jaw dropped. "Seriously??"

"Baby," Miriam sat forward in her seat, her thick-lashed brown eyes fixed on her niece. "I'm not trying to be insensitive. We all know you love Travis. But you're putting your life on pause while he's on fast-forward. Not everything lasts forever, despite how much we might want it to. Hell, you know I was married once before Tariq."

"Yeah, but your first husband died, though, Auntie. It's not exactly the same thing."

"Whatever. The marriage ended, nonetheless. And he and I were teenage sweethearts just like you and Travis were. I could've buried myself in grief and refused to get on with my life but I didn't. I cried, I grieved, but I moved on. And you have to move on, too, baby. Life has to keep moving."

"But what if I move on and Travis decides he wants me back?"

"Oh well. That'll be his own damn fault."

"Auntie."

"What?"

"She's got a point, sis," Enya gently chimed in. "Not to mention how you're making yourself look by sitting over here waiting for him. You never know, he might realize what he lost if he knows you've moved on with someone else, or just that you're happy and thriving without him. Don't let him hold all the cards. Love shouldn't keep you stuck."

Evelyn opened her mouth to protest but nothing came out. She knew what her sister and aunt were saying wasn't totally wrong. Maybe she *had* been too consumed with Travis, but getting over him was easier said than done. She honestly couldn't imagine herself with anyone else, and the image of Travis with his arm around that woman made her sick to her stomach. She just didn't understand how he could possibly want another woman when she was still there, just as in love and as willing as ever.

As she got lost in her own thoughts, Enya turned her attention back to her aunt. "So, Auntie, how come you didn't meet us at the mountain for the hike? You missed the New Year's party, too."

"Oh, yeah. Tariq and I were going to pop in but then we started playing with our sex dice. Once we got to acting all that stuff out..."

"*Gosh*, I envy you..."

"Girl, when the new year came in, we were in there on the kitchen floor spreading stuff on each other. It was a wrap after that, as far as going anywhere."

"Okay, well what about the next day, for the hike?"

"I quit trying to make up excuses to miss that last year. I love y'all more than fried fish but you know I always thought all these extra holiday traditions were a little corny. And I told my brother that when him and your mama started it when y'all were kids."

"Yeah, Daddy *did* always say you were stubborn."

"Call it what you want. I *bet* I had more fun here than y'all did trekking up a mountain."

"I don't doubt it. But I was so high off of my pregnancy scare being a fluke that I would've walked to China."

"Thought you were knocked up, huh? Sounds familiar."

"That was in college and many moons ago, Auntie."

"Uh-huh."

"But regardless, I don't wanna go through that again. From here on out I'm gonna be more careful. 'Cause I'm sure it'll only be a matter of time before one of those little swimmers actually makes it to the promised land and then I'll be stuck on mommy duty for eighteen years."

"I still don't understand how you're so against having kids," Evelyn piped up. "I'm looking forward to being a mother. And I bet none of their friends would have a zookeeper for a mother like mine will."

"I'd be fine not having any kids but if I do, I want it to be with someone I'm in love with and that *wasn't* Vaughn. The last thing I want is to be a single mother if I don't have to be."

"I guess I can understand that. Just don't go finding someone before I get back with Tr-uh, before I do. It would just figure."

"That's a very Emberly thing to say. And don't think we didn't catch that."

Evelyn blushed. "What if Que came back wanting to reconcile? Would this laid-back attitude stay put or would you fall back head over heels like you were back in the day? You were worse than I am with Travis."

"Nah, because when Que and I were over, I let it go. I didn't wallow in it like you are."

"Hmph."

"Snap," Miriam smirked, snapping her fingers with a flourish. Evelyn cut her eyes at her.

"And anyway, Que is engaged with, like, two kids," Enya added. "He and I follow each other on social media. He's doing his thing and I'm happy for him. So...nice try."

Evelyn just flopped against the back of the couch and folded her arms in a huff, with her amused sister and aunt looking at her.

WHILE HER SISTERS WERE visiting their aunt, Emberly was working up the nerve to visit Dallas's office.

She knew it probably wasn't the smartest idea to just pop up on him at work like this. But she had to get some answers. And it wasn't like she stalked him or did some deep dive to find out where he worked; he told her on his own during one of their initial conversations, along with his usual work hours. So she managed to convince herself that she wasn't doing anything wrong.

Checking her appearance for the fifth time in her compact then again in the visor mirror, and rubbing yet another layer of lotion over the tattoo sleeve covering her right arm (that Dallas had said was hot over their video chat), she took a deep breath and pushed open her car door. She had parked across the street from his office, and after looking both ways, trotted over to the building where he worked out of as a corporate publicist. She could see him stroll across the lobby through the glass door, his cell phone attached to his ear. Her heart started beating faster but she made herself keep her feet moving to the door, then pull it open.

"Hi, can I help you?" the receptionist greeted her politely with a smile. The name plate on her desk read Ari.

"Oh hi yeah...um, I'm here to see Dallas..." Emberly's voice trailed off and her eyes widened slightly, realizing she didn't know his last name. The embarrassment of the realization almost knocked her over.

"Sure, he's in the back," Ari confirmed, thankfully easing her sprouting humiliation. "Do you have an appointment?"

"I'm a potential client," Emberly lied, thinking quickly. "I'm not on his calendar but we've talked about possibly working together on some things and I just wanted to follow up, since I was in the area."

"Oh okay. He's always raking in new clients; in fact, he's pretty loaded up right now so I'm surprised he's considering taking on anyone else. What kind of business are you in?"

"I'm a pastry chef; I own Oh My Decadence. It's mostly catering and providing desserts for various restaurants but I also have an online store and my brick-and-mortar will be up and running in the next two years."

Ari's eyes lit up. "Oh my god! My cousin ordered some desserts from Oh My Decadence for her anniversary party and they were ridiculously amazing...there wasn't a crumb left by the end of the night. *You're* the genius behind that??"

Emberly smiled proudly. "That's me. And my staff, of course."

"Girl, your hands are blessed. We were fighting over the last of those apple strawberry bars with the toffee crust and that yummy crumble topping. And that triple-layer white chocolate cake with the dulce de leche filling and maple whipped cream? *Orgasmic*."

Her grin widening, Emberly reveled in the praise. She'd always loved to bake and had built her business from just making orders by herself out of the small kitchen of her previous tiny apartment to having a staff and more orders for her treats than she felt she could handle at times. Her business was booming and growing, and she never got tired of hearing raves over her creations.

Snapping out of her musings, she replied, "Yeah, that's been a popular item ever since I put it on my menu. I fear a revolt if I ever decided to discontinue that one." She fished a business card from her bag and handed it to Ari. "Thank you so much for those kind words. I hope you keep me in mind for any events you might have in the future."

"Events? I'll order your desserts just to pig out on right in my apartment." As Emberly laughed, Ari shook her head. "But I'm sure you have things to do so let me quit fawning. I'll page Dallas for you."

"I appreciate it."

Ari picked up the phone and pressed a button. "Yes, Mr. Cutler, you have a visitor. Sure, I'll let her know." To Emberly she said, "He'll be right out."

"Awesome." *Cutler...I'll have to remember that*, Emberly noted silently.

A couple of minutes later, Dallas emerged from the short hallway, looking at her curiously. Emberly noticed how his smile faltered slightly when he saw her standing there.

"Kimberly, hey," he greeted, going over to shake her hand. "What brings you by?"

Emberly hated that they were still standing in front of his receptionist, because not only was he giving her some cold handshake like she was a random business associate, he'd gotten her name wrong, to boot.

"I'm sorry to just drop by like this, but do you have a minute?" she managed to ask in an even voice.

"Uhh, yeah." Dallas glanced at his watch before looking at Ari. "What time is my next appointment?"

"You still have about thirty minutes," Ari confirmed after a quick check of the calendar.

"Cool. Follow me, Kimberly." Dallas headed back to the hallway and Emberly gritted her teeth as she followed.

As soon as they were behind the closed door of his small office, Emberly spewed, "Seriously? So not only do you stand me up, you forget my name?"

His eyes widened slightly. "It's not Kimberly?"

"No. It's *Emberly*. Emberly Holliday. The one you were *supposed* to be hanging out with on New Year's Eve? Or did you get me confused with *another* tattooed pastry chef with ass-length locs?"

Sighing, Dallas rounded his desk and dropped into his slightly worn chair. "Look, I'm sorry...I know it wasn't cool to leave you hanging like that."

"So why did you do it? Then you ignored me afterwards? I thought we hit it off really well; what did I do to deserve that?"

"Nothing," he quickly replied. "You *didn't* deserve that, Emberly, and I'm sorry. It's just...we had only had that one long video chat and then you invited me to spend the holiday with you and your family, and while it sounded all right when I was drinking spiked coffee, the more I thought about it, the more it just felt like too much too soon."

"Oh." Emberly hadn't considered that her invitation for him to join her and her siblings would be overwhelming. It wasn't like he was meeting her parents. Of course that was impossible, but still. "Why didn't you just tell me that, then? We could've hung out another day."

"I don't know...I didn't change my mind until the last minute and didn't know how to tell you without sounding like a jerk."

"So you just brushed me off and made yourself look worse?"

He briefly hung his head. "Yeah, I didn't consider that at the time. I punked out, I admit it. I really do like you, Emberly, but I wasn't ready to spend the holiday with you at a family gathering, especially since we hadn't even met up in person one-on-one yet."

Considering his words, Emberly nodded in concession. "I guess I can understand that. I just wish you'd been honest with me. I would've understood, if you had broken it down the way you just did."

"I know. I should have. Please, accept my apology, Emberly. It definitely wasn't anything personal."

"All right. So what about us hanging out now? I mean, not *right* now, but another time, just the two of us and away from any siblings or aunts or anyone else that might make you uncomfortable? I've really been enjoying getting to know you."

She eyed his boyish good looks as he pondered her suggestion, wondering how he would react if she dove across his desk and helped herself to a taste of his moist lips. He was so freaking cute, with his honey-colored eyes and faint mustache and brown skin so smooth she was actually jealous of it. Yeah, he would make an excellent mate for her.

"Sure," he finally responded. Emberly made herself ignore the fact that he sounded less than excited about it. "I've liked getting to know you, too, so, yeah, we can do that."

She grinned. "Great! I'm looking forward to it."

He just nodded, his lips stretching into a tight smile.

"Well, I'll get outta here and let you get back to work; I know you have an appointment shortly. Um, call me tonight?"

"Yeah. I mean, I'll try. If it's not too late when I get home."

"Doesn't matter what time it is. I'll look forward to hearing from you. And I'll even be sure to wear something extra cute for our video chat."

"Right. Well...I'll talk to you then, Emberly."

He remained seated, and Emberly realized he wasn't going to give her a parting hug. She wondered if he possibly imagined what she did; he'd take her into his arms, hold her tight, then after a few moments they'd each lean back and share a long lingering gaze before he eased down and took their first kiss. Then he'd slowly back her against the door-

"Emberly?"

"Oh!" Emberly jumped, startled, blinking away the fantasy. "Sorry about that; my mind wandered for a second, there. Talk to you tonight."

She turned and left, actually whistling as she crossed the lobby, waving at Ari before pushing open the door and strolling back to her car, feeling better than she had in a while.

Unfortunately she had to go back to work since she had several orders that still needed to be filled. She headed back to the commercial kitchen she rented where her main assistant chef Camilla was filling apple cider cupcakes with salted caramel frosting.

"How's it going?" Emberly asked her, stashing her crossbody hobo bag and grabbing her apron from the hook. She had four other assistants but one of them was mainly for administrative tasks, social media, and deliveries, two handled the abundance of online orders, and the last helped out wherever needed on any given day.

"Almost done with this batch," Camilla muttered, concentrating. She paused to twist the pastry bag in her hands to move the frosting down and resumed her cupcake-stuffing. "People are really loving these things. Someone ordered some more just this morning."

"Told you they'd be a hit. My brother Noah scarfed them down like he was trying to win a contest when I let him test some."

Camilla's movements stilled briefly. "Yeah? How is Noah?"

"He's fine. Still doing his thing running that analytics firm. We all teased him when he started that business but he's been on the grind with it for years and now he's more successful than all of us. He's so in demand and has even been offered millions of dollars for his company from some major players in the business."

"Really? Like who?'

"Girl, I couldn't tell you. I know nothing about any of that; it goes right over my head. Noah is the genius; of us triplets, Enya is the most like him, with all that corporate stuff. But regardless, I'm so proud of him."

"That's admirable. So...all he does is work, huh?"

"No, he loves to paint. That's how he clears his head. He's also a really good musician. Like, a savant. Hasn't taken one lesson in anything but can pick up any instrument and play it like he'd been studying it for years."

"Wow, that's impressive."

"Yeah, it really is. And he dates some, too. He's seeing some chatty woman now; brought her to the New Year's Eve party. Though I wouldn't be mad if he dumped her 'cause homegirl was a little annoying."

"Oh..." Camilla put the pastry bag down. "What about you? How did it go with that guy you were telling me about?"

"Went great; I just left from seeing him, as a matter of fact." There was no way Emberly was going to admit that she'd been stood up. She and Camilla were cool but not *that* cool. "Is it silly that I'm looking forward to our video chat tonight like it's a date?"

"No, that's not silly. You like him. Little things mean the world when you really like somebody."

"Very true." Emberly washed her hands before she took another tray of cupcakes from the cooling rack and began filling another pastry bag with the creamy salted caramel frosting. "What about you? I'm always going on and on about my stuff but I hardly know anything about *your* love life. Do you have a man? Crushing on anybody?"

"Uhhh..." Camilla shrugged, her long brown ponytail falling from her shoulder. "Nothing really to tell in that area. I live a kinda dull life, really; I just work and go home, pretty much."

"Why is that? You don't want to be in a relationship or something?"

"It's not that. I guess I just don't make much of an effort to meet anyone. I'm pretty introverted."

"Oh. Well, that's understandable. Maybe Enya can hook you up with somebody. She's, like, the queen of that. When she wants to be," Emberly couldn't help adding.

"Yeah? I think I'm okay for the time being but I'll surely keep that in mind."

They continued stuffing the table full of cupcakes, Emberly whistling and anticipating the evening and Camilla trying to quell the butterflies she always got at the mention of Noah's name.

Chapter 4

NOAH HAD JUST GOTTEN out of a meeting and was getting ready for another when he got a call from Kimmy. Sighing, he took the call, despite his temptation to let it go to voicemail.

"Hey, Kimmy, what's up?"

"Noah Love, hey! I'm so glad I caught you 'cause I know you said you had a bunch of stuff going on today, and I have about an hour before my dance class starts so I wanted to see what you had going on for next Monday."

"That's MLK day."

"Oh yeah! I totally forgot about that. Well, that's cool; you're not gonna be working, are you? I mean I know you're an entrepreneur and you don't exactly punch a clock or anything but I hope you'll be able to make some time to take a break on that day. I'd love to spend it with you, if I could."

"Oh...well, I'm usually with my sisters. And maybe my aunt if her and her husband can peel themselves off of each other long enough."

"What are y'all gonna be doing? Another hike? I wish I could've joined you. It would've been a great way for me to get my steps in. Not to mention what it does for my thighs."

"No, it's not another hike. We do something else." Noah hoped being vague would give her a hint, because he could sense she would probably be fishing for an invitation.

"Well, what is it?"

"Kimmy, I have a meeting I need to get to..."

"Oh okay, okay, I totally understand. Well, regardless, I'd love it if I could join you for whatever cool thing you all do. I know it's gonna be interesting. Your family is *so* cool. I wish we had those kinds of creative fun traditions when I was growing up but my parents didn't have that kind of imagination. All we did was the regular basic stuff, if anything."

"That doesn't have to be a bad thing. But like I was saying about needing to go-"

"Yeah, I know you have to go to your meeting. But real quick, am I gonna be able to go with you on MLK day? Whatever it is, I know that would be a fun thing for us to do together. And I'd get to hang out with your fascinating sisters again. They are such a hoot!"

Resisting the urge to sigh again, Noah gripped the pen in his hand a little harder than necessary. It was on the tip of his tongue to refuse her and hastily hang up, but he couldn't make himself do it. Kimmy was a nice woman and he enjoyed her company, but he was starting to wonder if he needed to move on from her. The fact that he wasn't gung-ho about spending more time with her had to be a sign, and not a good one.

"All right fine, you can join us next Monday," he made himself say, forcing pleasantness into his voice. "But I'll have to fill you in on the details later 'cause I really do have to go."

"Goody! Okay, go on to your meeting. I look forward to seeing you. Hopefully it won't be all the way until next Monday when I get to see you next, though. I miss you. We haven't gotten to cuddle in too long. I got a cute new nightie, too; I know you're gonna love it. But yes, yes, go to your meeting. Call me later?"

"Sure. Bye." He hung up the phone, feeling notably more drained than he had just minutes before.

Reminding himself that he didn't have time to worry about Kimmy at the moment, he gathered his folders and headed to his meeting, then continued on with his day. He enjoyed being a business intelligence analyst but there were days when it caused more stress than he liked. But he'd take working for himself over punching a clock for someone else any day of the week. His father was an entrepreneur and his ultimate role model when it came to that.

He was finally winding things down several hours later when he got a call from Sid Ledbetter, the man whose family was renting his parent's former home. The siblings had renovated it and started renting it out about a year after their parents' passing, since none of them wanted to sell it.

"Hey Sid, what's going on?" Noah greeted him, grabbing his keys and getting ready to close up his office. "Everything okay?"

"Hi Noah. Yes, everything is just fine. Am I catching you at a bad time?"

"No, you're good. How's the family?"

"Everyone's good. Our youngest, Suzette, just moved into an apartment with her friends off campus this past weekend. She was our last one to leave the nest, so now it's just me and Lily, being an old married couple here together."

Noah chuckled. "That's awesome; congrats."

"Thanks, Noah. That's part of the reason I'm calling, though. Now that the kids are gone, the house is a little too big for just me and Lily. We've been saving up over these past few years for a little bungalow, and we just got informed today that our offer was accepted for the one we've had our eye on. We're thrilled. So once our agreement is up at the end of the month, we're going to be moving out."

"Oh..." Noah's eyebrows shot up. He hadn't expected that. "That's great for you two. Yeah, that's no problem; I'll let my sisters know."

"We're excited about it. Though I can't say we love packing up everything. But we'll have the house in tip-top shape come the end of the month."

"Awesome, thanks. All right, well, congratulations again, and thanks for letting me know. I'll talk to you soon."

"Thanks, Noah."

Ending the call, Noah shook his head, though he wasn't upset. He didn't expect the Ledbetters to rent the house forever. He just didn't look forward to the process of finding new renters.

Once he was in his Lexus, he opened the group chat to let his sisters know this latest development with Sid.

*Noah*: **Hey. Just got a call from Sid; they won't be renewing their rental agreement with us at the end of the month. So we need to get someone else in there after they leave.**

*Enya*: **Did he say why they were leaving?**

*Noah*: **They bought a smaller house now that all their kids have moved out.**

*Evelyn*: **Good for them.**

*Noah*: **Yeah, it sucks for us but I'm happy for them. They were pretty ideal, as far as renters go. Rent was** always on time, the neighbors like 'em, kept the house in good shape. Whoever we get to replace them needs to keep that going.

*Enya*: Ugh, I don't wanna deal with all that...

*Emberly*: I'll handle it.

*Noah*: What? You?

*Emberly*: I don't understand the surprise. I help out plenty.

*Noah*: I know, E1, but we all know I usually deal with the renters directly. I'm just surprised that you want to take the lead but hey, have at it.

*Enya*: Thank god you volunteered, Emberly. Now I don't have to.

*Evelyn*: But you have no problem getting your cut of the rent, though.

*Enya*: Of course not.

Considering the matter settled, Noah headed on home. Though he was curious about Emberly's sudden desire to step up regarding the rental, he didn't have the energy to question it. It was one less thing on his plate and that was all he cared about.

After he had gotten home, showered, and heated up one of the ready-made meals that he had delivered every week, he turned on some Charlie Parker and went into his spare bedroom where he did most of his painting. In a watercolor kind of mood, he pulled out his materials and began, feeling more relaxed with the first stroke of his brush. Between the painting and the bourbon he was sipping on, the day's stress melted away and the tension in his shoulders eased.

Though some of it returned when he got a text from Kimmy, asking if he was home yet. He leaned over to read it but made no move to respond, only taking another sip from his glass. His friends thought it was crazy that he wasn't more hyped about her; she was a pretty, brown-skinned curvy sweetheart, even if she could be a little much at times. He wanted to be as into her as she was into him. But it just hadn't happened like that. And despite outside opinion, he wasn't sure that would change over time.

He was musing all of this when he heard the doorbell. Not in the mood for visitors, he frowned and clunked his glass on the desk, grabbing his phone on the way to the door to see if he had missed a message about someone coming over. The last person he expected to see on his security monitor was his ex, Monique.

"What the hell..." he muttered, unlocking the door and wrenching it open. His frown hadn't eased by the time he was standing face-to-face with his unexpected visitor. "Monique, what are you doing here?"

"Wow, that's how you greet me?" She chuckled, but Noah didn't.

"We haven't talked in months, since we broke up. And you made it clear we didn't need to see each other anymore, remember?"

"Yeah, I was in my feelings that night," Monique admitted, sticking a hand in her light brown microbraids and shaking her head. "As soon as I said that shit, I regretted it. But I figured you wouldn't want to talk to me yet, which is why I let some time pass before showing up again. I was hoping you'd have cooled off by now."

"I'm not mad at all, Monique, but I'm also not interested in going there with you again."

She actually looked surprised, shifting her weight. "For real, Noah?"

"For real. No hard feelings, but let's just leave things as they are. I'm seeing someone, anyway."

"Oh." Disappointment painted her face. "I guess I should've figured that. You *are* a damn good catch, after all, and you never seem to stay single for very long. Is it serious?'

"Doesn't matter," Noah replied, ignoring the comment about his love life. "I only deal with one woman at a time. I don't have the time or energy for more than that."

Monique chuckled as if that was a joke. "Okay, so what if we just hang out as friends, then? I miss those nights we used to spend together. We were buddies before we were anything else, remember?"

"Yeah, I remember. And I'm not trying to be cruel at all but I'm good on that, too. Let's just leave well enough alone."

Monique stood there eyeing him for a moment, her hazel eyes roaming his face. "I hear the jazz playing; you must be in here painting."

"I am."

"You look good, Noah. Tall and chocolate and as fine as ever."

"Thanks, Monique." He resisted the urge to return the compliment, but it definitely applied. He'd always loved her long legs and toned body and coffee brown skin that was as soft and smooth as butter. There were plenty of nights he spent massaging her with edible body oil because he couldn't keep his hands off her.

And with the way she was looking at him right then, she wanted his hands on her again. She stepped closer to him, leaning in and placing a hand on his chest. She bit her bottom lip and Noah had to will his body not to react, though it wasn't totally working.

"I want you, Noah," she boldly informed, rubbing her leg against his as she eased her face towards his, eying his lips. "We can have some fun together tonight, can't we? I'm already here and I can *feel* how much you want me."

Yes, he was aroused. And very tempted. But he still gently grabbed her chin and stepped back right before her lips made contact with his.

"I can't," he told her, his voice low. He bit his own lip as he tried to get his body to calm down, despite his mind replaying images of having Monique hoisted up against the wall or riding him on his back deck. "As good as you look and as much as I might be tempted physically, I can't do that, Monique. I'm not a cheater and you know that."

Her expression faltered a tiny bit. "But if your relationship isn't even serious-"

"I never confirmed if it was or not. All I said was it didn't matter."

"Noah." Her hand started to ease under his shirt but he stopped her. "You know if you were all in with whoever this woman is, you'd clearly make that known. The fact that you're being so vague must mean you're not into it."

She had a point. Noah *wasn't* that into Kimmy, certainly not as much as he'd been at first. And true enough, they weren't in love or even exclusive. But for the time being, they were still dating, and he meant what he said about being a one-woman man.

"Regardless, this isn't happening." He stepped back, gently prying her hands from his chest. "And anyway, I don't believe in going backwards; when my time with someone is over, that's it. And it was *your* choice to end things with me, so...I need you to leave, please."

Her hand dropping to her side, Monique looked sincerely floored. She hadn't expected Noah to resist her. But she just cleared her throat and stepped back.

"If that's the way you want it..."

"It is."

"Guess I have to respect that, then." She briefly touched his cheek. "Bye, Noah."

"Bye."

She turned and walked off, heading back to her black Audi. Noah watched her pull off, making sure she got on her way safely before closing the door and releasing a long breath. His body was already mad at him for not taking Monique up on her offer; he hadn't had sex in a few months. Even though he and Kimmy had been dating a little while, he hadn't wanted to take it there with her yet. The most they'd done was a lot of kissing and heavy petting, which she thankfully was fine with for the time being.

But that was just yet another sign that Noah wasn't as into Kimmy as he needed to be for them to continue. When he was really into a woman, he wanted her in every way, even if he didn't always act on every primal urge. He needed to go ahead and do what he knew needed to be done.

Right where he stood, he called Kimmy, for once praying she answered the phone.

"Hey, Noah Love!" she greeted after a couple of rings.

"Hey, Kimmy. Listen, I-"

"I am so glad you called because I was over here eating some potstickers and it made me think of the time we ordered those on our second date, and I was wondering if you'd gotten home yet and if you had, if you'd eaten already. Because I'd gladly bring you something to eat if you need me to. Or if you're still at your office, I can bring it there. I figured since you didn't respond to my text that you might still be at work but I'm guessing you're home now or at least on your way?"

He was tired from just listening to her. "Yeah, I'm home, and thanks for the offer but I already ate. Kimmy-"

"You want me to come over? I started to come by a little while ago but stopped myself; I know you're not crazy about unannounced visitors."

Noah wondered what would have happened if Kimmy had come by when Monique was there. He was glad that didn't happen.

"Look, Kimmy, I need you to listen for a second, okay? Can you let me say what I need to say without interruption?"

Growing uncharacteristically quiet, Kimmy eventually mumbled, "Okay..."

"Kimmy...I'm sorry but this isn't working, what we have going. I like you, I do; but if I'm honest with myself, I can't see any kind of future for us. And I don't want to insult or disrespect you by letting you think there is."

She gasped, clearly thrown for a loop. "Are-are you serious? You're ending this between us, just like that?"

"I won't waste your time, Kimmy. You deserve a man that's all in with you and that's not me."

"What could have happened to have you change your mind so fast? We were good a few hours ago! What is it, you think I talk too much? I know people have told me that before and I try to rein it in but sometimes I just have so much in my head and I'm not able to filter or organize all of it and just have to get it out as I think it. It's been like that ever since I was a kid; my parents even had me tested for ADD. Turns out I didn't have it. I'm sorry if that annoys you; my friends don't love it, either. But if that's *all* the problem is-"

"It's not just that, Kimmy," Noah gently interjected. "I mean, no, I don't love that but it's not the worst thing in the world, as far as flaws. I'm just not feeling it between us. As much as I sincerely like you, we're not right for each other romantically. I don't want to hurt you, but...that's what I'll do if I keep seeing you knowing my heart isn't in it. I'd rather just let you go so you can find the man you deserve."

Kimmy grew quiet for several moments, and Noah wondered if she was going to cry or beg him to reconsider, or curse him out. He'd never seen her get angry, but he didn't put anything past any woman when she might feel scorned.

"I, um..." Kimmy finally spoke, clearing her throat. "I can't say I'm not surprised to hear this and that it doesn't hurt but I appreciate you being honest with me about your feelings. If that's how you're feeling about us then you're right; I *should* move on."

Mildly surprised, Noah breathed a silent sigh of relief. The last thing he wanted was for things to end on an ugly note. "I wish you nothing but the best, Kimmy, for real."

"Thank you, Noah. Um, I should go. I'll miss you. Good night." She hung up.

It was one of the most mature, amicable breakups he'd had and Noah's respect for Kimmy increased several notches. It was too bad they couldn't work out but he knew in his heart and mind that she wasn't the woman for him. And until he found who was, it would just be him and his work, his jazz, and his paintings. And his bourbon.

Chapter 5

"WHAT THE HELL DID YOU just say?"

It was Martin Luther King Jr. day and the Holliday siblings were gathered at Evelyn's townhome, gawking at her after the news she tried to casually mention without anyone noticing.

"I said I invited Travis," she repeated with a shrug. Tucking some hair behind her ear, she went about her task of rearranging and fluffing the couch pillows. "What's the big deal?"

"Uh, the *big deal* is that you're supposed to be moving *on* from him, remember?" Enya reminded her. "How many conversations have we had about this?"

"How did you come to decide to invite him, E2?" Noah asked her. His sisters had been visibly pleased that he'd shown up without Kimmy, and even more pleased when he announced he broke up with her. Emberly had to pay Evelyn twenty dollars for losing the bet. "You called him?"

"I had to. I found something here of his that I needed to return to him."

"What?"

Evelyn averted her eyes. "His razor."

"It's only 'cause you're my little sister that I'm not clowning you super hard for that right now. Do you not hear how crazy that sounds?"

"I wanted to see him, okay?" Evelyn huffed, folding her arms. "It's not like I invited him over here for a booty call."

"Though I'm sure you wouldn't turn that down if he offered it," Enya muttered. Her phone chimed in her hand and she glanced at it, immediately breaking out into a huge grin.

"Looks like someone might be having their own booty call later tonight," Emberly commented, nudging her sister playfully. "I know that smile."

"I don't know what you're talking about," Enya weakly protested, trying to suppress her smile and failing. She moved her phone out of view. "It was just a random text message."

"Random text messages don't have you cheesing like that."

"You're seeing someone?" Noah asked Enya.

Enya shrugged. "Kinda..."

"Kinda?"

"Okay, I met someone. But it's not a big deal."

Evelyn eyed her. "Then why are you blushing?"

"Okay, so I like him. I can admit that. But it's still early. I don't wanna jump the gun too soon."

"What's his name?"

"That information will be divulged at a later time. It's too soon to be handing out those kinds of details."

"I didn't ask for the man's blood type."

"Well, at least you and Evelyn have something to smile about when it comes to men, even if Evelyn is still delusional about hers," Emberly said to Enya, earning a frown from Evelyn. "Can you believe that Dallas ghosted me *again*?"

Her siblings looked at her in alarm. "Seriously?" Noah asked.

"Yes! Even after I'd gone to talk to him and he told me what happened on New Year's Eve, which I understood, and then we had a long conversation that night. We were supposed to meet up the next day but he never showed up. And when I tried to call, I realized he'd blocked me."

Evelyn gasped. "What? Why would he do that??"

"Beats me. We didn't have an argument and he was talking like everything was good. Even went so far as to say he was looking forward to seeing me the next day. But I sat in that park for over an hour waiting on him, looking like a fool. I can't believe he would do me like that."

"Damn, E1," Noah sighed, sliding a comforting arm around her shoulders. "I hate to hear that."

"It was pretty embarrassing," Emberly admitted, half of her face buried in Noah's chest. "If he'd changed his mind again, all he had to do was say so. I don't know why people play with other's feelings that way."

"He's a punk, E1. There's no other way to put it."

"A really cute punk," Emberly muttered.

"Where does he work? You want me to go beat his ass?"

Unable to resist a smile, Emberly looked up at him gratefully. "Would you do it if I actually said yes?"

"Don't act like I haven't fought anybody for you before. You *know* I'd do it."

Grinning, Emberly hugged him around his waist. She loved how he always had her back. "As tempting as it is to sic you on him, I guess I'll just have to let it go. Although it really sucks, the search continues for someone more willing."

"What do you mean, more willing?"

Shaking her head, Emberly avoided Evelyn's curious look. "Just, you know...more willing to be all in with me. To be honest and see where things can go. That's all."

Enya, who had gone quiet during this exchange, cleared her throat. "You *do* deserve someone who won't punk out on you like that, Emberly. I'm sorry he hurt you."

"You and me both. But I'll just have to get over it, I guess."

Just then, there was a knock on the door. Evelyn jumped, then excitedly squealed as she scurried to the mirror in the foyer to check her hair and adjust her chest-hugging sweater to show a bit more cleavage before swinging open the door.

"Travis," she breathed, her smile widening.

"Hey, Evelyn. Sorry I'm late. All that construction has really jacked up the traffic."

"It's no problem. Come on in."

She reached out and grabbed his wrist, pulling him inside. As soon as the door was closed behind him, she launched herself into his arms for a tight hug, not caring that her enthusiasm practically doubled his. She was clamped onto him while his arms only lightly encircled her.

"Ahem!" Enya cleared her throat loudly, frowning at them.

Travis's arms dropped and he stepped back, though Evelyn kept a hold on his arm as they headed into the living room with the others.

"Hey, everyone," he greeted, giving a wave. "It's good to see y'all again."

"Hmph. Well, if only we could say the same about-"

"Let me take your coat, Travis," Evelyn spoke up loudly, shooting a pointed look at Enya. "We'll put it in my room."

"*Or* you could just hang it in the closet right there where we hung ours," Emberly suggested with an arched brow.

Her face tightening, Evelyn waved the comment off. "No more room in there. Come on, Travis. You can come with me."

Before Travis could respond, Evelyn grabbed his hand and dragged him behind her as she headed upstairs. Her siblings looked after them warily.

"I bet his coat won't be the only thing that ends up on her bed," Enya muttered, shaking her head. "She's gonna try to jump his bones, watch what I tell you. Bet y'all ten bucks."

"Please, I'm not trying to lose any money like that," Emberly retorted. "I was gonna bet y'all twenty on the same thing."

"Hopefully she wouldn't do that with us down here," Noah suggested. "If she does, though, I'm out."

"You can't leave! We haven't started the spades tournament yet."

"I do not wanna hear my little sister getting busy, tradition or no tradition. Y'all will just have to be mad at me."

"I'll bum-rush them before that happens. And, anyway, you know you're not gonna miss out on the MLK pie."

"What kind is it this year? And please don't say apple."

"I talked her out of it," Enya spoke up. "Though I practically had to pay her."

Emberly rolled her eyes. "Hush, Enya. Apple desserts are my specialty but it's not like I don't know how to do anything else. I made a rhubarb meringue, a spiced pear, blueberry, and almond shortcake pie, and a roasted strawberry and cream."

"Dibs," Noah called out immediately. Emberly chuckled.

"Well, we can get started on everything once Evelyn and Travis get back down here," Enya commented, just as her phone chimed again. A lovesick smile took over her face as she typed in a reply message. Emberly started to comment, but stopped herself. Clearly Enya wasn't going to tell them anything about her new boo-of-the-moment until she was good and ready.

Plus she figured that whoever it was wouldn't be around long anyway, knowing Enya's short attention span when it came to men. The thought made her relax a little.

Glancing at his watch, Noah moved over to the bottom of the stairs, seeing Evelyn's bedroom door was closed. He shook his head. "Y'all might be right about her making a move. Not sure why they need to be in there with the door closed just to drop his coat off."

"Oh hell no," Enya muttered, stopping mid-type and stomping over next to Noah. "Evelyn!" she yelled up the stairs. "Will y'all get your asses down here? We're waiting on you!"

"Start without us!" Evelyn yelled back from behind her closed door.

Despite that, though, the door quickly opened and Travis hurried out, almost as if he was escaping. Actually looking relieved, he trotted down the stairs. "Sorry to keep everybody waiting. Y'all are getting ready to play spades, right?"

"Yeah. And we can't start without Evelyn." Enya crossed her arms and looked at Travis suspiciously. "And just what were y'all doing in there with the door closed?"

"None of your business, Enya!" Evelyn exclaimed, emerging from the room at that moment. She trudged down the stairs, clearly not as eager to rejoin the party as Travis was. "Y'all didn't have to be down here worrying about what we were doing, anyway. You could've done something else."

"It's spades, then pie. You know this. Don't be trying to change up the program just because you invited a...*guest*."

"Whatever."

"Is Aunt Miriam coming?" Emberly asked, going to the drawer of the end table where Evelyn always kept the playing cards and the notepad.

"She said she might. But I wouldn't be surprised if she flakes on us again. You know how her and Tariq like to get all *preoccupied*." Noah shook his head.

"Just curious; y'all don't call him Uncle?" Travis asked.

"He and I are practically the same age. So...no."

"Plus, after catching him and Aunt Miriam in one too many compromising positions, calling him Uncle would make it more weird than it already is around him," Evelyn added. "I had to give her their emergency house key back. Got tired of catching them in the act."

"That's because they're damn near always *in* the act," Enya chuckled. "Even with an aisle's worth of vitamins, I could only pray for that kind of stamina. I'll Facetime her, see if she's on her way."

"Hand me the cards, Emberly," Noah requested with his hand out. "We can be on teams again."

As he shuffled the cards, Enya held her phone up as her video call to their aunt connected. Thankfully, she was fully clothed. Evelyn breathed a very loud sigh of relief.

"What's up, my beautiful family?" Miriam asked, grinning briefly before her face relaxed and she bit her lip.

"Hey Auntie," Enya greeted. "We just wanted to see if you and Tariq were coming over. We're at Evelyn's for MLK night."

"Yeah...I'm not sure we're gonna make that." Miriam shifted in her seat, trying to keep her face even. "We kinda lost track of time over here."

"Well, you still have time to get here. We haven't even kicked things off yet," Emberly informed. "We can wait for you."

"Oh, no...I wouldn't want y'all to be delayed because of us." Her mouth opened slightly and her eyes fluttered closed, a tiny moan escaping. She quickly tried to clear her expression. "Just, um...I'll catch y'all on Valentine's Day. Or...Tuesday."

"Auntie..." Enya began with narrowed eyes and a mischievous smile, "What are you doing?"

"Hmm? What you mean?"

"Where's Tariq?"

Miriam's eyes dropped down around her waist area below the camera, and Enya cackled gleefully. Evelyn and Noah groaned and quickly turned away, and Emberly just shook her head, though she was smiling. Travis's light brown skin was actually flushed as he tried to act like he wasn't paying attention.

"You should really write a book," Enya teased, still grinning.

"Hang up," Tariq's voice grunted from off camera.

"Gotta go, my babies. Have fun!" Miriam ended the call before any of them could respond.

"I swear she's my role model," Enya marveled.

"I'm not gonna be able to un-see that," Evelyn muttered. "I can't believe my auntie gets more action than me."

"She's married, Evelyn."

"Yeah, well..." Evelyn shot a pointed glare at Travis, who looked away uncomfortably. "That doesn't always have to be the case."

Grunting, Noah gave a final shuffle to the cards and tapped the deck hard against the coffee table. "We playing or what?"

"Yeah; Evelyn and Enya, y'all are on teams. As usual," Emberly muttered, sitting on the loveseat across the coffee table from her brother. "I've got Noah."

"Great," Evelyn smiled. She looked over at Travis. "Come on, you can sit with me."

Surprised, Travis remained where he stood. "That's all right. And there doesn't seem to be much room over there, anyway. I can just stay over here in the cut."

"Nonsense. Just sit on the couch and I'll sit on your lap."

Everyone looked at her, but she pretended not to notice. "Come on, Travis."

Even though he clearly wasn't thrilled about it, Travis hesitantly moved over and eased onto the loveseat next to Emberly, stiffening when Evelyn happily dropped onto his lap. One of his hands stayed plastered to the arm of the couch while the other jammed underneath his thigh. Noah and Enya just shook their heads as Noah began dealing the cards.

The game kicked off, with the siblings engaging in their usual banter and trash talk. Every now and then Evelyn would snuggle up against Travis or caress his face or touch him with a kind of affection that clearly made him even more uncomfortable than he already was. She was acting like they were a couple again, even calling him pet names like she used to do when they were married. Her siblings looked at her like she was nuts.

After a couple of games, Travis couldn't take any more. He bolted up from the couch, practically knocking Evelyn to the floor. "We need to talk. Can we go in the kitchen?"

Adjusting her glasses, Evelyn tried to look unaffected. She smoothed down her skirt anxiously. "Uh, right now?"

"Yes. Right now."

He stalked off without waiting for her agreement. Barely glancing at her gawking siblings, Evelyn finally trailed behind him.

Travis did not look pleased when she finally joined him in the kitchen, his face pinched in a frown and his arms tightly folded.

"Is something wrong?" Evelyn innocently asked.

"You know it is."

"What?"

"What do you mean, what? Why did you invite me over here?"

"I..." She hunched her shoulders. "I thought it would be fun. Why, you're not enjoying yourself?"

"No, I'm not. Maybe I would if you weren't acting like we're some kind of couple. We're *divorced*, Evelyn. And I'm dating someone. Did you forget about all that?"

Her face tightened. "You don't have to say it like that, like you're rubbing it in my face. It's not like I straddled you out there."

"No, but you *did* kiss me when we were up in your bedroom."

"*And* you kissed me back. Now, what?"

Travis's frown faltered, and he ran a hand down his face. "That was a weak moment, I admit it..."

"And you didn't seem to mind the hand job I was giving you, either. You weren't worried about who you were dating *then*."

"Evelyn-"

"So I don't see why you wanna come down on me for being affectionate in front of people when you were all for it in private. Are you trying to play me or something?"

He sighed wearily, giving her a look. "You know I wouldn't do that to you."

"Then what *are* you doing, Travis? Why are you sending all these mixed signals?"

"I'm not trying to do that either, Evelyn. I've never stopped caring about you and would never intentionally...okay, I admit, I still have some feelings for you. And clearly, I still find you attractive. But that doesn't change the fact that I still think we're better off as friends."

"How can you say that? We obviously still have chemistry, not to mention all the history between us. And

I'm standing right here, willing to give you my heart again. How is that not good enough for you?"

"Evelyn, don't do this to me...I'll always love you but it's like I've told you before, our relationship ran its course and I needed to move on."

"Just call it what it is. You wanted to sleep with other women."

"Okay, I'm not gonna lie; that's part of it. We'd been together since we were teenagers, Evelyn; we hadn't experienced anyone else. And over time you got so consumed with me and us that I started to feel smothered. You would barely even hang with your sisters because you always wanted to be up under me. I couldn't take that anymore."

Evelyn shrank slightly at his words. That was the part he never told her. She'd been thinking it was all about him wanting to sow his wild oats when in reality, she had driven him away. The realization made her skin burn.

"You never told me that," she practically whispered.

He looked at her, his expression remorseful. "I didn't want to hurt you."

"I've been hurt ever since you asked me for a divorce."

Sighing, he placed a hand to his chest. "I don't love hearing that."

"So? What are we gonna do about it?"

A few quiet moments passed as they faced off, looking at each other. Evelyn wanted him to take her into his arms and tell her that he wanted nothing more than to ease her hurt, and would be willing to give them another chance. She was more than ready to make compromises if that meant getting the love of her life back.

Travis finally spoke. "I think it's best if we don't see each other for a while."

Her eyes widened. "What?"

"Clearly, we still need some distance. I need to get past any lingering attraction for you and you need to learn to move on from me. It's the only way we'll be able to heal, Evelyn. Not to mention, it's not fair to my lady friend-"

"I don't care about her!" Evelyn practically yelled, throwing her arms up. "What about what's fair to *me*? You promised to love me forever but as soon as times got a little hard and you got frustrated, you bailed. Yet you claim to care about me *so* much. You're gonna stand here in my face in my house talking about some other woman when you *know* I want you back. I don't give a *damn* about that lady friend, Travis!"

"Evelyn!" He held up his hands, taking a couple of steps back. "Look, I can't keep doing this with you. Like I said, we need some time apart. I've told you how I felt and I'm sorry if it's not what you want to hear, but I have to do what I think is best for me right now." His hands fell to his sides. "So I'm gonna go."

Evelyn opened her mouth to ask him to stay, but she stopped herself. Despite the ache in her chest at what he was telling her, she wasn't about to beg. She had to have some pride about herself.

"Fine," she managed to say, hating how her voice broke. She turned her face away from him. "Go."

Travis just looked at her for another few moments before finally easing out of the kitchen. She heard him say good night to her siblings before the sound of the front door closing made her squeeze her eyes shut, fighting back tears.

In the next few moments, her sisters hurried into the kitchen, with Noah right behind them.

"What happened?" Enya asked, concerned.

Evelyn held up a tired hand. "I don't wanna talk about it right now. But clearly it didn't go well, seeing as how he left."

"Are you okay?"

"No. Is it time for pie?"

"You don't wanna finish the game?" Emberly asked.

"I'd much rather stuff my face."

"Say no more."

Emberly retrieved the pies from the refrigerator and began cutting into them, dishing large pieces of each out onto the plates Noah pulled from the cabinet. Evelyn snatched the plate with the huge slice of roasted strawberry and cream pie that was intended for Noah and immediately began digging into it, ignoring the dirty look her brother was giving her.

Enya's phone was still chiming away as they all sat around the kitchen table enjoying their desserts, and while she'd usually ignore it, opting to check the messages when she was alone, now she was eagerly grabbing her phone every time it went off, blushing and grinning like a schoolgirl. Evelyn was too in her feelings to worry about it, but Emberly and Noah looked at Enya curiously.

"Whoever that is sure has you sprung," Emberly commented.

Enya tried to erase her smile, but it didn't quite work. "It's just a crush."

"Seems like more than that. I've never seen you this giddy over anybody else."

Only shrugging, Enya just stuffed a forkful of pie into her mouth, keeping her eyes on her plate.

They continued to sit around eating and talking, reminiscing as they usually did about how this particular tradition got started so many years ago. Their parents didn't just let them goof off on MLK day; they'd usually go volunteer somewhere, and then go back home, watch the iconic I Have a Dream speech, then play cards and eat their mother's homemade pie. The volunteering portion didn't happen every year like it used to, but they always at least got together for the cards and the pie.

"Well, y'all, I have to go," Enya announced, shooting up from the table. "I enjoyed it, as always."

"Where are you going?" Noah asked.

"Got a date."

"With the mystery man, no doubt," Emberly smirked, taking her plate to the sink. "I still don't get why you're being so cagey about it. It's not like we'll know who it is, most likely."

Enya grabbed her glass and drained the rest of her white grape juice. "Once I know this is something real, I'll tell y'all everything. Until then, bye."

They threw their hands up in acknowledgement as she hurried out of the kitchen. Evelyn, having finally snapped out of her funk, sighed as she stood up.

"Just leave the dishes in the sink, y'all," she told them. "I'll deal with them tomorrow."

"You sure?" Noah asked.

"Yep."

"You want us to leave?" Emberly asked her.

"No, you can hang out, if you want. I could use the distraction. Just please don't ask me what happened with Travis."

"Cool, though to be honest, E2, we wouldn't have to ask too much," Noah admitted. "Y'all weren't exactly being discreet."

Evelyn's head snapped to them, looking back and forth. "You heard us?"

"Some of it."

"Great."

"Don't worry about it, though, sis," Emberly said as they trekked back into the living room. "You know we're the last people to judge. Though – and I know you don't want to hear this – I do think Travis had a point about you two needing some distance. You're way too consumed with him and it's not healthy."

"I just miss him, that's all," Evelyn protested, running her bare foot along the edge of the coffee table. "Everyone is acting like I'm obsessed or something."

"Hopefully when you come down off this emotion and are thinking clearly, you'll see what we mean," Noah stated. "Maybe you should consider going to therapy."

Evelyn balked. "Therapy??"

"Don't sound so incredulous. There's nothing wrong with it."

"I don't need therapy just because I want my ex-husband back. Don't try to make it seem like I'm crazy."

"Not what I said."

Just then, Emberly's phone chimed with a text. When she checked to see who it was from, her eyebrows shot up in surprise and intrigue.

"Don't tell me that's Dallas," Noah grunted, eying her.

"Hmph. No, it's Amari, that guy I dated a couple of years ago."

"What does he want?"

"Don't know yet. All it says is 'what's up?'" Emberly hesitantly put the phone back on the arm of the couch beside her. "I'll get at him later."

Which she did. As soon as she was back home a little over an hour later, she called Amari to see what it was he wanted, not even offended to find out it was basically a booty call. In most instances she might have been, but given the current slow state of her love live, she was willing to take the action, ideal or not.

Amari showed up at her door around midnight, looking finer than Emberly remembered. For the life of her, she couldn't remember why they broke up. At the moment, though, she didn't care.

"What's up, baby?" he greeted, eying her hungrily. "Since when do you answer the door naked? Not that I'm complaining."

"Hey, I'm covered," Emberly countered, biting her lip.

"Yeah, the locs over the chest is a nice touch. It's wild how long they've gotten."

"You gonna stand there ogling my hair or are you gonna come in?"

"Oh, I'm coming," Amari assured, stepping inside and yanking her to him. He brushed her locs aside and lightly tweaked her nipple, smirking when she sucked in a breath. "And you're about to be, too."

Chapter 6

"DID Y'ALL HEAR ABOUT Magnolia? Word is she snapped."

Evelyn's ears perked up at her coworker's comment but she didn't respond. She just sprinkled more hot sauce into her cup of ramen.

"Yeah, she went crazy over that man she was seeing," another coworker replied. "Homegirl was blowing up his phone, stalking his social media, sending threatening messages to any woman that even seemed like they were flirting with him on there. Then she started going by his house..."

"Oh yeah, I heard she actually broke in while he was out on a date and was waiting in the closet when they got back there," coworker 1 replied. "Was in there listening to them have sex. She was nuts."

"She even went so far as to try to get his dad to *make* him get back with her." Coworker 2 shook her head as she sat back in her seat. "I don't care; I've never met a man that made me want to do all that. And lord knows I loved my ex but when it was over, I just cried and gorged on pizza and ice cream like a normal person, then tried to move on with my life. I didn't *stalk* him."

"Yeah, like acting that crazy is ever gonna make them wanna take you back, anyway. Some people are so backwards."

"I get being in love. But getting that consumed with any one person just isn't healthy."

Evelyn's eating had slowed to a halt. Her face felt warm, and she knew it wasn't from her hot sauced noodles. Her coworkers might as well have been talking about her, and the realization was actually embarrassing.

She might not have gone so far as to break into Travis's house or harass the women he dated, but Evelyn was fully aware of her inability to accept their divorce and move on from him. It had been months, but she just hadn't wanted to believe it was really over. Her sisters and brother tried to tell her, her aunt tried to tell her, friends tried to tell her, and of course Travis...she hadn't listened to any of them. She thought she was being steadfast but she realized she probably just looked silly and delusional. Which was a word they used to describe her more than once.

When she thought about how she'd been all over him on MLK night, she actually winced. She knew full well he was dating someone, and she still made a move on him in her bedroom and was kissing and touching all over him downstairs in front of her siblings, cooing over him like a horny newlywed. No wonder he said they needed some time apart.

Once Evelyn left work, she called Enya to see if she was home yet. Enya was just leaving the office and said Evelyn could meet her at her place, and Evelyn offered to pick up dinner, eager to have some girl talk with her sister.

"Damn, who else is coming over here?" Enya joked as Evelyn unpacked several containers full of fried fish and sides. "They had a sale or something?"

"I might've gone a little overboard," Evelyn admitted, looking at all the food. "I've been a little preoccupied most of the day."

"What's going on?"

"Well..." Evelyn sighed as she began filling her plate. "I've realized how crazy I've been acting over Travis. I'm gonna leave him alone finally, for good."

Clearly surprised, Enya paused her action of reaching for some tartar sauce. "And what brought this on?"

"Listening to my coworkers talk about someone they knew that went all nuts over her ex, and it was like the light came on. I hadn't even realized how crazy I was acting over Travis until I heard that. I know y'all tried to tell me..."

"Yeah, we did, but sometimes it takes something or someone outside of your loved ones to make you see that light. It doesn't matter, though; I'm just glad you're finally ready to move on. Travis was cool but he's not the only man in the world."

"Yeah."

"You block him on social media yet? And his number?"

The thought didn't sit well with Evelyn, despite her decision. Cutting herself off from Travis like that still felt so extreme, even if she could see the necessity in it. "Not yet. I haven't done much of anything but make the decision to leave him alone."

"I know it's not easy for you, but it's best to just go ahead and do it. Who knows how you'll feel tomorrow; you might change your mind about all this and decide you want him back again."

"I don't think I'll do that. But I see your point."

"I won't push you on it, yet. I'm just glad you're finally making some progress towards moving on from him. In the spirit of that, my offer to hook you up with someone still stands."

Evelyn immediately shook her head, her mouth full of hush puppies. "No, thanks."

"Come on, why not??"

"I'm just not ready for that yet. It took a lot for me to even get to this point; I'm not in the frame of mind to start anything with somebody brand new."

"Don't you think meeting someone else will only help you get over Travis faster?"

"It could. Maybe. But still. I wouldn't even know how to act around anybody else."

"Because all you know is Travis. Which is another reason why you need to start dating. Get used to some fresh meat."

"I...I'll think about it. That's all I can promise right now."

Enya wanted to protest some more, but chose to leave it at that. She forked a piece of fried whiting and plunked it in tartar sauce with a shrug. "Fine."

"So what's been going on with you and this new guy you're seeing?"

An automatic smile came to Enya's face. "Things are really good."

"When are you gonna tell us who it is?"

"I...soon. Maybe. I'm still waiting for the right time."

"What do you mean, right time? What's the big deal? He's not married, is he?"

"Hell no, it's not that. It's just..." Enya gazed at her sister thoughtfully before putting down her fork and turning to face her. Sensing this was something heavy, Evelyn did the same, giving her full attention.

"I *really* like this guy; more than I've liked anyone ever, probably," Enya hedged, anxiously rubbing her hands up and down her thighs. "But there might be a problem."

"What kind of problem?"

"It's Dallas."

Evelyn frowned, knowing she'd heard that name recently but unsure as to where. Then it clicked and her eyes widened. "Emberly's Dallas? The one that ghosted her?"

"Yeah," Enya muttered.

"Wait, are *you* the reason he-"

"No! He and I met totally by chance, and I didn't even realize he was the same Dallas at first. It wasn't until we were exchanging New Year's Eve stories and he told me he was supposed to meet up with a woman but changed his mind that I started to wonder. Then when he said she was a pastry chef with super-long locs and three siblings, I knew he was talking about Emberly."

"And what did you say when you realized that? Did you tell him you're her sister?"

"Not at first. I backed up off of him for a couple of days, because I didn't want to get involved with someone who would do that, especially to my own sister. But he kept calling and we eventually talked, and when he explained himself and his reasons, it made sense. And then I told him who Emberly was to me."

"Then what?"

"He said he could understand if I wouldn't want to see him anymore, but that he felt a connection with me that he hadn't felt with anyone. I realized I felt the same way. Ev, he's *all* I've been able to think about since we met. I feel guilty but I also...I just don't wanna let him go."

Evelyn blew out a breath, sitting back in her seat. "Wow, Enya."

"I know, I'm terrible." Enya ran her hands down her face. "I'm not proud of it 'cause I know Emberly is gonna feel some kind of way once she finds out."

"Well, yeah..."

"But I can really see myself falling for this guy, Ev. Hell, if I'm honest, I'm already starting to fall for him. Am I supposed to just forget about that? It's jacked up, but it's not like he and Emberly were ever a couple. They weren't in love. They never even went out."

"Because he kept standing her up, Enya. Come on, you know this isn't right."

Enya slumped in her seat.

"I cannot believe that you randomly met the same man that ghosted your sister," Evelyn mused. "*Then* you went and fell for him. That's crazy. I mean, seriously, what are the odds? I'd seriously like to know that. I bet Noah would be able to figure out the probability of-"

"Evelyn."

"Oh, right. My bad. Look, I get that you have feelings for him," Evelyn continued, sitting forward and placing a hand on her glum sister's knee. "And in any other circumstance, I'd be over the moon for you. But this can only get messy. How do you think Emberly is gonna react when she finds out about this? If you're feeling him like you say you are, you're gonna have to tell her eventually. You're not gonna be able to keep him under wraps forever."

"I know. And yeah, I'm not thrilled at the idea of my sister getting hurt or pissed at me. But I just don't wanna give Dallas up. And I really think that over time, Emberly will come to understand. Especially since this isn't just some fling for me."

"I doubt it'll matter."

"Well, I'm just gonna have to risk it. I know it hasn't been that long, but Dallas is already feeling like one of the best things to ever happen to me, and I'm not ready to walk away from that simply because he met my sister first."

"So you're gonna keep seeing him."

"Yeah." Enya's large gold hoops twisted as she nodded. "I'm gonna keep seeing him."

"Okay," Evelyn sighed. "I hope he's worth it."

"I'm think he is. In the meantime, though, I need you to keep this to yourself. Please don't say anything to Emberly about this. Noah, either. I need to figure out how I'm gonna reveal all this on my own."

Evelyn didn't enjoy keeping secrets, but she reluctantly agreed. She knew, though, that it wasn't going to be pretty when all of this came to light.

MEANWHILE, EMBERLY was meeting with Gideon, the new renter of their parents' house. They'd already done the walk-throughs, the background and credit checks, signed all the agreements. Her siblings were aware of him and all of his information, and had no problem with him moving in. Emberly was just meeting with him to give him the keys.

"I'm so glad all of this is done," Gideon commented, holding the keys in his strong hand with a smile. "Moving is enough of a headache and the last place I was supposed to rent fell through at the last minute. This is one less thing to worry about now."

"I can imagine. We're glad to have you."

Emberly tried not to show just how glad she was. Gideon was hot. His dark skin, shoulder-length locs and tight muscles had drawn her eye from their first meeting, and she might have advocated to her siblings on his behalf a little harder because of it.

"I'm gonna start moving in tomorrow," Gideon commented. "Once I get settled, you should come over for a drink or dinner or something. Nothing special; just as a kind of celebratory, thank you kind of thing."

"Oh...yeah, that sounds nice." Emberly smiled at him, glad to have an excuse to be around him some more.

"You know, we have something in common."

"We do? What?"

"I remember you commenting that you and your sisters are triplets. I have a twin brother."

"Yeah? That's awesome. Does he live around here, too?"

"He doesn't but he will soon, from what he says. Unless he changes his mind. I never know with him sometimes; I love him but we're not as close as people think we would be."

"Yeah, I know what you mean. I absolutely love my sisters but I usually feel like I'm on the outside looking in with them. They've always been like best friends while I'm just...there."

"Wow. I get it, though. Well, hopefully *we* can become friends, then. Since we feel each other's pain and all." Gideon smiled at her, and she eyed him, biting her lip. "If, you know, you're cool with that."

"I'm totally cool with that."

"Glad to hear it. Would you want to maybe go to a movie or something tomorrow night? I haven't been out and about since I moved here and I have a feeling you'd be cool to hang with. You see I'm in no hurry to go on about my business even though all I was supposed to be doing was getting my keys from you."

Emberly grinned. She liked hearing that he was enjoying her company, because she was surely enjoying his. The little voice in her head reminded her that she and her siblings had agreed back when they decided to rent their parents' house out that they wouldn't date any of the renters, but she muted that. This wasn't a date. It was just hanging out. Nothing wrong with that.

"I'd love that," she replied, earning a wider smile from him.

"Great."

They made plans for the next night, and Emberly was already looking forward to it. After that whole mess with Dallas, it felt nice to be pursued, even if it wasn't a *date*-date. Gideon could be a fine prospect for her; it was a good idea to have more than one iron in the fire, she figured. Amari, her ex, wasn't totally back in the picture. They'd shared a passionate night together but had barely spoken since. Emberly needed something more absolute.

The next day at work, her excitement about Gideon hadn't waned. She was actually humming to herself as she glazed a batch of maple apple doughnuts, the smile playing on her lips as it had been all day.

"Somebody's in a good mood," her assistant Camilla commented, smiling, as she lugged a huge bag of flour in from the store room. "You've been walking on air all morning."

"Meeting a hot guy will have you like that," Emberly commented with a wink.

"Nice! Well, good for you. Where'd you meet him?"

Emberly didn't want to admit he was her renter. "Just around town. He just moved here."

"And you're crushing on him, huh?"

"A little bit. I'm supposed to see him tonight. Can't deny that I'm looking forward to it."

"I hope it goes well; it's good to see you so happy." Camilla thoughtfully wiped out the bowl she was getting ready to mix some cake batter in.

Emberly glanced at her. "You all right?"

"Yeah. It's just...well, between you and me, I'm kinda crushing on someone, too. He doesn't know it, though."

Emberly grinned. "That's wonderful! What's the problem? Why haven't you made a move yet?"

"I admit I've never been good at that; making the first move. And also, he's a little out of my league. In my head, anyway. I don't want to make a fool of myself."

"Girl," Emberly shook her head. "Sometimes you just have to go for it. You never know what could happen. You're a sweetheart, super pretty, gainfully employed, and handling your business. There shouldn't be *any* man that's considered out of your league. Go for yours."

Blushing at the assessment of her, Camilla stood up a little straighter. "Maybe I will. Thanks for that, Emberly."

"Of course!"

Later that night, Emberly met up with Gideon. They went to a movie, then for pizza, and then headed to the arcade, playing games for a couple of hours. They joined forces on some and were opponents on others, but the laughter and good time was constant. Emberly couldn't remember when she'd had more fun, or laughed harder. Gideon had actually chased her around the game room when she playfully swatted his behind after beating him at air hockey, snaking between the games and dodging people. They might have drawn some strange looks, but neither of them cared.

Emberly was already looking at Gideon as a buddy. A hot, hunky buddy, but still. There was some flirting, but it was mild, and she figured her mostly-platonic assessment was mutual. They had the kind of easy, effortless rapport that she'd never had with a man, and while she loved it, it wasn't exactly the result she wanted to be left with at the end of their night together. Another friend wasn't what she was looking for.

Nevertheless, she still asked him if he wanted to come back to her place after they closed down the arcade, being among the last to leave. Gideon readily agreed, and followed her there in his car.

"You have a nice place," he commented once they were inside her loft. "That's one huge kitchen, too."

"I get plenty of use out of it. I love it here. Do you cook?"

"Oh, I can get down. My mama made sure we knew how to cook. I appreciate it now but I used to hate when she'd drag us into the kitchen with her damn near every night."

Emberly chuckled. "Good for her. When I have kids, I'm definitely gonna be teaching them, too. I never asked if you have any crumbsnatchers."

"Nah, not yet. One day, though."

"Nice. You want something to drink?"

"I'm okay right now, thanks."

Gideon moved towards the couch but didn't sit; he just eyed Emberly as she dropped her purse into a chair and removed her jacket, licking his lips as he admired the way her breasts and butt and thighs filled out her jeans and fitted tee. She moved over to join him and as soon as she was within arm's reach, he yanked her close and pressed his lips against hers. The kiss was brief and she clearly hadn't been expecting it, looking up at him with surprised eyes.

"Too far too soon?" he asked her, his hand still clamped on her arm.

Instead of answering, Emberly grabbed the back of his head and pulled him down to resume the kiss, their intensity going from zero to sixty. She reached for his shirt and lifted it, and he stepped back so he could finish pulling it over his head, tossing it aside. Emberly's arousal roared at the sight of his strong chest, a huge tattoo covering the entire right side.

She couldn't get her own shirt off fast enough, and Gideon couldn't help roaming his hands over every newly-exposed area of her body.

"You are too damn sexy, baby," he muttered, diving for her neck as she tried to kick her pants off. "I've wanted you ever since I first saw you yesterday."

"Same," Emberly panted, desire flooding her body. "Absolute same."

They lunged for each other once they were both naked, Emberly jumping into his arms before they fell onto the couch. She swung her locs to the side as she tongued him down, grabbing the side of his face as she grinded on him. Gideon's hands gripped her behind as she did, matching all the energy she was giving him.

He rolled her over, sandwiching her between him and the back of the couch, and pulled her leg over his hip. Their intense, sloppy kisses continued as she reached between them and grabbed his manhood, loving how long and thick it was. They both moaned loudly when she began easing it inside her, their mouths falling open in pleasure.

Gideon gripped the top of the couch as he moved inside of her, lifting her leg even higher so he could get deeper. Emberly clung to him, loving how he covered her and pleading with him not to stop. Her couch had never seen so much action as they periodically switched positions on it, their sexual banter coming as easily as their playful, Emberly urging him to go harder and harder. He felt amazing inside of her and she didn't want him to stop.

Eventually, they ended up in her bedroom, where they went another round before laying spent in each other's arms.

Gideon made no move to leave, and Emberly wasn't even thinking about asking him to. She wanted him to stay so they could keep pleasuring each other into a coma.

*He might just work out after all*, she mused as Gideon held her from behind, snoring lightly. She smiled at the sound, proud that she'd tuckered him out. *I could certainly get used to this on a regular basis. He's definitely potential husband material.*

The more she thought about it, the wider her smile got. She felt she was finally making some progress.

Turning in his arms, she snuggled closer to him, rubbing her leg against his and already anticipating how she was going to wake him up.

Chapter 7

"BABE, YOU ALL RIGHT? You've been kinda quiet all night."

Enya looked over at Dallas and sighed. They were in his kitchen as he made her dinner, another first for her. They spent most of their time together at his place, since she was too paranoid to take him to hers. He'd only been there once, and she was worried one of her siblings would pop over unannounced the whole time.

"I've got some things on my mind," she admitted, setting her glass of wine on the counter.

"What's wrong?"

She leaned against the counter and crossed her arms, eying her bare feet against his slate tile floor. It was crazy how comfortable she already felt in his home. He'd already cleared out a drawer for her and everything. "I've been thinking about how all of this is going to go once Emberly finds out about us."

Putting down the spoon he was using to stir the mushroom gravy, he turned off the burner before stepping over to her, rubbing his hands up and down her arms.

"I wish you wouldn't stress so much. It's gonna be all right."

"You think so? You don't think she's gonna be upset to find out I'm dating someone that ghosted her? Twice?"

He sighed. "I acknowledge that I could've handled that situation better. It's not like I'm proud of treating her like that."

"So why did you?"

"I told you, babe; I just couldn't bring myself to tell her I'd changed my mind again. Emberly is cool but I just didn't think we were compatible romantically. That day she came to my office, as soon as I agreed to meet up with her again, it wasn't long at all before I was wondering how I could get out of it. I figured that had to mean something."

"I get it, Dallas, but you still should've just told her that."

"I know. I should've." He frowned slightly and tipped her chin up to where she was looking at him. "You're not thinking about ending this, are you?"

She looked into his eyes that always sent the butterflies into overdrive. "I don't *want* to...but that's my *sister*, baby. This just doesn't feel right, us sneaking around behind her back like this."

"We're not really doing that, though. She and I aren't a couple and never were."

"You know what I mean. She liked you. And you let her think that was mutual and then dogged her. And she doesn't know we're seeing each other."

"Well, let's tell her. Go ahead and get it out in the open."

"That's easy for you to say. You're not the one she's gonna hate forever."

"Babe, come on." He pulled her close and she went willingly, melting against him. He wrapped her in his arms. "I want to do whatever we need to so we can get past this and just focus on us. Yes, I'm sorry about how I did Emberly, and I need to tell her that. But I also don't want to lose you. She and I...wouldn't have worked. But me and you...this is something real. And I *know* you feel it, too."

"Yeah," she admitted, unable to keep the small smile from tugging at her lips. "I do feel it."

"Okay, then." He smoothed her short hair before leaning down and touching his lips to hers. She whimpered as she returned the kiss, her hand easing up to grip the front of his shirt. When the kiss ended, he rested his forehead against hers. "Please don't use this as an excuse to throw us away. I want this with you, Enya."

Enya wanted it, too. More and more each day. She'd lost count of the times she'd zoned out at work, fantasizing about Dallas, even doodling his name on random scraps of paper. Her body actually tingled when she knew she was going to see him, and time stopped when they were on the phone together. She'd never experienced that with any man and didn't want to give it up.

But at the same time, she still felt weird about the fact that Dallas was someone Emberly had wanted for herself. True enough, they'd never been a couple, but still. Enya knew she was breaking all kinds of sister codes by seeing Dallas, but every time she thought about ending it with him, it actually brought tears to her eyes.

Her mind was still on the fence but her heart knew she wouldn't be able to do it.

They went on about their evening, and Enya managed to temporarily put her troubled thoughts behind her as they enjoyed the dinner he prepared for them. They talked, they laughed, they held hands, they tangled their legs together under the table as they shared multiple kisses. Enya had never felt more in tune and in sync with anyone, and by the time they were washing dishes together, she felt a lot more at ease.

"You want to go get some dessert?" Dallas asked her once they were done. "I had some gelato but I ate the rest of that last night when we were binge-watching our show over the phone, and I'm admittedly not as good at making dessert as I am savory stuff."

"Yeah, we can do that. I wouldn't mind some doughnuts and there's a place about fifteen minutes from here that should still be open."

Of course thinking about doughnuts reminded Enya of Emberly, but she made herself snap out of it. She wasn't trying to get bummed again.

"Then doughnuts it is. Let's go."

They each put their shoes on and headed out. Enya couldn't deny how happy she felt as she perused the doughnut selections with Dallas's hand gripping her hip. Especially when she saw the appreciative glances the cashier kept sneaking at him.

*Yeah, you can look all you want but he's mine*, Enya thought smugly.

They stepped outside hand-in-hand a little later with their treats, chatting about what movie they were going to watch when they got back to his place as they gorged on their doughnuts. Then Enya looked down the street and gasped, stopping in her tracks. She felt like her heart had stopped.

"What's wrong?" Dallas asked, concerned.

"It's my brother," she muttered, seriously considering making a run for it. But she told herself to calm down. Noah didn't know who Dallas was; he'd only heard the name. And anyway, he'd already spotted her.

"It's gonna be all right, babe," Dallas assured her in a low voice as Noah approached. "No need to panic."

"Just please let me do the talking, okay?"

Dallas eyed her but agreed with a nod.

Telling herself to stay cool, Enya forced a smile as Noah approached with one of his own.

"What's up, E3?" He leaned down and gave her a strong hug.

"Hey, Noah. What are you doing over this way?"

"Had a meeting. I guess I don't have to ask *you* that," he teased good-naturedly, eyeing Dallas. He held out a hand. "What's up, man? I'm Noah, Enya's big brother."

"Hey, nice to meet you," Dallas replied, feeling Enya's eyes on him. "I've heard a lot about you."

"Yeah?"

"This is my friend, Rico," Enya jumped in, introducing Dallas by his middle name. "I wish we could hang for a minute but we have somewhere to be. I'll talk to you later, all right?"

"Okay," Noah replied easily. "Y'all be safe. Love you."

"Love you, too."

Enya scurried away, pulling Dallas by the arm and releasing a shaky breath. She knew she'd dodged a bullet because that could've easily been Emberly instead of Noah. She knew she was going to have to come clean with her sister.

EVELYN WAS NO PAINTER, and it showed.

"It looks like a kindergartner did this," she muttered, looking at her canvas. It was supposed to be an elephant but looked more like a gray box with a hose at the end. "I so suck at this."

"Doesn't matter," Noah replied, his eyes on his own painting. Evelyn marveled at the landscape portrait he was creating. He made it look so easy. She still couldn't believe he'd never had any lessons at all. "It isn't about being good; it's just for stress relief."

"Not sure how that's gonna work when I'm standing next to you over here painting like Van Gough while mine looks like I painted it with my feet."

"Stop comparing. It isn't a competition, E2."

"Hmph."

"Do you not feel more relaxed?" Noah looked over at her, pausing his brush strokes. "This is supposed to help take your mind off of everything that's bugging you. Nobody's gonna see it but you."

"That's for damn sure."

They continued their painting with faint jazz playing in the background. Evelyn had taken Noah up on his invitation to come over and join him in this activity because she was eager for anything to help get her mind off of Travis, even if just temporarily. She might have decided to move on from him, but that didn't mean it was easy. She still thought about him more than she wanted to, and missed him something terrible. More than a few times, she was tempted to peek at his social media pages or find some excuse to send him a harmless text, but she managed to refrain. She didn't want to keep being the desperate ex. It was time to move on, even though it was one of the hardest things she'd had to do.

"Enya set me up with someone," she finally revealed as she attempted to paint an apple next to her excuse for an elephant. "It did not go well."

Noah looked over at her. "What do you mean? What happened?"

"I mean, it's nothing he did...he seemed nice enough. I'm just not ready for dating yet."

"That's understandable. I'm surprised you'd even agree to see anyone else right now, really."

"I didn't really want to. Enya kept bugging me about it so I agreed to let her give the guy my phone number. We talked a couple of times and met up for drinks, but I wasn't into it. And I'm sure he could tell."

"Well, hey, don't force it. If you're not ready, you're not ready."

"Yeah. Well, let Enya tell it, seeing other people will force me to get over Travis faster; that I won't have time to think about him if I'm dating someone else. And I guess I can see her point. But I don't want to waste anyone's time. It would be one thing if I was interested in meeting someone new but I'm just not."

"Nothing wrong with that. Have you given any more thought to getting some therapy?"

Evelyn's hand stilled briefly. "I thought about it...but I guess I figured making the decision to move on from Travis was good enough and that I didn't need it."

"Couldn't hurt. Believe me, I'm proud of you for coming to the realization that you needed to leave him alone. But you're clearly still struggling. There's nothing wrong with seeing someone to help you along this process and get to the 'why' of things."

"What would that look like, me going to a shrink just because my husband left me? Folks go through way worse stuff than that."

"Who gives a damn what anyone else thinks about it? It's nobody's business, E2. And it's nothing to be ashamed of. People seek therapy for all kinds of reasons, and each one is as valid as the next. I'm just saying; the help is there if you need it."

"I thought I was doing all right. I'm not gonna act like I'm floating on air-"

"Let me ask you something," Noah put down his paintbrush. "If Travis called right now wanting to get back together, would you do it?"

Hesitating slightly, Evelyn adjusted her glasses and replied, "Probably."

"If he wanted a booty call-"

"Noah!"

"Let's not act like you don't have those, all right? We're grown."

"Fine. I mean, I don't know...I'm sure I'd be *tempted*..."

"And if he called just wanting to talk?"

"What's wrong with just talking?"

"It would leave you wanting more than that. How many times since you decided to break from him have you looked at old pictures of him, or you two together, or wore an old shirt of his or listened to music that reminds you of him?"

Evelyn hated to admit she'd done all that and more. "What's your point, Noah?"

"That it might not be as easy for you to move on from him on your own as you think. And getting some help and insight might help you get to where you're trying to go faster. *That's* my point."

Mulling over his words, Evelyn couldn't deny that they had merit. Quitting Travis cold turkey clearly hadn't worked; sure, she hadn't contacted him, but she was still reminiscing and yearning over him practically every night, crying herself to sleep over what she couldn't have. That wasn't healthy and she knew it, especially since it hadn't alleviated any.

"I see where you're coming from," she finally admitted. "I'll give it some serious thought."

"Good."

"I can just imagine what Enya will say."

"Again, it's none of her business. You don't have to get her approval for everything."

She looked at him in alarm. "Who said I needed her approval?"

"Please. Ever since we were kids, she's had a certain influence over you. You know, like convincing you to go out with someone even though you repeatedly said you weren't ready?"

Evelyn averted her eyes.

Noah wasn't done. "And you always seemed to feel like you needed to run everything you did by her, and if she didn't like it, you usually backed up off of it. This is something you're gonna be doing for *you*. Enya's opinion doesn't matter here."

Evelyn hadn't even realized she'd done that. She and Enya had always been close, but it never occurred to her that she sought her sister's approval like that.

"I doubt Enya has time to worry about what you're doing, anyway," Noah continued, dipping his brush into some green oil paint. "She's probably too wrapped up in her new dude that I saw her with the other night."

Alarmed, Evelyn almost dropped her brush. She placed it on the ledge of the easel and turned to him. "What? You know about him?"

"I mean, yeah..." Noah shrugged. "Though I'm sure she wasn't expecting to run into me. She looked a little caught when I saw them on the street. Guess she still wasn't ready for anybody to see her mystery man yet."

"I *told* her it was only a matter of time before someone found out she was seeing Dallas but she didn't wanna listen."

Frowning, Noah set down his own brush. "Dallas?"

"Yeah...that's who you saw her with, right?"

"The guy she was with, she introduced him as Rico."

"Rico?" Then Evelyn squeezed her eyes shut. She recalled being at Enya's recently and seeing the name Dallas Rico Cutler doodled on a piece of mail. She had teased her sister incessantly about that at the time, then forgot about it. "Crap..."

"What's going on?" Noah demanded.

Evelyn briefly covered her face with her paint-covered hands. Figuring the jig was up, she sighed, dropping them and leaving a red smear across her cheek. "Enya is seeing the guy that stood Emberly up on New Year's Eve."

"What?? Since when?"

"They met not too long after he ghosted Emberly. She's already feeling like he might be the one. If she's not in love with him already, she's on the way to it."

"Damn, for real? So she has no problem with what he did to Emberly, huh?"

"She's not happy about that," Evelyn defended. "She actually *does* feel bad about feeling like she's betraying Emberly. *But*...she also can't ignore the feelings she has for Dallas. Like I said, she thinks this is the real thing between them. And you know that's not something she usually says about anyone."

"True," Noah admitted. "So when is she gonna tell Emberly about it?"

"I've told her she needs to go ahead and do it. That it'll be worse the longer she waits. But clearly she hasn't." Evelyn shrugged, taking a sip from her glass of grape juice. "You know Enya is gonna do stuff how she wants to do it."

"Yeah. I see."

"Noah, *please* keep this to yourself. Enya will kill me if she knows I slipped and told you about this."

"Hey, you don't have to worry about me saying anything," Noah assured. He reached for his own glass, though his was full of bourbon. "It's jacked up, but I'm staying out of it. I just hope Enya comes clean sooner rather than later; I hate the thought of Emberly getting hurt over this. She's been hurt enough."

"You and me both."

Later that evening when Evelyn was back home, her childlike painting leaning face-first against the wall where she couldn't see it, she climbed onto her bed with a paranormal romance novel and tried to curl up and read, but her mind kept wandering. Try as she might, she couldn't stop her thoughts from straying to Travis, and wondering what he was doing at that very moment. Was he with that woman she saw him with on Buttercup Mountain? She still hated the thought of him with someone else, and tears began to sting her eyes.

Shaking her head to clear the thoughts, she tried to refocus on the book. When she realized she had read the same sentence four times and still couldn't relay what it said if asked, she gave up. Putting the book down with a sigh, she rolled onto her stomach, resting her chin on her arm. She never thought she'd be alone and divorced at age thirty-four, but there she was.

She'd tried to be a good wife. All she wanted was to make him happy. She was faithful, loyal, more than willing in the bedroom, attentive...apparently, according to Travis, *too* attentive. He felt she was smothering him, but instead of talking to her about it so they could deal with it and she could try to do better, he just left. What kind of husband did that?

When Evelyn allowed herself to acknowledge them, Travis had more than his share of flaws, himself. He could be very passive at times; he didn't love conflict, and instead of dealing with tense situations and moving on, he let things fester. Many times she'd try to get him to talk to her when something was clearly wrong, but he'd just stubbornly insist he was fine.

They never could agree on the issue of whether or not to have children. Evelyn had never wavered in her desire to have them, but Travis kept changing his mind; one month he'd be all in, then the next he'd claim they weren't quite ready. Evelyn kept reminding him that she wasn't getting any younger, and he'd promised they would have a child soon enough, insisting that he wanted a baby as much as she did, but now she wondered if he was ever telling the truth about that.

He could be a little too laid back and reserved. Evelyn liked to laugh and have fun and go out and do things, but Travis could never just let loose and enjoy the moment. It was like he felt he had to be the 'adult' in the relationship, steering Evelyn back to a place of decorum when she got too out of line. It was something that hadn't occurred to Evelyn until that moment.

Her mind ran down several other things she never cared for about Travis but had somehow mentally muted during their relationship; how he hogged the television, his surprisingly intense fear of dogs, the way he'd lecture her when she didn't put her shoes away or invaded his side of the bathroom sink, his absolute refusal to try avocados. And more. She never let it bother her in the past but now, she didn't know how she'd put up with it for so long.

Thinking about all this helped ease the pain of the divorce some, but the tears still streamed down Evelyn's face. She realized she hadn't allowed herself to grieve for the loss of her relationship; she'd been too busy trying to hang onto it. But it felt good to acknowledge what was wrong between her and Travis instead of idealizing him as she had been since he left her. He wasn't perfect. And for the first time, she could admit that he likely wasn't ideal for her. Maybe when they were teenagers and young adults, he had been. But not now.

She thought about her parents. Jessup and Wilona Holliday were as made for each other as two people could be, and Evelyn had always been in awe of their love and bond. They were best friends, clearly enjoying each other's company, even if it was just sitting in the living room together doing totally separate things. Evelyn smiled wistfully as she remembered all the times she could hear her mother laughing loudly at something her father told her as they made dinner together, the kisses they snuck when they thought no one was looking, or how her mother would grin and blush whenever her husband winked at her. Evelyn always knew she wanted a partnership like that. And that wasn't what she had with Travis.

The heaviness she'd felt in her chest ever since Travis left her started to ease with each second that passed. She began to feel at peace, which was something she couldn't have imagined just days before. Travis was in the past, and that was okay.

Just like that, she knew she was going to be all right.

Eying her phone for a few moments, she finally grabbed it and texted the guy Enya had set her up with, asking if he wanted to meet for coffee the next day. Despite still not feeling a hundred percent ready, she felt it was necessary to push herself out of her comfort zone. When he replied mere moments later agreeing to meet, Evelyn smiled, feeling like she was finally making some progress.

Chapter 8

"YOU THINK HE'S GONNA get here in time?" Camilla asked worriedly, checking her watch.

"He just texted that he's five minutes away," Emberly replied, doing her own time check. "He probably got delayed by the road work. I'll be glad when they're done with all that."

"Too bad that won't be any time soon, from what I've heard." Camilla anxiously smoothed her hands over her ponytail and adjusted her clothing.

"Calm down, girl; he'll be here," Emberly assured her, slightly amused. "We still have an hour. You don't have to look so nervous."

Blushing, Camilla dropped her hands and forced a chuckle. Emberly had no idea that her nervousness had nothing to do with the event they were trying to get to. "You're right. I should chill out."

They were getting ready to cater a corporate event and their company van wouldn't start. Emberly called Noah, knowing he had a huge Suburban truck that he rarely used. Thankfully, he wasn't too busy to come help them out, even agreeing to stay at the event with them until they were done. Emberly couldn't remember when she'd been more relieved; her big brother had come to her rescue once again.

"He's here!" Emberly exclaimed when Noah pulled up. She rushed outside while Camilla put on another coat of lip gloss.

"I expect a batch of scones for this," Noah was teasing Emberly by the time Camilla joined them outside. They had started moving the trays of desserts from the van to his truck.

"Brother, with the way you're saving our asses right now, you can get all the scones you want," Emberly assured him. "I don't know what's up with the van; it was working fine a couple days ago."

"It's no problem. Glad to help." His eyes turned to Camilla, and he stood up a little straighter. A smile came to his lips. "Hey, Camilla."

"Hey, Noah." Camilla couldn't resist her own smile as heat rushed to her cheeks. She hoped it wasn't obvious. "I'm glad you're here. I mean...that you're able to help us like this."

"Me, too."

He eyed her for another moment, and Camilla made herself move from where she was lingering and help them get the dessert trays transferred. Emberly didn't even notice the looks they were occasionally passing each other, since she was so focused on making sure the trays were arranged where nothing would get smushed or damaged during the ride.

Once everything was loaded, the three of them headed to the conference center where the event was being held. Camilla sat in the back to keep an eye on the food, and Emberly continuously fussed about the slowed traffic from the front seat, occasionally checking her phone. When one of her incoming messages resulted in a grin from her, Noah glanced at her curiously.

"What's that about?" he asked, smiling himself.

"Oh...nothing." Emberly tried to clear her face, putting her phone face-down on her thigh.

"If it's a guy, you can say it."

"It's a guy. But there's nothing to tell about him yet so don't ask me for any details."

"Everyone wants to keep secrets lately," Noah muttered, shaking his head. "All right; do your thing, then. I'm just glad you seem so happy, whoever he is."

"So far, go good. I'm still trying to determine if he's the real deal yet."

"Hmmm."

"At least he hasn't disappeared on me like that punk Dallas did, so he's already won major points because of that."

Pursing his lips, Noah kept his eyes on the road. He wished he didn't know about Dallas now seeing Enya. Even though he'd vowed to stay out of it, part of him felt bad for being aware of that when Emberly wasn't. "I feel you. So Dallas never at least called to explain himself, I take it?"

"Hell no," Emberly sucked her teeth. "That would've been nice, but apparently I didn't deserve that courtesy. If he wasn't interested, I wish he would've just told me that instead of leading me on, then blocking me when he didn't have the balls to tell me he apparently changed his mind. Hopefully I never see that bastard again."

Noah's brow furrowed slightly but he quickly erased it. He could only hope that Enya either broke up with Dallas or let Emberly know that she was seeing him soon, because he could see this turning into a big mess down the road. And he didn't want to be in the middle of it.

Thankfully Emberly got another text that took her attention, and the subject dropped. Noah glanced in the rearview mirror and saw Camilla already looking at him.

They shared another smile before he turned his eyes back to the road.

They managed to make it to the venue on time, and Noah helped the ladies get everything unloaded and set up. He mostly hung in the background once more guests started to arrive, since he was dressed in a simple t-shirt and jeans instead of the collared shirts bearing Emberly's business name and logo and black slacks like Emberly and Camilla wore. While Emberly schmoozed the guests, Camilla stayed quiet as she usually did, doling out desserts and business cards.

"Let me help you with that," Noah offered, moving over to grab an empty tray from the display table. His fingers brushed hers when they reached for it at the same time.

Camilla hoped he couldn't tell that she was practically vibrating, being so close to him. His light touch had sent currents all the way up her arm. She looked up at him, noting how he smelled yummier than the desserts they were serving. "Thanks, Noah. I appreciate it."

She could've easily moved the tray herself but she wasn't about to deny any opportunity to get closer to him. And he didn't seem to mind it, either, since he was in no hurry to step away from her.

"Whatever you need," he assured her, his voice low and as smooth as buttercream.

Camilla bit her lip, temporarily forgetting where they were. It was only when someone approached the table asking if there were any more apple pie eggrolls that she snapped out of it and made herself move.

The rest of the event went smoothly, with Noah and Camilla continuously stealing looks and smiles at each other and Emberly being too consumed in tending to guests and checking her messages to notice. When things started to wind down and the guests began to dissipate, Emberly stepped away to speak with the hosts, leaving Noah and Camilla alone.

"This went well, seems like," he commented, glancing at the nearly-empty table. "They surely gobbled everything up."

"They really did. Emberly's desserts are always a hit, though."

"True. She's always loved to bake. What about you?" Noah moved closer to her as she gathered the serving utensils. "Is this what you've always wanted to do?"

"Ever since college, yeah," Camilla replied. "At first, it was just something I did on the side to make some extra money, but I realized I actually loved it. So I changed my major to Business Administration, got my degree, then went to culinary school."

"That's awesome."

"Yeah, I'm glad I did it. Ultimately I'd like to have my own bakery, but I enjoy where I'm at for now."

"What else do you like to do?" Noah asked as he stacked the empty serving trays.

"Read spy novels, go to wine tastings, listen to live music. Nothing all that exciting."

"Sounds cool to me."

"What about you? I imagine you probably work a lot, running your own company and everything."

"I do, but thankfully I've built a team that I trust and can delegate to so I don't have to run myself ragged doing everything myself. My chill time is valuable; I usually can't wait to get home, get a glass of bourbon, turn on some jazz and turn my mind off."

"I *love* jazz!" Camilla exclaimed, grinning. "I usually go to sleep listening to it."

"Same. It's almost always on at my house. My friends actually tease me because I listen to that more than hip hop."

"You too? I know next to nothing about these current artists out now. I get plenty of 'old lady' teasing from my girls about that. But I like what I like."

Noah started to ask if one of the things she liked was him, but he didn't want to put her on the spot, especially not with so many people around. But his gut feeling told him she was feeling him as much as he was feeling her.

They continued getting to know each other as they got everything packed up, complete with a sufficient amount of mild flirting. Noah kept finding excuses to move closer to her, because she smelled like cake batter and he wished he could bury his face in her neck. He wanted to ask if she was seeing anyone, but again, figured it wasn't the time to ask. He'd surely be posing the question at the first opportunity, though, because he was interested in her and wanted to do something about it.

He hoped to get Camilla alone to ask for her number, but he never got a chance to. By the time they finally made it back to the kitchen and got everything unpacked and squared away, Emberly sent Camilla home, saying she and Noah would lock up. Camilla had hesitated, protesting that she didn't mind sticking around with them, but Emberly insisted. With a parting look at Noah, Camilla grabbed her things and headed out.

"Hold up, Camilla; I'll walk you out," Noah offered, heading over to her. To Emberly he said, "I'll be right back."

"All right." Emberly's attention was on her phone again.

Noah and Camilla were quiet as they headed across the parking lot to her car., walking close but not touching. She looked up at him, smiling.

"Thanks for seeing me outside," she said in a shy voice.

"Don't mention it. There's no way I'd let a lady walk out to her car by herself at night if I could help it. Though I admit I have kind of an ulterior motive, too."

Her eyes turned curious. "You do?"

"I wanted to ask if you were seeing anyone."

"Oh." An immediate flush came to Camilla's cheeks. "No, I'm not. Totally single. Umm, you?"

"Same. And I don't think it would be a total surprise that I'm interested in you."

Her face now flaming, Camilla grinned. "I'm glad to hear that, Noah. It's definitely mutual."

Now *he* was grinning. "We should talk about that, then. May I have your number?"

"Of course."

Noah handed her his phone and she saved her number into it. They stood there smiling at each other for several moments before Noah took a step back, though he really wanted to hug her.

"I'll call you later tonight, if that's all right," he told her. "Unless you think it'll be too late."

"No, I'm usually up late; feel free to call whenever," Camilla insisted. "I'm looking forward to it."

"Good. Well, I'd better get back in there before Emberly wonders what's taking me so long. Get home safe, Camilla."

"Thanks." Camilla wanted to step forward and hug him but didn't have the nerve, despite now knowing that her interest in him was mutual. She just eased into her car, started the engine, and waved before driving off.

Noah actually whistled as he headed back inside. There was an extra spring in his step. It had been a while since he felt so excited about a woman, and he couldn't wait to get home and talk to Camilla to see what other things they had in common. He felt in his gut that she could be different for him.

"What are you smiling so hard about?" Emberly asked him once he was back inside.

"Just got some good news."

"Yeah? One of your stock tips hit or something?"

"Nah, even better than that." Noah figured he might as well come out with it, since she'd undoubtedly find out eventually. "I'm interested in Camilla."

It took a second for what he said to register but when it did, Emberly dropped the paperwork she'd been holding onto the stainless steel workspace. "What did you say?"

"I said I'm interested in Camilla. And it's mutual. It's wild to say it like this but...I'm actually excited about getting to know her better and seeing where this can lead to. I haven't felt this amped about a woman in years, if ever."

Emberly tried to hide the slight frown that came to her face but Noah saw it. He eyed her. "What's the problem with that?"

"I just..." she hedged, eyes averted. "Well, you can't date her, Noah."

"Excuse me?"

"You can't date Camilla."

"Why the hell not?"

"Don't get upset. I just don't think it's a good idea for you to be dating my assistant. What if y'all break up?"

"Then we break up. We're adults; it happens. But I like Camilla more than I've liked anyone in a long while; it feels different with her. I'm more interested in focusing on what it can turn into than worrying about how it's gonna fall apart."

"And that's great, Noah, and I'm not trying to be a downer but I just don't need things getting messy. My brother and my assistant-"

"Really doesn't have anything to do with you," Noah interjected strongly. "Don't mistake my telling you about my interest in her as asking for your permission. If she and I are into each other – and we are – then that's all there is to it."

"So you're just gonna pursue her regardless of what I think about it?"

"Basically."

"Wow, Noah. This is really inconsiderate of you. So if you find something wrong with her – or should I say *when*, 'cause you always do with women – and dump her unceremoniously, then what? She's gonna be all in her feelings, will probably start acting funny towards me simply because you're my brother, and then leave me high and dry because she won't wanna risk running into you anymore."

Noah's face tightened, but he shook his head. "I see you just have me all figured out, huh? Don't try to paint me as some heartless playboy that just runs through women, 'cause that's not me. And it's an insult for you to even suggest it."

"That's not what I said, but...come on, Noah. You know you're a serial monogamist. You're all in until you decide you're not."

"And I'm always honest as to why. Leave it to you to try to put some kind of negative spin on things. I tell you I'm sincerely feeling someone and you can't wait to throw cold water on it just because things haven't been going well in your own love life."

Emberly gasped. "I can't believe you just said that, Noah!"

"Am I lying?"

"I'm just saying; why waste her time if-"

They heard a door close before Camilla appeared through the doorway. Emberly immediately wondered how much she'd heard.

"Sorry for interrupting," Camilla hedged, glancing back and forth between them. "I was down the street when I realized I forgot my phone."

"It's a good thing you came back because there's something we need to clear up," Emberly stated, folding her arms.

Camilla looked immediately nervous. "What's wrong?"

"When you told me you had a crush on someone the other day, were you talking about Noah?"

"Oh, umm..."

"I'm not trying to put you on the spot but I need to know," Emberly added strongly, glaring at her blushing assistant. "Are you trying to date my brother?"

Sensing that Emberly wouldn't like the true answer to that question, Camilla cleared her throat and muttered, "No."

Emberly glanced at Noah, who looked like he'd just had the wind knocked out of him. He stared at Camilla, whose eyes were on the floor.

"So you're *not* interested in Noah?" Emberly pressed. "You have no feelings for him at all?"

"I like Noah but we...we're just friends, that's all." Camilla didn't dare to look at Noah right then; she could only imagine what he was thinking of her. Not ten minutes ago, she'd told him just the opposite. It burned that she was likely blowing her shot with him but she couldn't afford to have Emberly upset with her, and she sensed she would be if she told her the truth.

"I'm just gonna grab my phone and go," Camilla muttered, keeping her eyes low as she eased over to the counter where she'd left her phone earlier. Practically snatching it, she scurried out of the room, wishing she could send Noah some sort of signal that she hadn't meant what she just said. Noah looked after her with a confused frown. He wanted to follow her to find out what was going on, but refrained.

Emberly could see the disappointment on her brother's face, and it didn't make her feel good. Camilla's response didn't sound very convincing, but Emberly was still glad to hear it. She didn't need Camilla and Noah hitting it off any time soon.

"Well, there you have it," she finally concluded, hoping she didn't sound too smug.

Noah just glared at her. "The next time your van breaks down, don't call me."

Her mouth fell open in shock. "Noah-"

He was already heading for the door. By the time he got outside, Camilla's car was down the street.

EMBERLY WAS HOME LATER that night, mindlessly playing with her locs as she laid in bed. She hated how things were left between her and Noah earlier. She'd tried to call him to smooth things over but he didn't answer. He was the last sibling she wanted to be upset with her, but she hoped that after a couple of days, he'd cool off. Or forget about whatever infatuation he felt he had for Camilla.

She frowned curiously when her phone rang. It was almost ten o'clock. When she rolled over to reach for it and saw Gideon's name, she smiled.

"Hey there," she greeted, rolling onto her back.

"Hey. Can you come by the house?"

"Why? What's wrong?"

"There's just something I need you to see. Some kind of issue upstairs. I could handle it but I wanted to run it by you first before I did anything."

Curious, Emberly sat up. "Okay, but I have to admit that I'm not very handy. Noah usually handles that kind of stuff."

"You don't need to be that handy for this. Can you come by?"

"Uhh, yeah, sure." Emberly was tired from the long day, but she was also now extremely curious as to what Gideon wanted. "I can be by there in about thirty minutes."

"All right."

Emberly slid off the bed to change out of the nightshirt she was wearing and into some leggings and a sweater. Thankfully she'd already showered when she got home earlier. After pulling her locs into a ponytail and spraying on some honey caramel body mist, she headed out.

Gideon had instructed via text for her to use her key to get in, and she cautiously looked around as she entered the darkened living room, part of her wondering if this was some kind of prank. She hoped he hadn't called her over there just to mess with her.

"I'm upstairs," Gideon called out.

Emberly ascended the staircase, her footsteps muted by the relatively-new carpeting. She saw the light from under the door of the master bedroom, though she couldn't hear anything. Stepping over to the door, she knocked lightly. "Gideon?"

"Come in."

She opened the door and before she could blink, a naked Gideon grabbed her and yanked her to him, and she yelped in surprise. He pushed the door closed behind her before backing her against it, taking a deep kiss that immediately had Emberly's panties soaked.

"Gideon, what-"

"Shut up," he ordered, jamming his tongue back down her throat. His hands were already sliding underneath her leggings, and when he stepped back and told her to take them and her sweater off, she didn't hesitate to obey. His forcefulness was a surprise but also a huge turn-on, and Emberly was eager to see what else he wanted her to do.

He grabbed her hand and placed it on his granite-hard penis, guiding her as they stroked it together. His other hand teased her dark nipple for a moment before he stepped closer to her, pressing himself between her quivering legs. His lips brushed hers when he whispered, "You get what I wanted you to handle, right?"

Unable to speak, Emberly just nodded. She leaned forward to kiss him but he evaded her.

"Don't play with me," she panted.

"Oh, I'm not." He stepped back, biting his lip as he eyed her up and down. "Get on the bed."

She was too horny to protest. Climbing onto his California king-sized bed, Gideon yanked her onto her back and pushed her legs up and open. Eying her wetness hungrily, he licked his lips before diving his face into it, earning a loud and long moan from Emberly. He eagerly feasted on her, lapping and sucking, taking his time as Emberly squirmed and writhed above him. He slid two fingers inside of her, still sucking her like candy, and Emberly's hands went from clawing at the comforter to digging in his locs to pulling at her own.

"I want you to come for me," he informed her, lightly biting the inside of her thigh. He curled his fingers inside of her and smirked as she let out a string of curses. "Four times."

Her head popped up. "You trying to kill me?"

"On the contrary. You'll never feel more alive as when you're with me. And you're not leaving here until I get it out of you."

He didn't have long to wait for the first one, because mere moments later, Emberly had clamped her thighs around his head so hard he thought she might've been trying to kill *him*. The orgasm hit her with more force than she'd ever experienced, and she didn't know how in the world he expected to get three more out of her that same night after that.

But he did.

He was still inside of her when she came down from orgasm number four almost two hours later. Clearly in no hurry to move, Gideon pressed leisurely kisses to her lips, pleased at how utterly relaxed Emberly looked. She could barely keep her eyes open.

"Feeling good?" he asked her, his voice low.

"That's one way to describe it," she muttered. "I don't know how I'm gonna be able to move after that."

"Good thing you don't have to any time soon. Unless you have somewhere to be."

"If I did, that would just be too bad. I can't even feel my bones right now."

"That's what I wanted to hear." Gideon smirked as he carefully withdrew from her and slid off her body, keeping a possessive hand on her damp torso. He rested his head on his bent arm. "I'm glad you could come over. I know you had that event thing earlier today."

She glanced at him. "You know, if you wanted a booty call, you could've just said that."

"That's not very creative, is it? Plus, I didn't want you to think that's all I called you over here for."

"If it wasn't, whatever else you wanted will have to wait. Unless you're about to propose and was going to suggest we elope, then I'll chug a Red Bull or something."

Gideon threw his head back and laughed. "See, that's why I like hanging with you, Em. You're hot but you have a sense of humor, too. I actually like talking to you, which isn't something I can say about most women I've dealt with."

Emberly looked at him, her mind focusing on one part of his statement. "You think I'm hot?"

"Hell yeah. You can't tell? Since we started getting down, I can barely keep my hands off you."

Emberly wondered if she was the only woman he was 'getting down' with, but she knew she had no right to ask. They weren't a couple. Though she didn't know how to tell him that her joke about them eloping wasn't totally a joke at all. It was something she'd wanted to talk to him about since their first date but didn't know how to broach the subject. She'd gotten to know him pretty well since they met, but wasn't sure if he was Team Marriage or Team Playboy. And she needed to find out because she felt she might be running out of time.

"Yeah, we've been having a good time," she finally mused, her hand sliding on top of his.

"It's actually refreshing to be with someone that I can be friends with, too," Gideon stated. "Sometimes the whole dating game can be a pain in the ass."

"You date a lot?" Emberly asked, trying to sound casual as she traced a finger along his knuckles.

"Some," Gideon shrugged. "I don't know a lot of women here yet, but before I moved, I had my share of dates. Nothing serious, though. Haven't really met anyone that made me want to take it to that next level, you know?"

"Yeah. But you *would* get married if you met the right person? You're not against it?"

"No, I'm not against it. Not in a hurry about it and can't say I'm looking for it right now, but not against it. If it happens, it happens."

"Hmm." Emberly tried to work up the nerve to say what she'd been wondering about since she met him. "So...since you said that, I have kind of a crazy question to ask. I mean, it's a little off the wall, so brace yourself."

"Okay..." Gideon looked at her, amused. "What's up?"

"What do you think about getting married for money?"

*NOAH*: **I need to go by the rental and check on some stuff.**

*Emberly*: **Why?**

*Noah*: **Because I need to.**

*Emberly*: **I already checked on everything over there. No need for you to go.**

*Noah*: **Again, wasn't asking for your damn permission.**

*Evelyn*: **What is going on with you two?**

*Noah*: **Nothing.**

*Enya*: You sure are eager to handle everything over at the house all of a sudden, Emberly.

*Emberly*: Just trying to do my part. Plus, the new renter doesn't care for a lot of disturbances.

*Noah*: Oh, you mean they like people that mind their own business? Not sure how they get along with YOU, then.

*Emberly*: Noah. When are we gonna talk about this?

*Noah*: We're not.

Chapter 9

"SO WHAT ARE WE GONNA do for Valentine's Day, babe?"

Enya looked over at Dallas, whose eyes were on the laptop perched on his lap. They were both working at home, his home, since it was thundering and pouring rain outside and would be for most of the day, and neither wanted to be bothered. They'd been side-by-side on the couch with their laptops and a slew of snacks, each more content than they'd ever been.

"We usually have something at Noah's," Enya replied, returning her eyes to her own screen.

Dallas's fingers stopped typing. "So we're not even gonna be alone on our first Valentine's Day together?"

"We'll be alone. As soon as I get back from Noah's, I'm all yours."

"Babe..."

"Dallas, you know the deal. You can't go with me. Emberly will be there."

"When are we going to handle this?" Dallas asked, moving his laptop off his lap and turning to her. "I thought you were gonna go ahead and tell her."

"I was. I am."

"So what's the hold-up?"

"It's not as easy as you're making it sound, Dallas."

"Okay, so it's a difficult conversation; I get that. But it still needs to happen. We can't hide out in my house forever.

You haven't wanted to go anywhere with me since we ran into your brother the other night."

"I know." Enya sighed. She absently ran her fingers through her short hair. "I'm not thrilled about it, either."

"So let's fix it, Enya. We can't have a relationship like this."

She gazed at him for a moment before moving her own laptop to the side and turning to face him, tucking her legs underneath her. "Dallas, if I'm gonna risk damaging my relationship with my sister, it needs to be worth it. I know we've said we have feelings for each other, but...are you really trying to go the distance with me? Like, for *real*? Because if you're not, I don't see the point."

"I am," Dallas confirmed without hesitation. He took her hand, stroking her soft skin with his thumb. "I'm in love with you, Enya."

Her breath hitched in her throat. "Y-you are?"

"Yes. And I'm totally sure about wanting you in my life indefinitely. Do you want the same thing?"

"Yes," Enya replied immediately. She inched closer to him, and he pulled her legs into his lap. "I absolutely want that. It seems so crazy since we haven't known each other all that long but I've never been surer about anything. Baby, I love you."

He grinned. "Come here."

She climbed onto his lap and they wrapped their arms around each other, sharing lovesick smiles and gazes. Dallas's hands roamed her back before one slid up to the back of her neck and pulled her closer for a kiss. They sank against each other, kissing with the familiarity of a couple that had been together for years. Enya's hand grabbed his face, her heart feeling like it was about to burst. She'd never been in love like this before but she knew it was the real thing now. And she wasn't going to lose it.

"I'll tell her," she promised once the kiss eventually tapered off. She rested her forehead to his. "I promise, I'm gonna tell her soon."

"Good. In the meantime..." Dallas bit his lip as he began easing down the zipper on the front of her sweatshirt. "What do you say we take a break for a while?"

Enya grinned, then her expression melted into slack-jawed ecstasy as Dallas began slowly tracing his tongue around her nipple. Her hips began winding on him. "I like the way you think, baby."

He stood, hoisting her in his arms, and carried her back to his bedroom. They didn't get back to work for the rest of the day.

THE NEXT DAY, ENYA, Evelyn, and Miriam were out doing some shopping. Enya hadn't been able to keep the smile off her face, still riding high from the day before with Dallas. She couldn't remember ever being so happy, and she knew she had to come clean with Emberly so she and Dallas could really move forward. She had to believe that her relationship with her sister would ultimately be all right, even if Emberly was upset with her for a while.

"Somebody must have gotten some last night," Miriam surmised, eying her smiling niece.

"It sure wasn't me," Evelyn muttered, snatching a fat scented candle off the shelf.

"I'm talking about your glowing sister over here," Miriam replied, jerking her head in Enya's direction. "That little naughty smile hasn't left her face all day."

Not bothering to deny it, Enya just shrugged. "Nothing like having a good man. You know how it is, Auntie."

"I surely do. So who is this man that has you walking around like you've got one of those candles shoved up your-"

"Auntie!"

"What?"

"Let's just say I think I've finally found the one," Enya answered, her voice taking on an airiness that had Evelyn looking at her in alarm. Wistfulness wasn't a trait that Enya usually exhibited. "I'm really happy. Like, over-the-moon, happy."

"Well, that's wonderful!" Miriam grinned. "I'm happy for you, because I was thinking you were going to be spending your life stubbornly single."

"It's like I always said; I wasn't pressed to find anyone but if I did, I wasn't gonna run from it. And I'm definitely not running from this."

"Maybe you *should*, though," Evelyn grunted, cutting her eyes at her sister. "Considering who it is and everything."

Enya glared at her while Miriam looked confused. "Really, Ev?"

"Am I lying? And I bet you *still* haven't told her yet, have you?"

Hesitating slightly, Enya turned her attention to a display of candle warmers. "It's not like I haven't tried. I called her this morning but she didn't answer."

"Try again."

"What the hell is going on?" Miriam butted in, her hands on her hips. "What are y'all talking about? Please don't tell me you're out here with a married man, Enya."

"No!" Enya immediately exclaimed. "Hell no, I wouldn't do that!"

"Then who is it that you're apparently not supposed to be with?"

Before Enya could answer, a cinnamon-colored gentleman came down the aisle the ladies were congregated in, his eyes fixated on Enya.

"Excuse me," he said to her, looking transfixed. "I'm sorry to interrupt you all, but I saw you and couldn't make myself keep walking. You're *gorgeous*."

Smiling politely, Enya just nodded briefly. "I appreciate that, thanks."

"I'm Cree and I would love to get to know you better, if that's possible."

"I'm flattered, Cree, but I'm spoken for," Enya informed him with a shrug. "Sorry."

"Damn. Guess I shouldn't be surprised, though." Cree sighed regretfully. "Too bad. It was nice to meet you anyway, though..."

"Enya."

"Enya. Beautiful name." He looked at Miriam and Evelyn, nodding politely. "Again, sorry for intruding. Enjoy the rest of your day, ladies."

"You, too," they chorused, eyeing him as he strolled down the aisle, turned, then went out of sight.

"Girl, your nose must really be open over whoever your new man is, because that brotha was ridiculously fine," Miriam marveled, looking genuinely floored. "Any other time you would've been all over that."

"Probably," Enya shrugged. "But not now."

"Okay, now you *really* need to tell me who it is you're so crazy over."

Figuring she might as well come out with it, Enya sighed. "Dallas."

"Who?"

"The guy Emberly met online that stood her up on New Year's Eve."

"And one more time after that," Evelyn added.

"I don't need any help telling it, Evelyn," Enya snapped.

"Wait a minute," Miriam held up a hand, frowning. "You're actually dating a man that dogged your sister?"

"It's not like I went *looking* for him," Enya defended, exasperated. "We met by chance and I didn't even know he was the same Dallas at first."

"And when you realized he was, then what?"

"I..." Enya's voice faded as her eyes fell to the ground. "Okay, fine, I kept seeing him. Maybe I shouldn't have without talking to Emberly first-"

"No *maybe* about it, sweetheart," Miriam interjected. "You shouldn't have."

"I admit that. But I didn't expect to fall for Dallas like this. What we have is the real thing, Auntie."

"All the more reason you need to tell your sister about it. If he's not going anywhere any time soon, then she definitely deserves an explanation. You wouldn't want her finding out from someone other than you."

"I guess. Though the only people that know are you two and Noah. Though he thankfully didn't know who Dallas was when he saw us."

Evelyn looked away guiltily.

"Look," Miriam strode over and gently lifted Enya's chin, waiting for her niece's eyes to meet hers. "I get that there are some things you can't really control, like who you fall for. And I know there was nothing serious between Emberly and this man. But at the end of the day, she's your sister; that should mean something. I'm not saying you need to choose between them or dump him, especially if you feel as strongly about him as you say you do. But there's no way things should have gotten to this point with all of us knowing before Emberly does."

Enya knew Miriam was right. Her other two siblings and her aunt now all knew about her and Dallas while Emberly still had no clue. Enya knew that wasn't right, and that she would feel some kind of way about it if the roles were reversed.

"I'll let her know," Enya assured with a strong voice. "I'll try to catch her when I'm on the way home, if I can."

"Good."

Evelyn just stood off to the side, listening. She almost wished she could be there when Enya told Emberly about her and Dallas. She was curious as to whether Emberly would feel betrayed or if she wouldn't care at all, having gotten over what Dallas did. Part of her wanted to ask Enya to let her be there when she told her, but she refrained. Emberly would likely pitch a fit if she realized she was the last to know about all this.

A couple of hours later, she headed home, her mind still whirling about the drama between her sisters. At least focusing on that gave her a reprieve from thinking about her own sad love life, or lack thereof. She was making strides in getting over Travis, but she knew she wasn't there yet. The guy Enya had set her up with, Caliph, was nice and she enjoyed his company, but she didn't see their relationship going beyond friendship. There were no butterflies around him to be found, but she wondered if it was even fair to expect any at this point.

When "Just Because" by Anita Baker came on the radio, Evelyn immediately started to turn it off, as it reminded her of Travis. It was the song she had playing the first time she prepared a romantic surprise for him, and the one that always brought thoughts and memories of him crashing to her mind. That was the last thing she needed.

But she had taken Noah's advice about seeing a therapist, and she remembered their advice about reassigning the association of things that reminded her of Travis instead of running from them. So she clamped her hand back onto the steering wheel and tried to think of anything else that she might be able to associate that song with. When she remembered that it would be played during school dances back in the day, before she met Travis, she smiled. She remembered first dancing to the song with a boy in her class that had braces and wore way too much cologne; his name escaped her, but it didn't matter. This was progress.

Conjuring up more memories about that night almost curbed any frustration from the slowed traffic. She hated that the city was re-working the roads, and that there was no telling when they'd be done. She sucked her teeth when the road she usually would have taken to get home was blocked off, and she had to take yet another detour, tacking ten more minutes onto her ride.

The route took her by her parents' old house, and she sat up in her seat, wondering if she would catch a glimpse of the new tenant maybe getting their mail or something. And she saw him, all right...with his arms tightly wound around Emberly.

Chapter 10

"MR. HOLLIDAY, YOU HAVE a visitor."

Noah frowned slightly as he continued typing the email he was drafting. He glanced at the door towards his assistant, Yetta, who insisted on calling him Mr. Holliday despite his repeated insistences that she could just call him Noah. She blamed it on her military upbringing.

"Who is it?" he asked distractedly.

"A Ms. Camilla Towns."

His eyes snapping up, the email was instantly forgotten as his hands stopped moving. He sat back in his chair and ran a hand down his face, feeling some mix of excitement and annoyance. What could she possibly want?

"Send her in," he finally instructed, the frown still furrowing his brow. Though now it was more from curiosity than distraction.

Yetta stepped out, and Noah heard her telling Camilla that she could go in. Noah stood, mindlessly checking his clothing, then stopped himself. He remembered Camilla telling Emberly she wasn't interested in him five minutes after telling him she was, so he didn't need to be preening for her.

Moments later, she was in front of him. Noah hated to acknowledge even to himself how his stomach fluttered upon being in her presence again. And he wished he could ignore how good she looked, dressed in a green jersey dress and white sneakers, with her thick brown hair down and flowing around her shoulders instead of in its usual ponytail.

Her makeup was simple, just mascara and lip gloss, but it was plenty. Her face was pretty enough on its own that she didn't need anything else.

"Hi," she greeted shyly, still hovering near the door. "Is this a bad time?"

"You're in here now," Noah shrugged, trying to hang onto his indifference. "You can close the door."

After doing so, Camilla took a few steps toward him. He was standing, but remained behind his desk, leaving some distance between them.

"What brings you here?" he asked, folding his arms.

Camilla wrung her hands together, clearly nervous. "I know you're probably wondering why I said what I said to Emberly the other day..."

"You mean when you lied about your interest in me? Though I'm not sure if you were lying to me or to her."

"It was to her," Camilla quickly clarified, taking a step closer. "Noah...I absolutely have a crush on you. A huge one. I did when I said it and I still do. I'd like nothing more than to see you and date you and get as close as I can to you."

"So why did you tell Emberly otherwise?"

"Because with the way she asked me, I knew she wouldn't have wanted to hear the truth. She clearly had a problem with it."

"So?"

"So I don't want her firing me over this," Camilla admitted. "I'd like to think she wouldn't, but I had no way of knowing. You're her brother..."

"Who is a grown man and can date whoever he pleases. And so can *you*, by the way."

"In theory, yes, but people don't always think rationally when it comes to family. And I can't afford to lose my job right now."

"Has Emberly ever made any kind of stipulations about who you can date, be it me or anyone else?"

"No, but..."

"I get being concerned about your job, but I seriously doubt Emberly would actually fire you if we went out. Whatever problem she has with it is hers, not ours. And I told her as much when she tried to tell me I couldn't date you."

Camilla's eyes widened. "Really? You told her that?"

"Among other things. She's worried about what'll happen if we don't work out, and how it'll affect her. That's really all it's about."

"Oh." Camilla rubbed her arm, her eyes fixated on the hardwood flooring. "I didn't know that."

"I guess you wouldn't, since you chose to lie instead of just being honest."

"Wow..." Her face flamed at his words. "So I guess I blew it and you're not interested in me anymore?"

Noah couldn't say that. Even though he'd been annoyed at that whole scene in Emberly's kitchen, he was more disappointed than anything. He sincerely liked Camilla, and had for a while; the fact that she was so easily intimidated by his sister, for whatever reason, didn't sit well with him. He'd sensed that day that she wasn't being honest with Emberly, just by her body language. Spineless women never appealed to him, and that's what he'd thought of her actions that day.

But, hearing her explanation now, he could understand why she said what she said, even if he still didn't agree with lying about it. It was easy for him to say that she should just be honest and let the chips fall where they may; he worked for himself so he didn't have to worry about anyone firing him. But Camilla seemed genuinely concerned about Emberly being petty enough to do that to her if she dated him, and he didn't want to be insensitive to that.

Rounding his desk, he went and stood in front of her, itching to touch her but refraining. Despite whatever annoyance he might've had with her, his interest in Camilla hadn't waned. There was something about her that intrigued him, and had since he first met her over a year earlier. She was quiet and understated, a departure from the kind of women he usually dealt with. She could easily get lost in the crowd if you didn't pay attention. Even though she didn't say much, she had a smile that spoke a thousand words, and after the few talks they'd had over the months he'd known her, he knew she had a sense of humor that became more pronounced the more comfortable she got with someone. It was like a child peeking around the corner, waiting for permission to come out and play. Noah realized he wanted to keep learning more about her, and to become someone she could really be herself around. He wanted to be there when she let her guard down.

"That's not the case at all," he corrected, looking right into her eyes. She still smelled like cake batter; in other words, delicious. "I'm still very much interested."

She flashed a relieved grin. "I'm *so* glad to hear that. I really thought I'd lost my chance with you."

"But you need to come clean with Emberly about it," Noah continued. "Because I'm not going to be sneaking around. It needs to be out in the open or nothing."

Camilla's grin faded as quickly as it came. "I see. I suppose I can understand why you want it to be that way, but I can't help still being worried about how Emberly will react. I'd like to think she and I have a good enough partnership to where it wouldn't matter, but-"

"Camilla," Noah took her hand and gathered it against his chest. "I get it. And I'm certainly not expecting you to choose me over your job. All I can tell you is that my interest in you and desire for us to get closer is as real as it gets. You've occupied space in my head for a while now, and I'm finally ready to do something about it. I want us to go out; I wanna find out more about you, see where you live, take you to my place, spend lazy nights with you listening to jazz. And don't even get me started on my desire to finally kiss these." He gently grabbed her chin, tracing his thumb along her lower lip. She whimpered in response, her hand tightening in his as she inched closer. "And if we get to that point, I want to proudly claim you as my woman. You just have to want the same."

Her heart felt like it was going to pound right out of her chest. Camilla had never been so touched or so turned on by a man's words before; no other man had presented himself and his feelings to her like Noah just did. Everything in her wanted to throw caution to the wind and jump into Noah's arms, then call Emberly and tell her everything. But as much as she might've liked to, she couldn't totally suppress her concerns.

"Noah," she hesitantly placed her free hand on his chest next to their clasped hands, "I've been crushing on you since the moment we met. And I absolutely want everything you just said. But..."

"But you still have concerns," he surmised. He didn't sound angry or annoyed, to her relief.

"I'm sorry."

Eyeing her for a few moments, Noah lifted her hand to his lips and kissed it. "Like I said, I get it. And it has to be your decision."

"Are you going to give me an ultimatum?"

He frowned slightly. "Absolutely not. Look, if it'll help put your mind at ease any, I'll talk to Emberly. I sincerely don't think you have anything to worry about, and I wouldn't tell you that if I didn't believe it. Emberly isn't cruel like that. Whatever issue she'd have with us dating would likely fade over time, especially if this turned into something real and our relationship actually worked out."

Camilla bit her lip, and Noah's breathing deepened. It did something to him when she did that, regardless of whether it was intended to be enticing or not.

"That means a lot, that you would do that," she commented, her hand taking a light grip of his shirt. "It means a whole lot."

"I meant it when I said I want you. I want us to have a real shot. And knowing that, hopefully you'll consider joining me at our Valentine's Day gathering at my place. I'd love for you to be my date."

Her lingering concerns be damned, Camilla nodded vigorously. "I'd love to."

Noah grinned, which caused her to grin. "I'm glad to hear that. But are you sure? Please don't feel pressured."

"No, I'm sure. Yes, part of me is still concerned about what Emberly's reaction will be, but the larger part of me doesn't want to miss out on the possibility of us. I've been bummed ever since that day I lied about my feelings for you, and knew I didn't want to leave things like that. I was hoping you would call me that night so I could explain, but I understood when you didn't. It took a lot for me to work up the nerve to come here and talk to you today, but I'm *so* glad I did."

"I'm glad, too."

They stood gazing at each other before Camilla suddenly leaned up and kissed him, sliding her arm around his neck and pulling him closer. Noah was startled for a second, but his eyes quickly slid closed as he willingly returned the kiss, releasing her hand and wrapping her tightly in his arms. She opened her mouth to him and he felt her soft tongue against his, and his body flooded with heat. His hand drifted up to grab the side of her face, his fingers tangling in her dangly earring and her hair. He'd never kissed a woman in his office like this before; Camilla had thrown him for another loop but this one was welcomed.

Everything outside of his office door faded out as the kiss continued, their holds on each other firm and unyielding. Camilla's soft moans and whimpers were driving him crazy, and Noah had to mentally tell himself not to get carried away. Every part of him wanted to pick her up and carry her over to the couch under the picture window in his office, but for now, this was more than enough. He was finally getting to hold her and kiss her like he'd imagined doing so many times since they met. And it was just as sweet as he fantasized.

It was several minutes before the kiss finally began to taper off. Camilla reluctantly eased back, keeping her hold on him as she looked up at his handsome face.

"I should probably go," she whispered, making no move to do so.

And he didn't want her to. "You sure?"

"No."

And just like that, their lips met again, their kisses now more impassioned. Noah eventually paused long enough to instruct Yetta to hold all of his calls and that he was not to be disturbed, then he took Camilla's hand and led her over to the couch, where they spent the next hour unabashedly making out like they'd both been fantasizing about doing for months.

EMBERLY KNEW IT WAS a risk to go by Gideon's unannounced. It was late in the afternoon and she finished her work for the day earlier than expected, and their last sexual romp had been on her mind so heavily that she couldn't resist seeing if she could get a repeat performance. She tried to call him but it went to voicemail; she wondered if he was busy or just ignoring her call for some reason, though she didn't want to think that was it. She knew he worked from home a lot, so the likelihood of him being there but just unable to talk at the time was high. She was tempted to try the lingerie-under-a-long-coat thing, but didn't quite have the nerve to be that bold.

She pulled up to the house, wondering if Gideon's Challenger was in the garage. Checking her appearance in the visor mirror, she got out of the car and strode to the door, trying to summon some extra confidence and hoping she wasn't about to make a complete fool of herself. She and Gideon were cool and had some great sex, but they hadn't established themselves as anything; she had no way of knowing how he'd feel about her surprising him like this.

When the door opened and a man that greatly resembled Gideon answered the door, her eyebrows shot up to her hairline.

"Yes?" the man greeted.

"Ummm..." Emberly was momentarily stumped. "I'm sorry; I was just stopping by...um, I'm Emberly Holliday. My siblings and I own the house."

"Oh yeah," the man smiled. "Gideon has mentioned you. I'm his brother, August."

"Oh!" Emberly had temporarily forgotten that Gideon had a twin brother. Her eyes scanned his textured tapered fro, faint mustache, and eyebrows that were thick and naturally arched. She could tell he and Gideon were identical, but thanks to their different hairstyles and the fact that August wasn't quite as muscular as Gideon, it was easy to tell them apart.

She didn't even realize he was holding his hand out to her, and she blushed when she finally did. Silently telling herself to get it together, she put her hand in his, feeling an immediate *something* shoot up her arm. "It's nice to meet you, August."

"Likewise." He stepped back when their hands fell apart. "Would you like to come in?"

"Sure, thanks," she replied, hoping she didn't sound too eager. Her body actually felt like it was tingling and she didn't know what to make of that. "If, you know, I'm not interrupting anything."

"No, you're good. I was just straightening up the kitchen. Come on in."

Emberly stepped into the house, feeling inexplicably nervous. The living room looked and smelled like it had been freshly cleaned, and she figured that was courtesy of August. It certainly never looked like this any other time she had come by to see Gideon. "It looks great in here."

"Thanks. I can be kind of a neat freak at times, I admit. I'm not too crazy with it, though. You want something to drink?"

"Oh no, I don't want to impose. Are you always this nice to strangers?"

August chuckled. "I'm a nice guy, generally, but you're not a *total* stranger. Gideon has mentioned you a few times. Said you were real cool to deal with."

Smiling, Emberly wondered if that was *all* Gideon told his brother about her. "I'm glad to hear that. He's not here, I take it?"

"No, he had some running around to do. There's not a problem or anything, is there?"

"Oh no." She shook her head emphatically. "Nothing like that." There was no way she was going to admit the real reason for her visit. "You moving in here, too? And before you ask, it's no issue, if you are; I'd just need to know."

"For the time being, yeah," August replied. He motioned for her to take a seat on the couch, following suit after she did. "I just moved to Terston and haven't had time to find a place yet."

"Well, there's certainly enough room for you here. I wondered why Gideon would want to rent a family home when it was just him but figured it wasn't my place to ask. And I guess it doesn't really matter, at the end of the day, as long as he can pay the rent."

"From my understanding, he would've preferred something smaller but the other places fell through. And the rent here was affordable enough that he couldn't pass it up."

Emberly was glad that was all it was; part of her wondered if he had a secret family that he was going to suddenly move in at some point. "Makes sense. You sure you don't want me to go?"

"Feel free to hang out for a while, if you want. I don't have much of anything going on right now. I don't start work for another couple of days."

"What is it you do?"

"I'm a pharmacist."

"Really?"

"You seem amazed," August noted, amused.

"Kind of. I've actually never met any pharmacists before. That's pretty cool. Is it, um…is it just *you* moving here or will other people be joining you?"

"Just me. I'm not in a relationship or anything and I don't have any children."

Emberly was surprised at the relief she felt upon hearing that. "Hmm. Okay, then."

"And what do you do, Emberly?" August asked her. "Beautiful name, by the way. And I love that tattoo sleeve. Are those baked goods?"

"Yeah," Emberly smiled, glancing at her arm covered in images of every kind of pastry imaginable, with various apples stuffed between them. "I'm a pastry chef and a lifelong lover of sweets, so it was an easy choice. And thanks for the compliment; I don't think anyone has ever said that about my name before."

"Really? That's surprising. Your name is almost as beautiful as your eyes."

He chuckled at the clear shock on Emberly's face at his comment. Her hand pressed to her flushed cheeks. She wasn't used to getting all this praise; men tended to appreciate her body but outside of her long locs, usually the things she got complimented on the most involved something she'd baked.

"That's really sweet of you, August," she commented, her hand sliding down to her neck and lingering there. "I'm gonna savor that compliment. I've never thought there was anything special about my eyes."

"You should take a closer look at them sometime. The brown reminds me of sweet tea, which I love. Their shape is mesmerizing, like an artist drew them; very sultry and piercing. And your lashes are no doubt the envy of most women. Those are all natural?"

"Yeah," Emberly concurred, her face flaming even more. "These are all mine. They're the main thing my sisters and I have in common; we're triplets."

"Yeah? That's interesting." He sat forward in his seat, eyes fixed on her. "I'm more interested in learning about *you*, though."

Emberly looked at him, their gazes locking. She felt something overtake her insides that she wasn't familiar with. Were these the butterflies that she always heard about? In all her years of dating, she'd never experienced them. But they were surely setting up shop now.

They continued to talk and get better acquainted, eventually facing each other on the couch. Emberly had even eased out of her slides at some point, at August's suggestion. They were so engrossed in their conversation that they were actually surprised when Gideon came in. And he was equally surprised to see Emberly there.

"Oh, damn."

"You don't have to look so shocked, brother," August chuckled.

"My bad. I guess I just wasn't expecting to see our landlord here." Gideon dropped his keys in the bowl near the door.

Even though that was technically her title, Emberly felt weird about Gideon referring to her as such. He'd seen her naked more than once. "Hey, Gideon."

He nodded at her and slid his hands into the pockets of his dark jeans, his eyes holding no tenderness or affection for her whatsoever."Emberly. You came by to check out that loose window pane upstairs?"

Her expression faltering slightly, she sat up a little straighter. Clearly, Gideon didn't want to let on about the personal nature of their relationship to his brother. The level of detachment he was treating her with was off-putting.

Figuring it was time to go, she slid her feet back into her shoes, then stood. August quickly followed suit.

"I'll be sure to let my brother know about the window issue," she informed Gideon, her voice as empty as his. "You can just deal with him on that. I'm gonna go."

"All right. See you later." He picked up the mail from the end table and began flipping through it, dismissing her.

Glaring at him for a split second, she pursed her lips and turned to his brother. "It was nice meeting you, August," she stated, the warmth returning to her voice. She smiled at him, part of her hating that she had to leave his company. She'd been enjoying their conversation and just...being around him. "I appreciate the hospitality."

"No problem. Here, let me walk you out."

After sliding his own feet back into his shoes, August stood and followed her to the door, his hand very gently touching her lower back. Emberly turned her eyes to Gideon as she passed, but he never looked at her; he just dropped the mail back onto the table and headed into the kitchen. Emberly didn't want to feel insulted but she did. She'd thought they were at least friends but he was treating her like she was nothing to him.

At least August soothed the burn a little with his kind words and lingering hug outside. Emberly had to make herself get in her car and drive off, because she wasn't quite ready to leave him. But she almost as equally wanted to get away from Gideon's standoffish attitude.

She was just pulling up at home when she got a call from him. Debating whether she should answer or not, she let it ring a few times before finally taking the call. "Yes?"

"Emberly," his voice rushed into her ears, already sounding remorseful. "Can we talk a second?"

"I haven't had a chance to talk to Noah about the window yet. I'll be sure to have him get back to you on that directly, Mr. Wheeler."

He sighed. "I'm sorry about all that, Em. Please don't take it personally."

"What, you acting like I'm nothing to you? Kinda hard not to. You were pretty convincing. But hell, I'm probably just a booty call to you, anyway."

"Come on, Em, you know better than that. I just didn't want to let on to my brother about me and you hooking up. There's been several times over the years where we've been attracted to the same woman; I just didn't want it to turn into a *thing* between me and him."

Emberly perked up at the thought of August being interested in her, because she certainly was feeling him. Her mind had already started whirling with excuses she could use to see him again. But she wasn't about to let Gideon know that.

"If you say so," she droned, his explanation not making her feel much better. "I need to go; I'll have to talk to you later."

"Are we cool?"

"I suppose."

"Come on, Em..."

"If I brushed you off like that in front of my sisters, you wouldn't be thrilled about it, either," Emberly stated. "Regardless of what my reasoning was. But whatever. It's not like we're a couple. You don't owe me anything."

"Can I see you later?"

"Why? Won't August still be there?"

"He said something about going out. And anyway, I could just come to your spot."

"I'll have to let you know. I'll text you." Emberly's mouth might have been saying this, but her mind was already replaying the things he did to her in the bedroom. There was no denying she enjoyed their sexual playtime. "Bye, Gideon."

He sighed. "All right. I hope I hear from you later. Bye."

Hanging up the phone, Emberly leaned her head against the headrest. This was quite the situation she found herself in; sleeping with one twin brother and immensely crushing on the other after just a couple of hours. She supposed she could understand Gideon's explanation; the truth was, she *didn't* know the nature of his relationship with his brother. And she barely knew August. Was it irrational of her to feel slighted by a man she was only having a sexual relationship with?

Not knowing how she was supposed to feel, Emberly knew she needed to talk to someone with more experience. Her mind strayed to her Aunt Miriam, who she knew would give it to her straight, but then she thought about Enya. Surprisingly, she wanted to confide in her sister about all this (excluding the part about Gideon being their tenant). Enya had way more savvy when it came to men and would likely be able to give her some insight. Plus, she hadn't seen her sister in a while.

She tried to call Enya but it went to voicemail. Glancing at the time, Emberly figured Enya would be home from work soon, if she wasn't already there. She worked from home at times. Figuring she'd just take a chance and swing by, she pulled out of her parking spot.

Enya still hadn't called or texted her back by the time Emberly made it to her house. There was an unfamiliar car in the driveway, and Emberly wondered if her sister had company. Before getting out of the car, Emberly sent her a text letting her know she was there and would be knocking on the door in a couple minutes; she figured that would be enough time for Enya and her visitor to get their pants back on.

When Emberly finally rung the doorbell, it was a while before she heard any movement and she wondered if Enya was even awake. She rung the doorbell again, pressing harder on it this time.

Finally, she heard footsteps. When the door eased open and Enya saw Emberly standing there, her eyes widened, almost in panic.

"Emberly," Enya greeted, tugging on the t-shirt she wore that clearly belonged to a man. It was several sizes too big for her. Her face was devoid of its usual makeup and her short hair was skewed, as if someone had been running their fingers through it. "What are you, uhh...I didn't know you were coming by."

"Hey, yeah. I tried to call." Emberly attempted to peek around the door. "And text."

"Oh, you did? I don't even know where my phone is, come to think of it...I didn't have it back in the room with me."

"I'm sorry for just dropping by like this but I needed to talk to you about something. And I haven't seen you since MLK day. I know you've called a couple of times and I tried to call you back but kept missing you. You've gone kinda scarce lately."

"My bad on that. I've just been kinda wrapped up." Enya anxiously glanced behind her.

Emberly looked at her sister expectantly. "Do you...need me to come back another time?"

"Could you?" Enya looked relieved at the suggestion. "I'd like for us to sit and hang but I have some-"

"Babe, have you seen my charger?"

Enya's eyes squeezed shut and Emberly frowned. That voice sounded familiar.

Then she saw Dallas walk through Enya's living room, shirtless and with the comfort and familiarity of someone who had been there many times. Emberly's eyes narrowed as they turned to Enya, who was looking as guilty as Emberly was furious.

"Is that *Dallas*?" Emberly asked, her voice heavy with accusation. Of course she already knew it was; she just wanted to hear it confirmed.

Enya stepped forward, her hand pressed to her chest and eyes shining with apologetic tears. "Emberly-"

"You're *fucking* the guy that ghosted me??"

"It's not like that! I swear, I-"

"What's it like, then? Because from what *I* see, my sister is hooking up with the bastard that ghosted me *twice*! *This* is the secret man you didn't want to tell us about? Well, I guess I see why. What, he stood me up so he could get with you? He was just jerking me around the whole time?"

"No! Emberly, please listen, okay? I should've told you sooner and I'm sorry about that. I just...we didn't-"

Enya screamed when Emberly hauled off and slapped her. She held her face, looking at her fuming sister in shock. They hadn't struck each other like that since they were kids. Emberly couldn't help it; the idea that her sister had chosen some man over her made her lose her head.

Dallas came running out from the back, looking concerned. When he saw Emberly standing there, his expression morphed into alarm.

"Emberly..."

"Yeah, *Emberly*. At least you got my name right this time."

He sighed. "I deserve that. Look-"

"You know what? Your punk ass can keep whatever you're about to say 'cause the time to talk would've been *before* you ghosted me, blocked me, then started fucking my sister! And Enya, I guess what he did to me doesn't matter, huh? You *saw* how upset I was over how he played me and said nothing, *knowing* you were seeing him?? I *bet* you wouldn't have done no shit like this to Evelyn but clearly *I* don't matter! So fuck *you* and fuck *you*!" She jabbed her finger in both of their faces, itching to punch them both. "To hell with *both* of you!" Unable to stand the sight of them a second longer, Emberly turned and hurried back to her car, her hands visibly shaking with anger.

Enya started to follow her before Dallas grabbed her arm in a silent reminder that she was wearing nothing but a t-shirt. "Emberly, wait!"

But it was no use. Emberly was already in her car, screeching off down the street.

Chapter 11

EVELYN WASN'T SURE when it happened, but she had begun actually looking forward to her therapy sessions. Despite her initial doubts, she was making significant progress towards moving on from Travis. Her thoughts about him had decreased. The temptation to find excuses to contact him had lessened. And when he did cross her mind or she came across reminders of him, she didn't feel the pang in her chest like she used to. She even went ahead and got rid of everything that Travis had given her over the years; all the gifts, letters, doodads, jerseys and hoodies, and cards were now gone.

"What about the pictures?" Dr. Meyer, her therapist, asked once Evelyn revealed this.

"Those, too," Evelyn replied proudly. "Though, to be totally honest, I couldn't bring myself to destroy them. I just put them all in a box and left them on his doorstep when I figured he wouldn't be home."

"Interesting. Has he contacted you since then?"

"Surprisingly, yes. He called the day after I dropped the stuff off but I didn't answer. Didn't respond to his texts, either. Hopefully he'll get the hint."

"It says a lot that you took such a step. And I'm pleasantly surprised about you not acknowledging any of his efforts to reach out."

"I don't want to tempt myself," Evelyn admitted. "I can't say with all certainty that I'm strong enough to deal with him directly yet."

"But you're getting there."

"True. And anyway, I'm not sure what he could have to say, anyway. This is what he said he wanted."

"Sometimes what we think we want isn't what we actually want. Maybe he didn't expect for you to actually cut him off like you have."

"Oh well."

"Are you still finding other ways to occupy your time?"

"Thankfully, yeah. I've taken up drawing, even though I suck at it. And I went out with that guy Caliph again."

"The one your sister set you up with? How did that go?"

"It was fine, but that's *all* it was; fine." Evelyn sighed and adjusted her glasses before burrowing against the back of the overstuffed tan couch in Dr. Meyer's office. "He's a nice guy and real cool to hang out with, but I don't see any romance happening there. And I realized I'm okay with that. Maybe it's too soon to expect anything more than friendship from anyone."

"Well, there's no timetable; only you will know when you're ready for something more than a platonic relationship."

"Yeah. Part of me wants to keep trying and the other part is fine just taking things as they come. I don't know if the issue with Caliph is that I'm ready but he just isn't the one, or if I'm not ready and it wouldn't matter *who* I went out with."

"There's nothing wrong with taking the time to figure that out. You've been in a relationship with the same man for more than half your life; maybe you should get comfortable being alone before venturing into another serious relationship."

Evelyn thought about that. She never realized just how much of her life had involved Travis. She could see Dr. Meyer's point, but she also couldn't deny the merit to Enya's argument about basically using one man to get over another one. Clearly, she still had some things to figure out.

Over the next couple of days, Evelyn just focused on her work as a zookeeper and her new drawing hobby. She actually chuckled at how bad her drawings were, but it didn't matter. She enjoyed the activity. It gave her something enjoyable to focus on; and after a long day of working around smelly animals, families with touchy-feely kids, and chatty coworkers, that's what she needed. No one would see the drawings but her.

She almost forgot about her upcoming date with Caliph. She'd had every intention of going home after work, taking a shower, eating some jambalaya, and curling up on the couch with her sketch pad. It wasn't until he texted her that she remembered she'd agreed to meet up with him.

Quickly changing into a matching steel gray sweater and leggings set and some sandals and brushing her hair up into a bun, she headed out. He offered to come pick her up but she still hadn't wanted to let him know where she lived.

"You look adorable," he greeted with a smile when she approached him outside of the movie theater. He stood and leaned in for a hug, which she obliged with a smile of her own. His low-cut sandy brown hair and skin of almost the same color beamed underneath the street lights.

"Thanks. I like your hoodie," Evelyn commented, eying it. *Unapologetic* was across the chest in a graffiti-like design.

"I appreciate it; my boy started a business and I was just trying to support."

"That's nice."

"Ready to see the movie?"

"Yep."

They headed inside, and since Caliph had already gotten their tickets, they stopped at the concession stand for popcorn and slushies before heading into the theater. Evelyn sat next to Caliph, feeling the occasional brush of his arm against hers and smelling his cologne and listening to him laugh at what they were watching, and she wished she was home with her jambalaya and her sketch pad. She just wasn't in the mood for this tonight.

Once the movie was over, she and Caliph headed outside.

"You want to grab something to eat?" he asked her. "I know I kinda hogged the popcorn in there."

"Hogged it, ate ninety percent of it; tomato, tomahto," she teased. "But I'm all right."

"You sure?"

Her stomach chose that moment to remind her that she'd barely eaten in hours, and growled loudly. Pressing a hand to it, she peeked at Caliph's amused face.

"Okay, maybe I wouldn't be mad at a burger right now," she admitted, hoping her cheeks weren't as red as it felt like they were.

"Sounds good to me. Let's go; you can follow me, since I already know you're gonna insist on driving yourself."

Evelyn just smiled, not bothering to dispute that. He was right.

They headed to Dink's, a popular diner and the spot in Terston for late-night grubbing, where they pigged out on bacon burgers, steak fries, and thick milkshakes. Caliph even enticed her into sharing a huge slice of vanilla cake. By the time they left, Evelyn was pressing her hand to her stomach for a whole different reason.

"Geesh, I am *stuffed*," she mused, blowing out a long breath. "Guess I was hungrier than I thought."

"I like that, though. I've been out with enough women who try to eat like birds while they're eying what's on my plate the whole time. It's cool to see a woman just go at it like you did."

"Damn, was I that bad?" Evelyn chuckled. "Ah well. It's late and I was too hungry to try to be cute."

They headed to her car, making easy conversation. She yawned, holding the side of her fist to her mouth.

"Long day?" Caliph asked.

"Yeah. And I guess it's catching up with me."

"Understandable. Well, I won't bother asking if you want to do something else. Go home and get some rest."

"I appreciate it. Wouldn't want you to have to pick me up and carry me after I fall over from exhaustion."

He chuckled. "I'd have your back but yeah, it's probably best we avoid that."

They stood there smiling at each other for a moment before Caliph leaned down and gently pressed his lips to hers. His hand took hold of her forearm as he stepped closer, their lips moving against each other's slightly.

Evelyn eased back, eying him as he rose back to his full height. It was their first kiss. She stood there looking at him thoughtfully before a frown began forming all on its own. She was waiting for the butterflies or the fireworks or *something*, but they never came.

"Is something on your mind, Evelyn?" Caliph asked, looking down at her. He was tall, almost too tall for Evelyn's taste. She was five-eight herself, and he had to be almost a foot taller. She didn't want to have to get a step stool every time they decided to hug.

Glancing at his concerned face, Evelyn sighed. She figured she might as well tell him the truth.

"Actually, yeah," she admitted, scratching behind her ear. "I'm not sure this is going to work."

"What's that?"

"This," she verified, waving a hand back and forth between them. "It's got nothing to do with you; this is all me. I'm still reeling from my divorce and was trying to put myself back out there, but I just don't think I'm ready to date yet. I've enjoyed hanging out with you, but I don't want to waste your time if you're looking for something deeper than I can give you right now."

Caliph just eyed her as he processed her words, then rubbed his chin. She wondered if he was going to go off on her and steeled herself for anything.

"I guess I can respect that," he finally said. The disappointment in his eyes was clear, and Evelyn felt a pang of guilt. "I can't say I love hearing it, but if you're not feeling it, you're not feeling it."

"I'm sorry."

"Was the kiss that bad?"

Not sure if he was joking or not, Evelyn smiled but didn't laugh. "It wasn't bad at all, Caliph. If I was in the right frame of mind, I'd probably be climbing you like one of those gym ropes right now."

That made him smile, to her relief. She sincerely liked him and didn't want them to part on bad terms.

"At least let me know you made it home safe," he finally requested, stepping back. His soft brown eyes gazed at her before dropping to the pavement. "If you don't mind."

"I'll absolutely do that."

"Good night, Evelyn."

"Good night." She shyly stepped forward with her arms partially extended, and to her relief, he granted her with a firm hug. He lingered for a moment, squeezing her shoulder before finally releasing her. With a wave, Evelyn got in her car and drove off.

She was mentally processing her evening as she drove home when she got an emotional call from Enya.

"You will not believe what your sister did!" Enya exclaimed.

"What?" Evelyn was alarmed; she couldn't remember the last time she'd heard her sister so riled up. Enya was the one that usually let things roll off her back.

"Emberly *hit* me!"

"She what??"

"She slapped me! In my *face*! Hauled off and did it right in my front door; can you believe that??"

"What in the world happened? Oh, wait a minute," Evelyn sighed, realization hitting her. "Did she find out about you and Dallas?"

A quiet moment passed. "I didn't know she was coming by here. Apparently she called while Dallas and I were in the shower, then when we got out, the last thing I was thinking about was checking my messages. She got here and I admittedly didn't know how to handle it. And it didn't help that I was in Dallas's t-shirt when I answered the door."

"Ouch."

"Yeah, *ouch*; that's what I said when she slapped me into next week. That shit *hurt*!"

"Okay, she shouldn't have done that. But I tried to tell you that you should've told her about you and Dallas sooner."

"Yes, I know you did, Evelyn. Now is not really the time for an 'I told you so.'"

"So now what? How did y'all leave things? Did you at least get to talk to her after she calmed down?"

"She wasn't here long enough for all that. After she slapped me and cussed both me and Dallas out, she left."

"Wow." Evelyn shook her head as she turned onto her street. "I hate to hear that but I can't say I'm all that surprised."

"And of course, she's been ignoring my calls," Enya continued, her voice losing some of its fire. "I was hoping she'd hear me out after she had some time to cool off, but no such luck."

"I'm sure she will, though. Once she comes down off the shock of catching you two together, she'll remember that she and Dallas were only a blip on the radar, if that. Then you two can have a drink and hash all this out."

"That would be nice but I don't see it happening any time soon. I know it's not about whether they were an actual couple or not; it's the principle. In her eyes, I chose Dallas over her and she's not gonna just get over that. You know how Emberly can hold a grudge."

"Yeah..." Evelyn pulled up to her townhome and turned off the engine. "She *does* have a tendency to not wanna let stuff go. But maybe since she seems to be seeing someone else, she won't hang onto this that long."

"What? She's seeing somebody?"

"I mean, I guess. I saw her and some guy hugging and it seemed pretty intimate."

"When was this? And where?"

"A few days ago, I guess. I've been losing track of what day it is. You know I used to count the days since Travis left me? So I made myself stop looking at the calendar-"

"Evelyn."

"Oh, yeah. I saw them outside of the rental house."

"Wait a minute...is she seeing the guy renting our house? Have you met him?"

"I haven't. You know I don't get that involved with the renters. Most of my input came in when we were doing the renovations."

"Yeah, yeah." Enya's voice sounded thoughtful. "I thought we all agreed not to date anyone we rented to."

"We did, but let's not forget that all I saw was a hug between her and some random man. For all I know, it could've been a guest or friend of whoever is renting the house, or somebody else. We shouldn't jump to conclusions about anything."

"You're the one that told me about it."

"I was just trying to take your mind off the slap. Maybe I should've told you how I think Noah has a new girlfriend." Having grabbed her purse from the passenger seat, Evelyn closed the car door with her hip and headed to the front door, keys in hand. She let herself in and closed the door behind her, flicking on the light. "You know how he tends to go radio silent when he first starts seeing somebody. I wonder who it is this time."

"Doesn't matter; she probably won't be around that long. Now, back to Emberly and the renter..."

Evelyn sighed, already regretting telling Enya about what she saw. "I don't have anything else to say about that, Enya. I told you I don't know who the man is."

"Uh-huh."

Knowing her sister was already probably plotting how she could find out the real deal about Emberly and this mystery man, Evelyn shrugged. She was mildly curious herself, but she figured if their sister was seeing someone and it was anything worth mentioning, they'd hear about it soon enough. It didn't usually stay quiet when Emberly was into someone.

She texted Caliph while she was still on the call with Enya, kicking off her shoes. She was heading upstairs when there was a knock on the door. Frowning curiously, she backed off the bottom step and headed over, only half-listening to Enya rattle on about Emberly's nerve and how they could get her to spill the beans about her hugging partner.

Evelyn officially tuned out, though, when she looked through the peep hole.

"Uhh, Enya, I need to call you back," she muttered distractedly, still marveling at who was on her doorstep. Not bothering to say goodbye, she absently hung up the phone while Enya was still talking and unlocked the door.

"What are you doing here?" she asked, wishing she could sound angrier about it.

Travis stood there with his hands in his pockets, looking relieved. "I almost thought you wouldn't answer the door."

"What do you want?"

"Can we talk for a minute?"

"About what?"

"Please?"

Her mind screamed for her to close the door in his face, but she felt herself step back and open the door wider, allowing him entry. He stepped inside, eyes on her.

"You've been on my mind a lot lately, Evelyn," he informed her, watching as she closed and locked the door. "That's part of the reason I've been calling you."

Stalling so she could gather her words, Evelyn moved further into the living room. She started to rub the back of her neck, but didn't want to appear as nervous as she felt, so she dropped her hands. "I don't know what I'm supposed to say to that, Travis."

"It really threw me when you left all that stuff at my place," Travis admitted, following her. He stood near her, but she stepped away from him. "I wasn't expecting that at all."

"Well," she hunched her shoulders, still not really looking at him, "It's what I needed to do to move on from you."

"You've moved on from me?" He moved closer to her again.

"I had to." She again stepped away, almost wondering if she was dreaming all this. "You said you wanted distance and to not see me so you could focus on your *lady friend*. Said all this stuff about needing to do what's best for you. You don't remember standing right there in my kitchen *telling* me I needed to move on?"

"Yeah, I remember." He sighed. "But I guess it hit different when you made it clear you were actually doing it."

"So, what, you expected me to keep pining for you while you went on with your life? You can't handle it that I'm doing fine without you?"

"That's not it." He reached out and grabbed her hand, noticing how she stiffened at his touch.

"Then what is it, Travis?"

"Maybe...maybe I'm not as ready for you to be out of my life as I thought. Maybe I just miss you."

Her eyes finally drifted up to him, and he looked so sincere and frustratingly handsome that she had to look away and will the tears that were pushing against her eyes to stay put. She did not want to be affected by his words. It had taken a lot of effort for her to progress past the pain of losing Travis and she didn't want to forget about that just because he was apparently starting to realize what he threw away.

"That's too bad," she finally replied in a barely-there voice. She pulled her hand from his and put it behind her back, taking another tiny step away from him. "You got what you wanted."

"No," he adamantly shook his head. "It's one thing to want a little space so we can adjust to our new reality, but it's another for you to totally cut me out. I never wanted that. Do you know how it felt, getting that box with every single *everything* I've ever given you? Just because I asked for a divorce doesn't mean I don't still love you, Ev. And maybe it's unreasonable, but I need to know you still love me, too."

Marveling at him, she buried her burning face in her hands as she paced in front of her rarely-used fireplace. There was a teeny tiny part of her that was touched by his words, and she hated that. How many nights had she wished and prayed for him to show up like this, saying these things?

"You really have a lot of nerve, Travis," she made herself spew. Stopping her pacing, she looked at him, mentally forcing a montage of everything she didn't like about him in an effort to wipe out any flattery from what he just said. "Whatever way you're feeling about me moving on from you, that's your problem. I don't owe you anything. And I don't appreciate you jerking me around like this." She stalked towards the door. "You need to go."

Seeing that she was serious, Travis hurriedly rushed over to catch her, grabbing her arm and pulling her around to look at him. "Evelyn, look at me."

She shook her head. "*Go*, Travis!"

"Evelyn! Come on, I'm not jerking you around!" His hands slid up to her shoulders, squeezing them affectionately as his eyes sought out hers. "Maybe I'm handling this all wrong but I need to hear you say that to me. Can you please just tell me you still love me? I can't leave here until you do!"

"Why? Why do you even care?"

"Haven't you been listening? I still care about you. I still *love* you!" He hesitated for only a second before yanking her to him and kissing her trembling lips, his arms wrapping around her back. She feebly pushed against his torso, hating how she automatically responded to his kiss. It was nothing like Caliph's kiss from earlier; *this* one gave her butterflies. And they were fluttering at full speed.

"Tell me, baby," Travis muttered against her lips, his hold on her tightening. "Tell me you love me, Evelyn."

Whimpering at both Travis's kiss as well as her rapidly-vanishing self control, Evelyn felt her mouth ease open wider almost on its own as he backed her against the nearest wall. Her tongue met his, falling into the familiar tangle that always left her panties soaked. Pretty soon, their somewhat-frantic kiss melted into an erotic reacquaintance with each other. Evelyn's hands went from trying to push Travis away to easing underneath his shirt. Travis slid his own hands down and around his ex-wife's body, grabbing handfuls of her behind before sliding them underneath her leggings, wanting to feel her skin. He pulled her towards his bulging erection and she groaned, pressing closer to him as her hands eagerly grabbed hold of his butt.

"I love you," she finally whispered, unable to hold back anymore. "Oh god, I still love you, Travis..."

Grunting loudly, Travis picked her up and rushed towards the stairs towards her bedroom. They quickly shed their clothes before Travis dove on top of her on the bed, kissing her hungrily and grinding his hard manhood between her quivering legs.

"Condoms," he muttered between kisses, his hand squeezing her moderate breast. She shuddered when his thumb teased her hardened nipple.

One hand blindly pointed while the other removed her glasses. "Nightstand."

Briefly retrieving the protection and then covering himself, Travis wasted no time getting inside of her, not having the patience for tortuous foreplay or ramping up. He buried his face in the crook of her neck as he stroked her urgently, as if on a mission, his voice breaking occasionally as he grunted and breathed in time with his thrusts. Evelyn clung to him, wondering if she was dreaming. She never thought she'd feel Travis inside of her again, but here he was. He had come back to her because he wanted to, not because she'd begged or plotted to get him there. Emotion surged through her, battling with her desire, and she concentrated on giving him the best she had.

"You always get so wet for me," he whispered into her ear, his hips still pumping frantically. "You still miss this, don't you?" When she nodded, he insisted, "Nah, baby. Say it."

"Yes," she breathed, not bothering to hesitate. "I absolutely miss it."

"You touch yourself at night, thinking about me?"

"Yes." She actually hadn't let herself do that in a while, but he didn't need to know that.

"Tell me you love me again." He grabbed a handful of her hair. "I need to hear it."

"I love you, Travis. I've always loved you."

"Damn right. This is still mine," he grunted before sucking her neck so hard she was sure it would leave a mark. "*You're* still mine, Evelyn."

Travis flipped her over and entered her from behind before she could respond or process his words, grabbing her hips and immediately increasing his speed. It didn't take long for him to announce his oncoming orgasm, his voice getting louder with every hard stroke.

"Dammit!" he yelled, his hips shuddering and slowing considerably. "You feel so amazing..."

He pulled out of her and they fell onto their sides on the bed, facing each other. Evelyn hadn't gotten hers, but she was too happy about Travis being there to worry about getting her turn on the orgasm train. She figured once he got his second wind, he'd surely rectify that.

"I needed that," he panted, brushing a hand along his sweaty forehead. He flashed her a satisfied smile.

Evelyn's own smile grew into a grin. "So did I. More than I realized."

His hand reached for hers. "Thank you, Evelyn."

Her brow twitched slightly in confusion about being thanked right after sex, but she made herself brush it off. It was probably just sex-drunk blabbering. "It was my pleasure."

Keeping hold of her hand, Travis closed his eyes and was snoring within minutes. Evelyn laid there for a while just gazing at him, unable to wipe the smile from her face. She wondered what Dr. Meyer would have to say about this.

It didn't matter, she told herself. This was a good thing. Travis had gotten the time apart he wanted, but now he was back. And now they could move forward together.

She scooted closer to him and snuggled against his lean body, sighing as her own eyes slid closed. The smile was still on her lips as she drifted into a euphoric sleep.

All of her good feelings went up in smoke, though, when she woke up in the middle of the night in bed alone. She thought maybe Travis had just gone to the bathroom or downstairs to get something to drink or watch television; it was something he used to do when they were married, so as not to disturb her. But when Evelyn slid on her glasses and a bathrobe, she realized all of his clothes were gone from where they'd been tossed onto her bedroom floor pre-romp. Her heart now pounding, she quickly checked the adjoining bathroom before snatching her bedroom door open and running down the stairs. Everything was dark. And a peek out the front window confirmed that his car was gone.

Telling herself not to freak out, she began looking for a note explaining why he'd left without waking her. *Surely* he left a note. He wouldn't just sneak out without some kind of word, right?

But she was clearly wrong, because after practically tearing through her townhouse checking every logical place where he might have left one, twice, there was no note to be found. She hurried to find her cell phone, thinking maybe he'd texted her an explanation. But she came up empty on that, too.

He'd just...left.

Realization hit her like a brick to the face. Travis had used her. He felt he no longer had the upper hand and decided to come over and get her to admit to still having feelings for him, and she stupidly fell for it. She'd actually told him she still loved him, and opened her legs to him like some eager naïve adolescent. Her head replayed him declaring that she was still his, and her hand drifted to where he'd left his mark on her neck. He didn't want her. He just wanted her to still want him. Wincing at what an idiot she was, she dropped onto the couch, her head in her hands.

She fell to her side, hugging a couch pillow to her chest. Not even bothering trying to stop the tears, she let herself cry for as long as she needed to, feeling stupid and embarrassed.

Chapter 12

*ENYA*: I just want to remind everyone about what we agreed on, as far as NOT dating anyone we rent to.

*Noah*: That's out of the blue. What brought that on?

*Enya*: Just saying.

*Evelyn*: Men aren't worth the goddamn trouble, anyway.

*Noah*: Whoa. What's going on with you?

*Evelyn*: Nothing. Men just suck.

*Enya*: You need to talk, sis?

*Evelyn*: No.

*Noah*: Clearly you do. But I'm not concerning myself with who dates who anymore, E3. People should be able to be with who they want, as long as they're not hurting anyone else.

*Enya*: Oh yeah, I heard you're seeing somebody now. That must be what inspired this one-eighty, 'cause you were the main one stressing the no-dating-tenants rule at first.

*Noah*: That was then and this is now.

*Enya*: Emberly? You're being awfully quiet.

*Emberly*: I'm busy. But I'm with Noah. As long as nobody is breaking the sister code.

EMBERLY WAS TRYING her best to keep her mind on the task at hand and not on what she saw when she showed up at Enya's. She still couldn't believe her sister was actually sleeping with the man that ghosted her. And what's worse, she didn't say one word to her about it. Emberly might have taken it better if Enya had come to her up front and told her she was seeing Dallas.

She was in her rented kitchen with Camilla and one of her other employees testing some new recipes. There wasn't a lot of talking going on; just faint music from the headphones her other employee wore as she worked. Emberly knew what was on her own mind, but she didn't know what had Camilla so tight-lipped. She sensed it might have something to do with Noah; Camilla had been tense and reserved ever since Emberly confronted her about her feelings for him.

Finally, she couldn't take it anymore. She put down the spoon she'd been using to stir the spiced sautéed apples and looked at her assistant.

"Camilla, I think we need to talk."

Emberly couldn't help but notice how startled Camilla looked at that statement. Really, she looked panicked.

"Um, what about?" Camilla asked, clearing her throat. She kept her eyes on the pistachios she was chopping.

"You haven't been the same since the night I asked you about your feelings for Noah, so I can only imagine your recent standoffishness has something to do with that."

Camilla shrugged. "I've just been doing my job."

"Yeah, you have." Emberly wished Camilla would look at her. "But we used to talk and joke around and stuff while we worked, and lately you only speak when you have to. I don't want things to be like this."

Pulling her lips in thoughtfully, Camilla finally put down her knife, glancing at her coworker as she grabbed a stack of dirty mixing bowls and danced out of the room. Taking a moment to gather her words first, Camilla finally turned her eyes to Emberly. "Well, I can't deny that it didn't sit right with me how you approached me about Noah."

Emberly's eyebrows shot up. "Just because I asked if you liked him?"

"It's *how* you asked, Emberly. It was clear you'd have a problem with it if the answer was yes. It was almost like you were challenging me."

"Well...okay, maybe I shouldn't have been so...*combative* with how I came at you that night. But I'm not gonna lie; I *would* have had a problem if you'd told me you were feeling him."

"Why?" Camilla placed a hand on her hip with a tinge of uncharacteristic attitude. "Am I not good enough for your brother?"

"That's not it at all. Look, this isn't anything you should take personally. You know I think you're great; or at least, I hope you know. It's not about you; it's about Noah."

Camilla frowned slightly. "What *about* Noah?"

"Look, I love my brother. Out of my siblings, he's definitely my favorite. But he's a serial monogamist. He'll jump into a relationship with someone, everything will be all good for a while, and then he'll decide he's over it and dump them. It's like he just gets bored with women after a while and then they're gone. I wouldn't want him to do that to you."

Clearly surprised by this information, Camilla's eyes fell to the nuts on her cutting board. "So...Noah doesn't take relationships seriously? Is that what you're saying?"

"Don't take this as me dogging him 'cause I'm not; like I said, I *love* Noah," Emberly insisted. "But I'm just keeping it real with you 'cause I care about you, too. He doesn't cheat or mistreat women at all. And when he's in, he's all in. It's just that there's no telling how long it will last. And I wouldn't want you to get with him, fall for him, and then get dumped when he decides he's had his fill and is ready to move on."

This didn't sound like the Noah that Camilla had been getting to know in the last couple weeks at all. He didn't strike her as the flaky type. But Emberly was his sister and Camilla knew how close the two of them were; why would she say that about him if it wasn't true?

"I just don't want you two to get into some kind of messy drama," Emberly continued, picking her spoon back up. "You would get hurt and it might also mess up our working relationship. It would just be best if you steered clear of him, as far as anything romantic goes. Save yourself the trouble."

Camilla didn't know what to feel or what to say. Her head was spinning with this revelation about Noah. If he was just going to toss her aside eventually, maybe she *shouldn't* get involved, regardless of how much she wanted him. The last thing she needed was to fall for him and get hurt.

What sucked, though, was that she felt like she'd already *started* falling for him. Their time in his office had kicked off the emotional snowball of her feelings, and it just grew the more time they talked and spent time together. Camilla already craved him more than any of the desserts she and Emberly crafted in that kitchen. It wouldn't be the easiest thing to walk away from that.

But she wasn't going to be a fool for him. So if that meant walking away, so be it.

WHEN EMBERLY'S PHONE rang later that evening, she hoped it wasn't another impromptu booty call from Gideon. She still felt some kind of way about how he treated her in front of his brother August. Even though he had explained, she hadn't been as high on him as she was prior to that whole scene. But if she was honest with herself, she knew it was mostly because of August.

He'd been on her mind since the day they met, and she wanted to see him again. But especially after what Gideon said about their tendency to go after the same women, Emberly didn't know how she should approach him, or if she should at all. Involving herself in drama between twin brothers wasn't exactly ideal. But if she was going to get what she wanted, she'd have to put herself out there. Especially since she couldn't be sure how much time she had left.

She felt like she hit the jackpot when it turned out to be August calling.

"I hope it's okay to call," he stated. "I asked Gideon for your number."

Emberly's brow quirked at that. "Did he ask you what you wanted it for?"

"He did. I might have said something about wanting to get you the sinus medication info you asked for."

"Sinus medication?"

"I'm not proud of lying but I knew I'd have to equate it with work or he'd ask a ton of questions," August admitted. "I was already kicking myself for not asking for your number before you left here that day."

Emberly grinned so hard her face started to ache. "Really? You were interested in me?"

"Very much so. Which is why I'd like to ask if you're busy this evening; I'd love to take you out."

"Oh, wow..."

"But I guess I should make sure you're even available first. Are you in a relationship with anyone?"

What she had going on with Gideon didn't count as a relationship to Emberly; they were just buddies who slept together, and they hadn't even done that since he verbally stiff-armed her in front of his brother. And Gideon had clearly expressed he had no interest in getting married any time soon, so they'd only be able to go so far, anyway. So as far as Emberly was concerned, she could do as she pleased.

"No, I'm not," she replied, the smile still on her face. She was already tingling with anticipation, knowing she'd be seeing August again shortly. "And I'd love to go out with you, August."

"I'm glad to hear that." She could tell he was smiling, too, which only made her own smile widen. "I'm still not that familiar with the city so I admit I'm not sure where to take you yet. Maybe I should've thought of that before extending the invite but I guess I got a little ahead of myself. I was looking forward to speaking with you again."

Emberly felt like a teenager. She actually did a happy twirl in the middle of her bedroom, giddy as she could be.

"That's all right; we can figure all that out later. I'm just...*so* glad you asked."

"Me, too."

What Emberly kept herself from saying was that she didn't care what they did; she just wanted to be around him again. Her mind was already racing with visions of them holding hands and laughing and hugging and sharing their first kiss. The images were so clear that it almost freaked her out, but she wanted to see more of them. And she wanted every one of them to come to fruition.

They agreed upon a time for August to pick her up before ending the call, with him promising to have a plan for their date in place by the time he showed up. Emberly couldn't remember when she'd been so excited for a date. She rushed to her closet and agonized over what she was going to wear, wanting to be cute but effortlessly so. And since they still weren't sure where they were going, she wanted to be comfortable enough. She didn't really do heels; she only owned one obligatory pair for any business or formal functions she occasionally had to attend. Most of her shoe inventory was Crocs, sneakers, and slides. Her 'cute' footwear was mostly various styles of flats.

She had just decided on an off-the-shoulder sweater and some hip-hugging jeans when her doorbell rang. Glancing at her watch, she figured it couldn't be August showing up already; he wasn't supposed to be there for another two hours. Tossing her locs over her shoulder, she walked quickly to the door, determined to get rid of whoever this unannounced visitor was. She had a date to get cute for.

The last person she was expecting to see standing there was Enya.

"What do *you* want?" Emberly asked, frowning.

"I figured if I called, you'd just keep ignoring me," Enya stated. Her hands gripped the strap of her purse hanging from her shoulder. "Are you ready to talk now?"

"Actually no, this is not a good time."

"Well, when *is* it gonna be a good time? I'd like for us to talk about this thing with Dallas and get everything out on the table."

"Wouldn't the time for that have been *before* you started sleeping with him?"

Enya sighed. "I fully acknowledge that I should have done that. When I realized who he was, I should have nipped it in the bud."

"But you didn't."

"No, I didn't. I developed feelings for him." Enya shifted her weight, glancing behind Emberly into the loft. "Look, can I come in? I'd rather not discuss this in the doorway."

Emberly hesitated. She wanted to get ready to see August but she also wanted to hear how Enya would try to justify all this. "You've got five minutes. I'm in the middle of something." She turned and walked further into the living room, leaving her sister standing there.

"Fine." Enya stepped inside and closed the door, then adjusted the collar on her brown leather jacket. Emberly was no clothes expert but she knew it was expensive, knowing Enya's tastes.

Plopping onto the couch, Emberly looked at Enya expectantly. "You were saying?"

Joining her, Enya continued. "Dallas and I aren't just sleeping together, Emberly. This isn't a fling. We have real feelings for each other. I've fallen for him."

That cooled Emberly's annoyance just a little. She hadn't expected that.

"Are you serious?" she asked, peering at her. "Or are you just saying that to get me to chill out?"

"If I was gonna lie about a man, it wouldn't be claiming I'm in love with him. How many times have you even heard me say that?"

"Just once," Emberly admitted, thinking of Enya's ex Que from years before. She'd been head over heels for him but he dumped her after visiting his hometown and realizing he still had feelings for his ex.

"Exactly." Enya looked at her sister pointedly, trying to convey how sincere she was. "For what it's worth, I went back and forth a hundred times about whether I should stay with Dallas or not; I felt *so* guilty for seeing him, knowing what he did to you. At the same time, though, I've never felt for anyone what I feel for Dallas. But I get that I should have told you about it when I started feeling him. I guess part of me thought it wouldn't matter."

With a frown, Emberly asked, "Why would you think *that*?"

"Come on, Emberly, you two never even went out. You only talked on the phone a few times and had a couple of video chats. I'm not saying this to try to excuse how I handled it, though; I know he stood you up, and I *did* tell him he was wrong for that."

"Hmph. And he said what?"

"He agreed. He fully intends to apologize to you for that."

"I'm touched. I guess he left out how he blocked me after ghosting me the second time without giving me the courtesy of an explanation."

"Yeah...he did, actually," Enya admitted, frowning slightly. She made a mental note to address that with Dallas later. "And if he did that, he was dead-ass wrong for that, too, and he's gonna hear about it. Please know that this isn't about me choosing Dallas over you; it's just an unfortunate situation. You're my sister and I love you more than anything. You know that, right?"

Emberly rolled her eyes. "Sure."

"Emberly...seriously? Are you now doubting my love for you just because of all this?"

"Do I believe you have love for me or whatever as your sister? Yeah. Do I believe you 'love me more than anything'? *Hell* no. Everybody knows you're closest to Evelyn and you'd probably put Noah ahead of me, too. And if I *did* ask you to choose between me and Dallas, I'm willing to bet my business you'd choose him, simply because I'll still be your sister regardless, even if I'm pissed at you. But it's different if Dallas disappears. If we're gonna talk, let's keep it a buck."

Enya looked hurt by her sister's words, but Emberly didn't care. Enya certainly wasn't worried about her feelings when she started seeing Dallas without a word to her. She'd be willing to bet Evelyn already knew about the two of them, too.

"I can't believe you actually feel that way, sis," Enya eventually murmured, her eyes falling to her hands in her lap.

Sucking her teeth impatiently, Emberly sat forward. "Let's not, okay? This dynamic has been in place since we were kids. You know it and I know it."

Enya wanted to delve more into this subject but she didn't put it past Emberly to physically put her out, so she reluctantly got back to the main topic. "Look... I hope that this won't be an issue between us, Emberly. Because I meant it when I said I've fallen for Dallas. And I don't want to give him up."

They peered at each other for a moment before Emberly turned her eyes away. She wondered just how petty she wanted to be over this. Should she just let it go and be happy for her sister, or keep holding a grudge about the proverbial sister code being broken?

"Surely you can understand where I'm coming from, right?" Enya went on, eying her. "The part about getting so caught up in the whirlwind of something new and fun and exciting that you're not thinking straight...it becomes your delicious little secret. Of *course* you know how that is."

Something in Enya's voice made Emberly's antenna go up and she fought to keep her face even. Enya almost sounded like she thought she had something on her. Emberly hadn't been out with August yet so she couldn't be hinting about him. That only left his brother. There wasn't any way she could know about Gideon...was there? Was that behind Enya's random text to the sibling group chat reminding them about not dating their renters? But where would she have even seen them?

Emberly had no way of knowing if Enya actually knew anything or if she was bluffing, but she wasn't about to take any chances. She definitely wasn't going to admit to anything unless she absolutely had to.

But then she decided that she didn't care if her siblings found out. If Enya could date Dallas after what he did to Emberly, then Emberly could date whoever she wanted, sibling agreement be damned. What would they do about it, anyway? She deserved to be happy.

"Your five minutes is up," she finally concluded, slapping her thighs with a little too much force. "If you say you're that happy with Dallas and you feel he's good for you and all that, more power to you. You're clearly gonna do what you want, anyway."

Enya's eyebrows lifted in surprise. "So what does that mean for us?"

"I'm not gonna mention you and bitch-ass again. I could be petty about it but I don't have the energy or the time. And it's not like I don't have my own stuff to worry about. I just look forward to the day when this lovey-dovey head-in-the-clouds newness wears off and y'all start dealing with some *real* shit; we'll see how y'all hold up then, since you like to keep secrets and he seems to have a problem with hard conversations. You better hope he doesn't punk out on you like he did me."

"Emberly-"

"Does Evelyn know about you and Dallas already?"

Enya's eyes widened before falling to the ground, and Emberly shook her head, not surprised.

"I'm so sorry," Enya whispered.

Emblery sucked her teeth. "Sure you are."

"No, really, sis. I know it's jacked up that everybody knew before you did-"

"Everybody? So Noah and Auntie know about y'all already, too? I'm the last to know?"

Enya winced at her slip-up.

"I guess next you're gonna tell me you confided in Tariq and Travis and Perla too, huh? Might as well scrape up every adjacent relative to help keep ol' Emberly in the dark," Emberly taunted, fighting her re-igniting ire as she glared at her sister. "Who else did you tell? The mailman? The pastor? The lady who does your nails?"

"No! Emberly, please, I...it was a mistake and I own that. I'm totally in the wrong and I won't make any excuses."

"As if you could. You have *no* idea how badly I wanna knock your ass out right now. But I'll keep my hands to myself 'cause I'm sure whoever you run and tell would just blame me, as usual. Look, I'm done talking about this shit. I'm not thrilled about how all of this went down but at the end of the day, it is what it is. Enjoy."

"I don't love leaving things like this. You're clearly still upset."

"Well, I'll just have to deal with it, won't I? Like you said, you're not giving Dallas up." Emberly stood, glancing at her watch. "Now, I don't mean to rush you, *sis*, but I have something I need to get back to. We'll talk whenever."

"Hmm. All right." Enya stood, giving Emberly a lingering look before turning to leave. Emberly just chewed her lip as she watched her.

"Emberly..." Enya said before she walked out the door. "Are you sure there's nothing else we need to talk about? Nothing else you wanna tell me?"

"No."

"I get that you're still upset with me but I'm still willing to listen if you have something you need to confide or...admit to."

Emberly glared right into her sister's eyes. "I think I'll follow your lead and keep my business to myself. I'm more than used to it. Just know that whatever I'm doing, I'm not the least bit ashamed of it nor am I worried about any repercussions from you, our siblings, or anyone else. So take from that what you will. *Good night.*"

Enya blinked, clearly thrown, before flashing a tight smile and leaving.

Once the door was closed behind Enya, Emberly released a long breath. That could've gone worse, but she told herself to shake it off. She was no more thrilled about Enya dating Dallas than she had been when she slapped her across the face about it, but she'd have to find a way to let it go. And even though she defiantly decided she didn't care about the 'no dating renters' rule she and her siblings established, she didn't need Enya deciding to go digging and find out about her and the hot Wheeler twins. There was no telling what kind of headache that would turn into.

At the end of the day, Emberly figured it didn't matter, anyway. Enya didn't do long-term relationships. She was talking like she was in love with Dallas, but Emberly didn't place a whole lot of stock in that. She gave it a few months, tops, before Enya was over it. Enya had said time and time again that she wasn't thinking about getting married, so Emberly told herself to not worry about it. Let them have their little...whatever.

With that resolved in her mind, Emberly went back to her room to get ready for her date with August.

IT WAS CORNY TO EVEN think, but Emberly didn't want this night to end.

She was having the best time with August. They'd decided to go roller skating, of all things, before having a nighttime picnic by the lake. There were several other people out there enjoying the nice evening, but they were just faceless blobs to Emberly. All of her attention was fixed on August.

"I know what you mean about not feeling that bond you always hear about with multiples," August commented, sliding the last beef empanada over to her. "Gideon and I have always been good but I can't say we're best friends at all. There's plenty I don't share with him and I know he doesn't tell me everything."

*You don't know the half of it*, Emberly thought to herself, thinking of her and Gideon's sexual past. "Yeah, I wish my sisters and I were closer. I love them immensely, don't get me wrong, but I've always been closer to my brother, Noah. He was the one that always looked out for me. Evelyn and Enya...they have their own thing."

"Do you wish it was different?"

"Sometimes," Emberly replied thoughtfully, cutting the empanada with her plastic knife and holding half of it out to August, which he accepted with a smile. "I used to wish they'd include me more. But that faded over the years. If anything, I've kinda resented them, if I'm honest."

"Why is that?"

"I don't know...Enya has always been the stylish one that got all the guys without even trying, and Evelyn can be kinda goofy so everyone usually wanted to be friends with her just for that. Things seemed to always come so easy for them. I was the outsider; not just with them, with everyone. I used to be overweight while they've always been thin, and when I was younger I made it my mission to get that weight off, thinking looking more like them would make us closer."

"Wow...I hate you felt you had to do that. Did they know that was your motivation?"

"Oh, no. I wasn't about to admit that; in the back of my mind, I always knew that wasn't a good reason. And thankfully, I quit worrying about being like them and embraced any differences I had, almost defiantly. I love my body now, and I do that while still enjoying the sweets I make for a living."

"That self-confidence is invaluable. I'm glad you realized how beautiful you are, just the *way* you are."

"Thank you, August," Emberly blushed. "But not much has changed, in regards to my sisters. They don't usually try to include me in things unless they have to. That was the case back in the day and it kinda still is."

"That has to be rough." August took a bite of the empanada. "Have you ever told them any of this? How you've felt over the years?"

"Nah. I figured there was no point; that maybe that's just how things were. Us being triplets didn't guarantee that we would all be super tight. The way I saw it, if they wanted to include me in things, they would have."

"Maybe it couldn't hurt to get it out on the table, though. Just because you all weren't close back then doesn't mean you can't be now, if you hash everything out. Maybe their excluding you wasn't a conscious thing."

"I guess that's possible," Emberly mused. "But I know it can't be said that I've never kept anything from them, either. We're just one big happy family, huh?"

August chuckled. "Hey, no family is perfect. Trust me, I've heard of a lot worse."

"I guess I shouldn't make it sound so terrible. When I think about it, I didn't have it *that* bad."

"It's amazing how our perspective evolves as we get older, isn't it? Things that seem like the end of the world when we're young seem so minor once we mature."

"Oh my god, you're so right about that."

While Emberly agreed with August's statement in general, she didn't want to admit that there were still some childhood grudges she was holding onto. Yes, she loved her sisters. But it always stung that they clung to each other like they did and left her as an afterthought. She always wondered why she was never good enough to be included. Was it because she was overweight then? She'd like to think her sisters weren't that shallow. Before she started growing her locs, her hair had been a wild mess of thickness that she refused to straighten, while Enya and Evelyn couldn't wait for their monthly appointments at the salon for their mane-taming relaxers. They bonded over things that Emberly didn't care much about, and they never seemed interested in learning about her interests. Emberly felt like the black sheep of the family, despite the fact that her parents loved her unconditionally and Noah always had her back. It just hit different that her fellow triplets didn't embrace her like they did each other.

She'd never gotten over it.

But hopefully now, she'd be able to turn the tables on them. She knew something they didn't, and remembering that always sent a rejuvenating rush through her. And hopefully, August being in the picture would help get her closer to getting what she wanted.

Pushing all of that out of her mind for the time being, Emberly just focused on the man in front of her that had her daydreaming and smiling to herself at random moments since they met. Yeah, August could be the one. She just hoped that his views on marriage were another thing he didn't have in common with his brother.

But all of that almost didn't even matter at the end of the night when he took her into his arms and asked if it was okay to kiss her while he looked tenderly into her eyes. Emberly's body lit up as she eagerly agreed, then felt his lips on hers for the first time. Their arms wasted no time sliding around each other, their grips tight as they got acquainted with each other's tongues and strokes and rhythms. He took his time with her, like he was savoring every second, and

Emberly never got the feeling that their kiss was nothing more than a prelude to what he really wanted. His hands roamed her back and arms and slid behind her head and dug into her hair, but they never went to her intimate areas, despite Emberly's desire for them to.

When he finally and reluctantly eased away from her and wished her good night with no attempt to go inside her place for more, part of Emberly was disappointed. She wanted August, in every way. But it touched her that he seemed to want her for more than just sex. That alone made him different than most of the men she'd dated recently, including his brother.

When she finally went inside, kiss-drunk and on shaky legs with a goofy smile on her face, she was even surer that August was the one she needed.

Chapter 13

NOAH SMILED AS HE OPENED the door for his Aunt Miriam.

"There's my handsome nephew," she greeted with a smile, reaching up to briefly caress his face before entering his house. She carried a large canvas bag in her manicured hand. "You have a woman in here? Do I need to keep my voice down?"

"No, Auntie," Noah chuckled, closing the door behind her. "I told you when you called to let me know you were coming that I was alone."

"Yeah, well. A lot can change in twenty minutes. What are you doing?"

"Just looking over some stuff for this meeting I have tomorrow."

"Have you eaten?"

"Not yet. I was going to order something in a little bit."

"That's what I figured." She handed him the bag, and that's when Noah noticed the delicious aromas wafting from it. "You're always eating out, so I wanted to bring you a home-cooked meal. Eat some *real* food, for once."

"I cook every now and then. And I usually order prepped meals every week. But I'm damn sure not gonna turn this down." He leaned down to kiss her cheek. "Thanks, Auntie."

"No problem, baby."

"Come on in," Noah offered, leading her into his spacious kitchen where he began unpacking the bag. His stomach growled when he saw the containers of oxtails in gravy over wild rice, charred green beans and onions, sweet potato soufflé, and honey butter cornbread. There was also a huge slice of cherry pie.

"*Damn*, Auntie!" he exclaimed, hurrying around the kitchen island to give her a grateful hug, lifting her off the ground.

"Put me down, boy!" Miriam laughed, playfully swatting him on the behind when he did. "You know I'm gonna make sure you're good."

"I surely appreciate it." Noah commented, grabbing a fork from a nearby drawer to start digging into the still-warm food. He took a bite of the soufflé and moaned his approval, nodding vigorously as he went in for another bite.

Miriam beamed. She loved the triplets as if they were her own daughters and always had, but she especially had a soft spot for Noah. She knew it was tough on him growing up, being the older brother to triplet sisters, though she never heard him complain about it. When they were born, all of the attention that had been solely on him for four years was snatched away. Her brother Jessup – their father- and his wife Wilona had done the absolute best they could, but four children under the age of five was a lot. It was Miriam who stepped in to help get Noah to his science fairs or baseball games when they had their hands full with the girls. And she babysat him more times than she could count. Over the years, they'd developed a special bond and even though he was knocking on forty, she still made it her business to see about him.

"What have you been up to?" Noah asked her as he continued eating. He dug into the oxtail, which had always been his favorite. "I tried to call you a couple times the other day and it went to voicemail."

"Oh yeah, Tariq and I were out of town. We decided to drive over to Sugar Lake for the weekend."

"What was the occasion?"

"Since when do I need an occasion to go with my husband to fu-"

"Never mind." Noah didn't need to hear the rest of that sentence. He didn't want to think about what his aunt and her young husband were likely doing in a secluded cabin for two days.

"You asked." Miriam took a seat on one of the cushioned barstools in front of the island. "What else has been going on with you? Please tell me you've been doing something other than working and painting."

"Bought a saxophone the other day."

"Since when do you play the saxophone?"

"I've always wanted to. It's been pretty cool, fooling around with it. I've already learned a couple of songs."

Miriam didn't know how in the world Noah was able to just pick up an instrument and teach himself how to play it in seemingly no time. She took years of piano lessons when she was young and still couldn't play anything if you paid her. "You'll have to let me hear that sometime, then. I've always loved the sax; it's incredibly sexy."

He dropped his hands, looking at her. "Auntie."

"What?"

"Anyway," he resumed eating. "I've also started seeing someone. Well, kind of. You remember Camilla, right?"

Miriam frowned thoughtfully. "I feel like I should...where have I heard that name?"

"It's Emberly's assistant."

"Oh, yeah. So you're seeing her now? That's wonderful. I didn't even know you liked her like that."

"I've had my eye on her for a while, really. Always thought she was pretty but more than that, there was just something about her. And when I broke up with Kimmy, I realized I wanted to quit wasting time and make something happen."

"And the feeling was mutual, I take it?"

"Thankfully. Even though she was nervous about making that known, thanks to Emberly."

"Emberly? What does she have to do with it?"

"She doesn't think Camilla and I should date, since she believes it could lead to some kind of drama between her and Camilla once I leave her, which Emberly is sure I'd do at some point. So basically, she's just worried about how it all will affect her."

"Hmm. And what, she said something to Camilla about it?"

"She told me that nonsense when I first mentioned having an interest in Camilla, not that I listened to her. And she basically dared Camilla to admit that she was into me, to the point where Camilla straight lied about it. But she came to see me and we hashed it all out, though she *has* been harder to reach these past couple of days. I wouldn't be surprised if Emberly has put some more bullshit in her head again. Camilla was already worried about Emberly firing her if she dated me."

"I can't imagine Emberly would be that petty. But then again, I don't put anything past anybody."

"Yeah. I suppose."

"I'll tell you, though, baby; if you *do* want to seriously start something with Camilla, you'd better make sure it's worth it," Miriam advised, lightly tapping her long crimson nail on the island. "Whether or not you take Emberly seriously, don't dismiss Camilla's concerns. You never know what trouble Emberly might give her if she knows the two of you are dating against her wishes."

Noah didn't want to believe Emberly would actually take any frustration about them dating out on Camilla. He figured she would pointlessly fuss at him about it then eventually get over it.

"And I know you're not gonna want to hear this, but it's not like there's zero merit to what Emberly said," Miriam continued, looking at her nephew intently. "Whatever your reasons, you *do* tend to up and leave relationships at the drop of a hat. It's not unreasonable that Emberly would be concerned about that, whatever her motives are. Maybe you should examine why you're so abrupt to jump in and out of these relationships like you do, especially if you really like Camilla. If you only want something casual, be up front with her about it. But if you're talking about making her your woman, I suggest hitting pause to decide if that's what you *really* want or if you're just satisfying some temporary urge."

Noah's chewing slowed as he thought about his aunt's words. Yeah, he tended to dive in with women headfirst, taking advantage of the initial high that came with having a new crush. And yeah, he always took solace in that when that high wore off, he was up front about it and just ended things rather than treating the woman differently or cheating. But maybe his way wasn't the best way.

"You've given me something to think about, Auntie," he commented solemnly, raking his fork through his wild rice.

"It's what I'm here for." Miriam reached over and patted his other hand before sliding off the stool. "Now, I need to use your restroom real quick before I head out. Maybe while I'm in there, I'll send *Tariq* something to think about."

"Oh my god..."

"Lighten up. I'm just kidding."

She wasn't. Noah knew she wasn't.

She strutted off to his guest bathroom, and Noah marveled at how she could move around so fluidly in those tight skinny jeans. Enya had definitely gotten her affinity for wearing heels all the time from Miriam; they went to the grocery store in pumps.

He shook his head and dug into his pie, trying to pretend his aunt wasn't about to be sexting in his bathroom.

IT WAS THE DAY BEFORE Valentine's Day and Camilla asked to see Noah. He was glad to hear from her but had a feeling her reason for wanting to meet up wouldn't be something he wanted to hear.

"I'm out doing some running around right now," he told her, pulling up to a red light as he spoke to her on Bluetooth. "You want me to meet you somewhere?"

"Yeah, I have to run some errands before a work event tonight. Are you anywhere near Forrest Park?"

"I'm not too far from it."

"Can you meet me there in, say, twenty minutes?"

Glancing at the time, Noah replied, "Yeah, that'll work."

"Okay, see you soon."

Noah arrived to the park first, but Camilla was only a couple minutes behind. He watched her bright green Kia Sorrento pull up beside him, absently wondering if she'd had it painted that color or if it came like that.

He motioned for her to join him in his truck, and she did, climbing into the passenger's seat. Her usual cake batter scent immediately filled the interior. Noah had come to love that scent.

"Hey," she greeted him, tucking some hair behind her ear.

"Hey. It's good to see you."

"I'm sorry that I've been a little distant these past couple of days. But there was a reason."

Noah turned his body towards hers. "And that is?"

"I had a talk with Emberly," Camilla informed him, facing him. "And what she told me left me with a lot of...concerns."

"What kind of concerns? What did she say?"

"In a nutshell, she said I shouldn't date you because you get bored with women easily and will just leave me high and dry eventually."

The immediate frown that came to Noah's face was so intense that it actually ached. "She seriously told you that?"

"Yes." She peered at him, her eyes roaming his face. "Was she wrong?"

Noah remembered his talk with Miriam the day before regarding how he handled relationships, and made himself calm down. There was no point in getting defensive. Even though part of him felt like his sister had thrown him under the bus, he chose to focus on Camilla's concerns instead.

"In essence, she has a point," he admitted, holding her eye contact. "Though it's not as cut-and-dry as she probably made it seem."

She drew away from him slightly. "Then how is it?"

"It's not that I get bored with women and dump them unceremoniously, or even cruelly. I simply realize they're not the ones for me and don't want to waste their time."

"It could be said that's just semantics, Noah."

"It's not, though. It's all about the intent. I don't date women I don't care about. And it's *because* I care about them that I let them go if I don't see a future, especially if I know they want one with me. I'm always honest about it, and respectful. And I'm always careful about what I say because the last thing I want to do is hurt them. So it's not as heartless as I'm sure Emberly tried to spin it to be."

Camilla looked at him thoughtfully before turning away, resting her back against the seat. Noah wondered what was going through her mind, and steeled himself to hear that she didn't want to take the risk and get involved with him. It was the last thing he wanted her to say. Ever since his talk with Miriam the day before, he'd been reexamining how he handled things with women. It kept him up all night, because he certainly didn't like being thought of as someone that treated women as if they were expendable. It hadn't occurred to him that his actions over the years had led to such an impression.

When she still hadn't spoken after a few moments, Noah tentatively reached over and took hold of one of her slowly-wringing hands. She glanced at the action before looking up at him.

"I *really* like you, Camilla," he told her, the intensity in his voice surprising even him. "And I can understand why what Emberly told you made you rethink some things, even after I just explained myself. It's not the easiest thing to start something with someone only to be worrying about when it's gonna end."

"No, it's not."

"And I don't want you to constantly be on edge around me, waiting for the axe to drop. Camilla, please know that if you and I get together, I'm all in. You would get all of my attention, all of my affection, all of my effort towards making it work. And I sincerely hope it *does* work."

"What if you decide it doesn't, though?"

"I'd rather not even think like that. I've been giving a lot of thought to how I go about things with relationships, and I wouldn't even get involved with you if I didn't think there was the high likelihood that we could go the distance. But the truth is, we never know how things are gonna turn out. Hell, you might be the one to dump *me*."

A smile tugged at her lips. "Maybe. Though I've never been much of a heartbreaker."

"I can't imagine that. I know *I'd* be highly disappointed if you decide you don't want to bother getting involved with me."

Her eyes softened, and her grip on his hand tightened. "I guess I just...don't want to make the wrong decision."

"I get it. But there's no way to predict the future." His thumb stroked her skin. "I guess you just have to decide if you want to take the risk."

"Yeah," she mused, her own thumb tangling with his.

"So I take it you're not sure if you're going to come to my place for Valentine's Day?"

"I'm still on the fence, honestly. And I like your sisters, but I don't know that I'd want us to spend our first Valentine's Day with them."

"That's why we kick things off kind of early in the evening; it leaves plenty of time for if anyone has a significant other they want to be alone with."

"Oh."

"So how about this. Everyone should start showing up around six. You have an open invitation. If you decide you want this to happen," he lifted her hand to his lips, planting a lingering kiss on her soft skin as he gazed at her, "Then show up. And if you don't, then I'll know you've moved on and I'll respect your decision. Fair?"

Camilla nodded. "Yeah, that sounds fair."

"I hope to see you. But I'll understand if I don't."

They shared a look, each wanting a kiss but neither making the move. Noah felt a pang of disappointment when she leaned away and gently slid her hand from his.

"I should go," she said, placing her hand on the door handle. "I still have some things to do before I head back to the kitchen. Emberly will be expecting me back soon."

"Yeah." Noah tapped a fist against his thigh. "Speaking of Emberly, is she going to factor into this decision?"

"No," Camilla replied with a shake of her head. The answer surprised Noah. "It's in the very back of my mind, but my main focus is just on the two of us. At the end of the day, I can get another job if I need to. There's only one of you."

Noah actually felt his face flush at her words. He couldn't remember a woman ever making him blush like that, and was glad his skin was dark enough to hide it.

"I'll do my damndest to make it worth it."

Camilla was touched by the tenderness in his voice. Resisting the urge to dive over the console and clamp herself to him, she just briefly reached out and touched his face before making herself open the door.

"Bye, Noah."

He just looked at her with soft eyes as she eased herself out of the truck, closed the door, got into her own car, and drove off.

EVELYN DIDN'T EVEN want to tell her therapist how she'd slipped up with Travis.

She was still kicking herself days later. Every time she thought about how she'd succumbed to his advances, letting herself be swayed by all his talk of love and missing her and all that, her eyes squeezed shut as if in pain. She couldn't believe she'd been so gullible.

And to make matters worse, he hadn't even called. After seducing her, sexing her, then slipping out in the middle of the night with no note or message of any kind, he still had yet to reach out to explain himself. Maybe he'd gotten what he wanted and there was nothing more to say. But Evelyn didn't want to believe he was that kind of guy. Travis had his flaws, but he would never deliberately use her like that...would he?

Seeing as how he had yet to call or text her, clearly he would.

The more Evelyn thought about it, the angrier she got. She'd been doing just fine on her own, *finally*, moving on from Travis and getting on with her life. The tears and pining had stopped. She was focusing on other things and enjoying herself, getting used to being on her own. And just because she got rid of a box of his things, he had to come and throw a wrench in all that. She felt like she'd just been knocked back ten steps in her progress.

Knowing Travis likely wouldn't call her, Evelyn took a few shots of tequila and made herself call him. She needed some kind of explanation, and if she had to make the first move so she could get it, then so be it.

She was crouched on her couch like a cat ready to pounce, with the phone lying in front of her. With a nod of resolve, she dialed Travis's number, putting it on speakerphone and rocking back and forth as she waited for him to answer, going over what she was going to say in her head. She hoped she'd be able to resist the urge to go off as soon as she heard his voice.

Only she didn't hear *his* voice. It was some woman's.

"Hello?"

"Oh..." Evelyn's mouth hung open, momentarily stumped. She poked at her phone. "I'm sorry, I must have dialed the wrong number. I was looking for Travis?"

"Oh yes, this is his phone. He ran to the store and forgot it. I'd be happy to take a message."

"Hmm. Well, yeah, I guess you can tell him...I'm sorry, who am I speaking to?"

"This is his fiancée, Perla."

Evelyn fell off the couch. His *what*? Since when did Travis get engaged?? Did he have this fiancée when he was at her house kissing on her and talking about how much he loved her, and sexing her to sleep?

Evelyn remembered meeting this Perla on New Year's Day on Buttercup Mountain. It wasn't her style to dog other women, but she couldn't help but wonder what this older, plain-looking woman had that she didn't. More gray hair?

"Hello?" Perla called out when Evelyn didn't speak for a few moments.

"Sorry," Evelyn muttered, scrambling back onto the couch and smoothing away the wisps of hair that had escaped her bun. She cleared her throat. "I guess I *do* have a message. Please ask Travis why he came over unannounced and uninvited the other night and seduced me like he did. Oh, and that if he's going to sneak out in the middle of the night, he should really work on getting dressed in the dark. He forgot his sock."

She hung up, blocked his number, and pushed the phone away, a hard scowl on her face. Then she started to laugh. She laughed so hard that she actually fell off the couch again, but she was feeling no pain. Maybe that was mean, but she wasn't going to feel bad about it. Perla's feelings getting hurt was Travis's problem, not hers.

After she calmed down, she took off her glasses and wiped her eyes, trying to ignore the ache in her stomach that was starting to intensify. She knew it wasn't from all the laughing. The realization of everything was hitting her, and it didn't feel good. Tears pricked her eyes, but she vigorously rubbed them away. She refused to cry over that man anymore. Anyone who would do what he did didn't deserve her tears. She wanted to brush it all off and forget about it, but she wasn't there yet.

Scratching her scalp through her haphazard bun with one hand, she grabbed her phone with the other and sent a text to the sibling group chat letting them know she wouldn't be going to Noah's for the Valentine's Day gathering, and that she didn't want to talk about why yet. The replies came immediately, but she just tossed the phone over her shoulder onto the couch without any further reply, letting her head fall back next to it. She'd tell them what happened at some point but for the time being, she just wanted to be left alone.

When her mind started to wander back to her trifling ex-husband, she pushed herself off the floor. She needed to find something to occupy herself with.

Not in the mood to draw, she grabbed her keys and headed out, not even sure where she was going. Her mind thought *bar* but her car somehow ended up in front of an animal shelter.

Chapter 14

"WHO THE HELL..."

Emberly poked her head from underneath the covers at the sound of knocking at her front door. She groped for her phone, looking at the time. It was barely five o'clock in the morning. She didn't need to be up for another half hour and being awakened before that injected her with instant attitude.

She started to ignore it, but figured it might be Noah or one of her sisters. Throwing the covers off of her, she adjusted her bonnet before hurriedly heading to the door, her bare feet gently slapping against the hardwood floor.

"Who is it?" she called out.

"It's Amari."

"Amari?" She stepped forward and wrenched open the door, looking at him like he'd lost his mind. "What the hell are you doing here this time of the morning? Did you call and I missed it?"

"I'm sorry for just showing up like this but I've been out of town and I wanted to see you."

"And this couldn't have waited until a more alert hour?"

"I always get up early, you know that. And I figured you'd be heading to work soon."

The one thing about owning a baking business that Emberly didn't love: having to start her days so freaking early. "I still had another thirty minutes of sleep. You kinda wrecked that so this better be damn good."

"I think it is." He leaned against the doorjamb. "I want us to get back together."

That woke her up. "What?"

"I've been thinking about our last hookup a lot since it happened and for the life of me, I couldn't remember why the hell we even broke up-"

"You said things were getting too heavy and you needed some space to 'do your own thing,'" Emberly informed him, making air quotes with her fingers before folding her arms. The memory had come back since their last romp, because she initially hadn't remembered, either. At his shocked expression, she continued, "Oh believe me, *I* remember."

"Okay, well that was then and this is now," Amari replied after a tense moment. "A lot has changed since then."

"Yeah? I also recall you saying back then that you weren't sure you ever wanted to get married." She eyed him pointedly. "Is that still the case or have you changed your stance?"

He hesitated. "I...well, you could say that. I actually no longer believe in marriage at all."

"You don't *believe* in it?"

"No. It's become an empty institution that people only go into to show off, and the ceremony is more important than the-"

"Yeah, yeah, yeah. We're done here." Emberly started to close the door.

He jutted a hand out, stopping it. "Emberly! You're just gonna shut the door in my face like that?"

"Basically."

"Just because I said I don't believe in marriage? What, you on some kind of desperate husband-finding mission now? Think your biological clock is ticking or something?"

Her face hardening, Emberly's grip on the door tightened. "I'm not desperate, hence me about to close this door in your face, but I *do* want to get married someday. So we're clearly not compatible. And my clocks and my ticks are no longer your concern. This isn't happening. So you can go ahead and get away from my door." She pushed the door closed, locking it.

So, Amari was out. Emberly hated to be down a prospect but she told herself that Amari wouldn't be someone she could ultimately put up with long-term, anyway. He could be flaky and selfish, which was an issue when they were together the first time. So she didn't need to be wasting time with him.

Knowing there was no point in laying back down, Emberly shuffled to the kitchen so she could make herself some breakfast before getting ready for her day. She had a lot to do before going to Noah's for their family Valentine's Day gathering that evening.

She pulled out the ingredients for apple pie oatmeal and paused, frowning. Enya would likely be bringing Dallas, and the realization was enough to tempt Emberly to skip the whole thing. She didn't want to see him. Whether or not she was supposed to act like she was fine with them dating or not, that didn't mean she wanted to see them together. It would be nice if she could have a date of her own to save face.

Dumping the Honeycrisp apples in her hand onto the counter, she hurried back to her room to get her phone. She wondered if August had any plans for the evening. As much as they'd been talking since their date in the park, the subject hadn't come up. And Emberly found herself a little shy about inviting him to join her that night; what if he pulled a Dallas and decided it was too soon to be around her family? She couldn't handle that again.

Her mind drifted to Gideon. They hadn't talked much recently, but they weren't totally out of touch; she'd started back responding to his texts after making herself get over what happened at the house. He kept asking her to hook up but she hadn't taken him up on it. Maybe he'd be willing to be her platonic date for the night?

For Emberly, August was her top choice. She was still majorly crushing on him, especially after their date. But she needed some kind of insurance, just in case.

So she texted both brothers, separately, asking if they had plans for the evening. It didn't take long for Gideon to reply that he was busy, but it took a little longer for August to respond. She wondered if he was up yet, and went ahead and continued making her breakfast, eying the phone for his response. When it finally chimed with a text, she almost cut herself with the knife in her hand, trying to grab the phone.

*August*: **Funny you should ask; I was actually going to ask you the same thing. I'd like to see you, if possible.**

Letting out a squeal, Emberly excitedly bounced on her toes as she typed her response, letting him know she'd love to.

*Emberly*: **We're having a get-together at my brother's house; it's just my siblings and maybe my auntie, and** whoever anyone brings with them. Are you okay with that?

She chewed her lip nervously but August's response was quick.

*August*: **Sounds cool. What time?**

*Emberly*: **Six o'clock. That way we can go do something on our own later, if we want.**

*August*: **Even better.**

Emberly grinned, the anticipation already buzzing through her. They exchanged a few more messages before they each needed to finish getting ready for their days. She wished she could press fast-forward on her work day and get on to the part where she got to see August.

An hour or so later, she was headed to work when she thought about her siblings, namely Noah and Enya. She wondered if they were still upset with her. She didn't want a lot of tension when she brought August around. Figuring it wouldn't hurt to try to mend fences, she dialed Enya, but got no answer. Emberly knew that Enya should've been up by then, so she was likely ignoring her call. It briefly crossed her mind that Enya might have been occupied with Dallas in some way, but she pushed the thought away.

Telling herself that Enya would call her back when she could, Emberly dialed Noah's number. He was the main one she was worried about, as she hadn't exactly let go of all of her frustration towards Enya, either. But again, her call went to voicemail. Noah must have still been salty about her telling him not to date Camilla. A slight frown marred Emberly's brow, and she wished she had time to go over and see him, but he was clear across town and she was already running behind. She hated when Noah was upset with her and wanted them to get past this.

She got to the rented kitchen before Camilla and her other employees, so once she stashed her things and hung her apron around her neck, she reached for her phone yet again to call Miriam. She wanted to see if she'd be at Noah's that night but also, if she'd heard anything about him being upset with her.

She got her answer as soon as her aunt picked up.

"Well, if it isn't the shit-starter."

Emberly's jaw dropped. "What are you talking about?"

"Don't try that."

"Okay, fine," Emberly sighed. "So I guess you've been talking to Noah."

"And Enya. She told me how you flipped out when you found out about her and that Dallas boy."

"Well, can you blame me? I shouldn't have found out about them like that. She should've told me they were together."

"You're right, she should've. And I told her as much. But regardless, you don't get so upset over some man that you hit your sister in the face. Especially a man you weren't even with. That was some bullshit and you know it."

Emberly was glad this conversation was taking place over the phone and not in person. She felt herself shrinking slightly under Miriam's reprimand, like she had since she was a child. "You're right."

"And now you're trying to tell Noah who he can and can't date, too?"

"It wasn't like I said that to be mean. If Camilla wasn't my assistant, I wouldn't care. But come on, Auntie, you know how Noah is when it comes to relationships."

"Yeah, I do. And I can even understand your concern about how it might affect your working relationship with Camilla if things went downhill between them. But how you handled it was all wrong. If you were that concerned, then you sit your brother down and talk to him about it, not give him an order. And *definitely* not ambushing Camilla in Noah's face and demanding answers like either of them owes you explanations about their personal business. 'Cause despite your concerns, sweetheart, they *don't*."

Her face burning, Emberly regretted calling her aunt. She should have known she wouldn't take her side. Hardly any of them ever did.

"I get it," she admitted, because she felt she should. "I could have handled things better. But it would've been nice if my *family* considered how that stuff would've affected me."

"Girl...I get that they're your brother and sister, but they have a right to live their lives like they want. Enya was plenty worried about how you were gonna take her being with Dallas. And I can guarantee that Noah would have been a lot more receptive if you hadn't tried to boss him around, telling him what he could and couldn't do. At the end of the day, all y'all are grown. And y'all don't have to like everything each other does but regardless, you're still family. Nothing should come before that."

"You sound like Mama and Daddy," Emberly muttered.

"I might not be as high on holidays and finding any excuse to get together like they were, but I definitely agree with them on that."

"All right. Point taken. But in my defense, the only reason I got so emotional over those situations is..."

"Is what?"

Emberly realized she was about to tell too much.

"Um, never mind. Like I said, I could have handled it all better and I own that. On another note, are you coming to Noah's tonight?"

"I doubt it. Tariq and I went to the sex shop yesterday so we have to test out everything we got."

A smile twitched at Emberly's lips, and she couldn't fight it if she wanted to. "Auntie..."

"What?"

"Y'all can't just do that later?"

"We need the whole evening. Plus, Tariq and I aren't too hyped about playing corny Valentine's games and gorging on chocolate and wine while we make homemade cards for each other."

"We stopped doing the cards last year 'cause we decided it was a little played out. This year it's paint and sip, and karaoke."

"Oh, I'm surely not coming, then. I don't wanna hear y'all try to sing. Catch me on the fourth of July."

"Come on, Auntie. What happened to family over everything? It's not like you and Tariq *never* get to do...what you're planning on doing. Just stay for an hour or two and then go home and play with your...purchases."

Miriam was quiet for a moment, considering her niece's words. "All right, fine. I'll talk to Tariq about it and we'll likely show our faces for a minute."

"Good. And I'll have some of those stuffed cookies you like, in appreciation."

"The brownie cookies with the dulce de leche filling?"

"Yep."

"All right, I expect to see them when I get there. And don't let anybody else have any; those are *mine*."

"I know. We all know."

"What else are you baking?"

"Nothing. Noah's handling the food. Which is just as well because I'm swamped today."

"All right then, well go on and handle your business. I need to get to work, myself. I'll see you later on, baby. Love you."

"Love you too, Auntie."

Emberly hung up the phone feeling pensive. She could kick herself for almost telling her aunt about the document she'd found in her parent's attic. It was the whole reason she'd been acting like she had.

Part of her also wished she hadn't promised Miriam her favorite cookies. She already had a ton to do before she could go to Noah's and didn't know how she was going to squeeze that in, too. But she'd have to now.

Her employees arrived a few minutes later, Camilla coming in last, eating a breakfast sandwich with one hand and thumb-typing on her phone with the other. She barely looked at Emberly.

"Good morning, Camilla," Emberly greeted, after speaking to the others.

"Morning."

Emberly figured she was still miffed at her. She started to comment on it, but decided she didn't have the energy. She'd explained her position. Camilla was her employee but Emberly also considered her a friend, and she hated that she was still being distant with her. For the time being, though, she couldn't worry about it. They had some huge orders they needed to complete that day for some corporate and private parties and a slew of online orders to fill, not to mention Emberly getting Miriam's cookies made. That was all she could afford to worry about for the time being.

So she just turned on some music to fill the silence and got to work, with Camilla joining her once she finished her breakfast, the tense expression hardly leaving her face all day.

SINCE THEY WERE HYPER-focused and not distracted with a lot of conversation, Emberly and her employees managed to get everything done slightly earlier than expected. Emberly wanted to ask Camilla if she had any plans for the evening, but figured that might not be received very well. She couldn't imagine Camilla was over Noah already, and likely wished to spend the evening with him. So Emberly just left well enough alone and kept her mouth shut.

After the orders were delivered, shipped out, or picked up and everything was cleaned and prepped for the next day, Emberly headed out. She wanted to go on home and get ready to see August, but first, she needed to check on Evelyn. She'd been kind of quiet lately, not to mention her announcing in the group chat that she wouldn't be going to Noah's that night. Emberly was worried about her sister, and wondered if her recent scarcity had anything to do with Travis. She hoped to high heaven that Evelyn wasn't planning on spending the evening holed up in her house getting drunk and reminiscing about her ex-husband.

Checking the time, Emberly headed over to Evelyn's townhouse, calling her on the way. She almost expected it to go to voicemail, given the trend of her siblings lately, but Evelyn answered.

"What's up, Emberly."

"Hey, sis. I just wanted to check on you."

"I'm fine. Thanks, though."

"What's going on with you?"

"Just dealing with some stuff. I don't have the energy to talk about it."

"Are you alone?"

"Kind of."

"Evelyn..."

"Travis is not here, if that's what you're thinking."

"Well, I need to see for myself. Open your door."

"What?"

"I'm pulling up. Open your door."

"Is this really necessary?"

"Yes."

Evelyn sighed. "Fine. The door will be unlocked."

A few minutes later, Emberly walked through Evelyn's front door, her eyes darting around for signs of man. She almost screamed when a brown and white Beagle puppy came scurrying out at her.

"What the hell??"

Evelyn appeared, donning a pink tank top and blue sweats. Her feet were bare, and she was clearly between pedicures because her white toenail polish was severely chipped. "Hey."

"Since when did you get a dog?"

"The other day."

"Why?"

Evelyn shrugged as she dropped onto the couch, the puppy immediately trotting over to join her and resting its front paws on her leg. It was rewarded with a smile and a gentle scratch behind the ears.

"So..." Emberly hedged, "A dog, huh?"

"Yep." Evelyn was still rubbing the puppy's head. "His name is Savior."

"Savior?"

"I didn't name him but it kind of fits." Her smile faded. "Especially now."

"What do you mean?" Emberly eased onto the other end of the couch, hoping the dog didn't jump on her. She only liked animals from a distance. "What's going on?"

"I..." Evelyn sighed, her hand falling to her lap. "I did something kind of stupid."

"What?"

"It's hard to talk about..."

"You don't have to be embarrassed around me. I've certainly done my share of stupid stuff."

Evelyn took her time responding, deciding whether or not she wanted to divulge her shame. It had been a few days but she was still reeling from what happened with Travis. Every time she thought about it, her skin burned.

"If I tell you about this, Emberly, I need you to please not clown or judge or berate me," she warned with a pointed finger. "I don't need that right now."

"I won't. I promise."

"All right." Taking a deep breath, Evelyn blurted, "Travis came over the other night after I had sent all the stuff he'd given me over the years back to his place, and he was saying all this stuff about how he missed me and loved me and blah blah blah, and then he kissed me and we ended up in bed. But he snuck out in the middle of the night without a word and of course, wouldn't respond to any of my texts."

Emberly was floored. "Are you kidding me?"

"Not at all. Then I come to find out he's engaged to that woman we saw him with on New Year's. She answered his phone and apparently hadn't gotten the memo about ignoring me. But who knows what name Travis has me saved under in his phone."

"Oh my god," Emberly marveled, flopping against the back of the couch while looking at her sister in amazement. Anger surged through her. If she knew where Travis was right then, she would have made a beeline to him and thrown something heavy right at his face. "I can't believe he would do that to you. If nothing else, I at least thought Travis still respected you, even if he didn't think you should be together."

"Yeah, that's what I thought, too. But clearly we were both wrong."

"And you still haven't heard from him?"

"No. I blocked his number after spilling the beans to his fiancée how he came over here and seduced me."

Emberly's eyebrows flew up in surprise that her sister would do such a thing. Evelyn wasn't typically vengeful, but clearly anyone could be pushed too far. Emberly felt the laugher bubbling in her throat.

"I thought I asked you not to clown me," Evelyn reminded with narrowed eyes when Emberly couldn't hold the laughter in.

"I'm not laughing at *you*; I'm laughing at how you called his trifling ass out," Emberly clarified as Savior trotted off to the kitchen, apparently bored with them. "I can't believe you would do something like that but I'm damn proud of you for doing it."

Evelyn couldn't resist a smile. "I'm kinda proud of myself, honestly. Thinking about the conversation they probably had after I told her that eases some of the sting of him leaving me hanging."

"Ooh, I'd give *anything* to have been there when she confronted him about that!"

The sisters shared a laugh, then were startled by a loud knock at the door. They looked towards it, then at each other, both having a sense of who it probably was.

Without a word, Evelyn pushed herself off the couch and headed towards the door, the knocking just getting louder and more insistent.

"Evelyn!" Travis barked from the other side, going from knocking to banging the door with his fist. "Evelyn, open the door!"

Swinging open the door with an indifferent expression, Evelyn droned, "If this is another booty call, I'm all used up. Plus, Emberly is here."

"Yep. And I'm crazier than her so I suggest you calm down some of this anger you have going on right now," Emberly added, standing and folding her arms. She looked angrier than Evelyn did.

Travis was clearly thrown that he and Evelyn weren't alone, but he quickly turned his angry glare back on his ex-wife.

"You want to explain to me why you told Perla what you told her?" he demanded.

"Not really."

"Evelyn. You totally threw me under the bus with that."

"You expect me to feel bad for you? You're the one that showed up here uninvited because you got in your feelings that I wasn't crying my eyes out over you anymore. I was minding my own business and you came and seduced *me*. I didn't even know you had a damn fiancée."

"Regardless of what I did, Evelyn, what *you* did was just petty. And I don't appreciate it."

"Oh really? Well, *I* didn't appreciate how you got me into bed, got yours, then dipped out like I was some meaningless side piece. Left me in here feeling stupid and embarrassed. What you *didn't* leave me with was an orgasm, though, so I can't even say the sex was worth it."

Emberly didn't even try to control her loud guffaw at Evelyn's comment. Travis glared at her.

"Can you please give us a minute?" he asked Emberly.

"No, I cannot."

Travis looked to Evelyn as if expecting her to back him up, but she just quirked a brow at him. He sighed.

"Evelyn," he began, a lot of the venom now absent from his voice, "I get that I was wrong for what I did. You're right; I didn't like the idea of you being done with me. It was always my intention that we remain friends at the end of the day, and-"

"I can't be friends with you, Travis," Evelyn shook her head. "There's no way. Not after all this."

His expression faltering, he took steps towards Evelyn but Emberly quickly moved closer, her eyes warning him not to try anything. He shot her a wary glance before looking back at Evelyn.

"You can't mean that," he told her, reaching for her hand but she evaded his touch. "We have too much history to just be...*done* like that."

"I don't know what it is you want from me, Travis. You asked for a divorce, and you got it. You asked for distance from me, and you got it. You said we both needed to move on with our lives, and that's happening. Hell, you went and proposed to another woman! What else do you *want*??"

"Evelyn, I-"

"Maybe if you hadn't handled all this like you did, we could have gotten to where friendship was an option sometime down the road," Evelyn interjected, again shrugging off his attempt to touch her. "But for you to treat me like that...to come over here, *knowing* you're engaged to someone else, and seduce me like it meant something, like you care about me-"

"I *do*!"

"No, you don't. You can't! This was all about your pride; you just wanted to prove that you could do whatever the hell you want with another woman yet still have me under your thumb, too. I felt *so* used after that, Travis; I can't even tell you. And then for you to not leave a note or a text when you left, then not reach out to me? Yes, I was stupid for letting my guard down and giving in to you. But I would *never* have played you like that, Travis."

"Evelyn, I am sincerely, *so* sorry," Travis urged, clasping his hands in front of him. "I was wrong, I get that. And I don't even have a good excuse; like you said, my pride was bruised and I came over here almost without thinking. And when I saw you, it was like all the old feelings rushed back, and I got lost in the moment. Part of me actually thought we might be able to try again. But then I woke up in the middle of the night knowing I'd made a mistake, and I admit I didn't have the guts to tell you that to your face."

"Or over the phone. Or in a text..."

"I was a coward. I own that. But regardless, I don't want you to be out of my life completely. There has to be some way we can work this out."

"There isn't any working this out. I'm done. Any man that would do something like that to me isn't a man I want anything to do with. But you got one more thing you wanted, since I was in here crying after you left like you did. So, congratulations."

His face looked pained upon hearing that. "That's the last thing I want, Evelyn."

"Whatever. You need to leave, Travis."

"Can we please talk about this?"

"Nothing else to talk about. Now go."

"Evelyn-"

"She said get out, Travis!" Emberly exclaimed, exasperated. "Don't you have a fiancée to go home to? Does she know you're over here?"

"Yeah, Travis, go home to your woman," Evelyn added, stepping around him and heading towards the door. "You know, the one you chose over me?"

"Evelyn!" Travis pleaded.

"This is my third time asking you, Travis. Don't make me get my weapon."

He froze at her words, his eyes narrowing slightly. "You don't have a weapon."

"Wanna try me?"

They stared each other down for a moment before Evelyn finally yelled, "Savior!"

When the dog came running from the kitchen, Travis actually yelped in surprise, skittering away from it.

"When did you get a dog??" he exclaimed, frantically dodging Savior's advances. He looked absolutely petrified as the dog barked and jumped at him. Emberly clamped a hand over her mouth, laughing at the whole scene.

Evelyn opened the door. "Still don't wanna leave?"

Without another word, Travis practically ran out of the house, and Evelyn caught Savior before he could chase him outside. She kicked the door closed before setting him back on the ground, unable to resist joining her sister in a hearty laugh over what just happened.

NOAH HATED FEELING this anxious, but he couldn't help it. He kept eying the time and the door, wondering if Camilla was going to show up. It was a strange feeling, being so worked up over a woman like this; he was usually the one to hold all the cards. But the more he waited, the more he hoped to high heaven to see Camilla come through that door and essentially say yes to him and their relationship.

He was so preoccupied with that that it barely fazed him when Emberly arrived with a man he'd never seen before. Usually he'd be in protective big brother mode, grilling the guy and finding out everything he could about him, but he was still a little miffed at Emberly for running her mouth to Camilla so for the time being, he was hanging back. When Emberly introduced her date to everyone, Noah just grunted and went back to getting the easels set up for the paint and sip.

"I didn't know you were seeing anyone, Emberly," Evelyn, who had changed her mind and decided to come after all, commented. She was feeling much better after her showdown with Travis.

"Yeah, well," Emberly replied with a coy shrug. "It's still kinda new."

"Are you two dating? Like, officially?"

Before Emberly could come up with a cleverly evasive answer, August replied, "Absolutely," and slid an arm around her waist. Emberly was caught off guard, but couldn't resist the grin that shot across her face. They hadn't discussed being exclusive but she was thrilled that he wanted to claim her like that. She just hoped he really meant it and wasn't just saying it for her family's benefit.

"Nice..." Evelyn grinned, nudging her sister's arm. Leaning in, she whispered, "He's cute, too."

Emberly just grinned harder, nodding enthusiastically before the sisters giggled amongst themselves. August, having heard Evelyn's comment, smiled and shook his head.

90's R&B love songs were playing from Noah's Bluetooth speakers, and he'd provided an array of alcohol selections, which Evelyn had wasted no time diving into when she arrived. There were also various appetizers like teriyaki salmon spring rolls, smoked sausage-stuffed mushroom cups, bacon wrapped shrimp, and spicy crab dip. There was also fruit with chocolate and caramel dipping sauces, mini cheesecakes, red velvet cupcakes and white chocolate truffles.

"Has anyone heard from Enya?" Evelyn asked, taking a sip from her glass of chardonnay. A spring roll was clamped between her fingers like a cigarette, since her other hand was holding a cupcake.

"I haven't, but she didn't say she wasn't coming," Noah replied. He began unwrapping the painting kits. "She'll get here when she gets here, I guess."

"What about Aunt Miriam?"

"She texted that she and Tariq were on their way."

"Good." Evelyn turned to August. "Our auntie can be a little...*uninhibited* at times, just so you know."

"Oh, I've already warned him," Emberly assured with a chuckle. "I told him to be prepared for anything."

"She sounds like a hoot," August commented.

"Oh, you don't know the half of it, believe me."

Everyone continued to converse and get better acquainted with August, with Emberly trying to hide her anxiousness that someone would discover he was staying at their rental house. Even though she'd decided she didn't care if her siblings found out, she didn't want to subject August to any tension over it, or give the impression that he was causing some kind of problem. Surprisingly, no one asked where they'd met, and Emberly figured they probably assumed she'd met him online like her last few dates.

Despite Noah clearly avoiding Emberly, the room was full of good vibes. Miriam and Tariq arrived, and August got an immediate demonstration of what Emberly and Evelyn were talking about when Miriam immediately pulled Tariq into another room so they could 'finish what they started in the car.' Emberly couldn't help but laugh at how shocked August looked.

"Told you," she muttered.

They were still chuckling about that when the doorbell rang again. Since Evelyn was closest, she went to answer it. Noah slightly lowered his glass of merlot, nervous about who was (or wasn't) on the other side.

"Oh, hey!" Evelyn exclaimed happily. "I didn't know you were coming! Get in here!" She reached out and grabbed Camilla by the wrist, pulling her inside with a grin. "Everyone, look who-"

Noah was already making a beeline over to them as soon as he saw Camilla cross the threshold. He yanked her into his arms, laying a kiss on her that left no doubt about his intentions. And with the way Camilla was eagerly reciprocating, she didn't want any ambiguity on her part, either.

"Oh, my..." Evelyn marveled with a hand on her chest and her eyebrows practically up to her hairline. She was actually blushing a little bit.

"I don't ever want y'all to say anything else about me," Miriam told them all, pointing a finger at her shocked nieces. "At least Tariq and I left the room when we did our stuff."

"*This* time," Emberly muttered.

"That wasn't my fault. Y'all were supposed to be paying attention to the movie."

"Wow," August mumbled. He leaned closer to Emberly. "Does that mean what it sounds like?"

She took a huge gulp of her Riesling. "Honey...I've tried to block that out."

Their kiss finally tapering off, Noah grabbed Camilla's hand and walked her over to where Emberly was sitting on the black suede couch. Looking right at her as he snaked an arm around Camilla's shoulders and pulled her close, he stated, "Clearly, this is happening, Emberly. So hopefully you can find some way to deal with it."

Emberly eyed the two of them. Camilla had a hold on Noah's waist and was looking as determined as Noah, each of them daring her to challenge them. Feeling she had no choice, Emberly forced a smile.

"Well then, I'm happy for you two," she made herself say. "If you like each other that much, hey...I wish you nothing but the best."

Camilla smiled gratefully but Noah just pulled her away to the kitchen, undoubtedly for appetizers and more making out.

Deciding not to wait on Enya, everyone opted to go ahead and kick off the paint and sip. Noah had set up several easels in front of his picture window overlooking the city, which was in full view since his floor-to-ceiling curtains were pulled back. Miriam was manning her easel with Tariq holding her waist from behind and whispering things in her ear, earning naughty smiles or playful nudges in his groin with her bottom. Evelyn nursed another glass of chardonnay while she focused hard on emulating the country house they were supposed to be painting. Emberly and August had their own easels, though they were moved closer together, in a playful competition with each other as to who would paint the best house. Noah wasn't even thinking about painting anything, as he was too busy nibbling on Camilla's neck from behind as she giggled and barely concentrated on her painting, happily receiving Noah's affection. Emberly was trying her best not to keep glancing at them; part of her couldn't help but seethe a little, but she told herself to let it go. She tried to concentrate on how Noah had never looked happier with anyone and not how any possible implosion (or long-term success) of their relationship would affect her.

Things were in full swing when Enya finally arrived, her hand firmly grasped in Dallas's. Both of them were all smiles.

"Geesh, what are you two so happy about?" Evelyn asked, glancing at them as she adjusted her glasses and turned her eyes back to her painting. "You're almost glowing."

"What can I say, sis; we're pretty delirious with the happiness right now," Enya replied, grinning up at Dallas. He tweaked her chin lovingly.

It was Miriam who noticed it first. She plunked down her brush and disentangled herself from Tariq, rushing over to her niece and grabbing her left hand.

"What the hell??" she exclaimed, holding up Enya's hand displaying the one-carat round diamond ring. Everyone else in the room (except August) gasped once they noticed, their paintings forgotten. "You're engaged?"

"Actually, Auntie," Enya hedged, throwing another lovesick smile at her man, "We got married."

"*You what?!*"

Chapter 15

EMBERLY HADN'T REALIZED how loudly she yelled, but at least she wasn't the only one floored by this news. But she might've been the only one literally shaking with anger.

"What the hell do you mean, you got married?" Evelyn exclaimed. "Since when have you been planning that??"

"Hell, since when have you *wanted* to get married?" Miriam asked. "You never seemed to care about it before."

"What can I say, Auntie? It's like you always used to say; it was just a matter of meeting the right man," Enya replied. "And I've met mine."

"So you just decided to run off and elope?"

"Basically." Enya rubbed Dallas's arm affectionately, her ring gleaming. "We've been talking about it more and more recently and finally decided that we didn't want to wait. So last night, we just jumped in and did it. I'm now Mrs. Dallas Cutler."

"Well, I'll be damned..."

"I know this is crazy and spontaneous and totally not something I'd usually do, but it just feels *right*," Enya continued. "I've never been surer about anything."

"And I just couldn't wait any more to make her my wife," Dallas added, gazing down at his new bride. "I've never fallen so hard for anyone. Enya is it for me."

"That's all I need to hear, then. Welcome to the family, Dallas!" Miriam commented, smiling and opening her arms. "Come on and give me a hug. I'm your auntie now, too!"

Dallas gladly went into Miriam's arms while Evelyn rushed over and hugged Enya, the two of them happily squealing and jumping around in a circle before Evelyn grabbed her sister's hand to get a closer look at the ring. Noah then came over to hug them both, followed by Camilla, offering them their congratulations and well wishes. Emberly tried to make her feet move, but she felt like she was stuck in cement.

"You okay?" August asked her, concerned. "You look shell-shocked."

That was one way to put it. "Kind of."

"How come you're not as happy as everyone else is about this?"

Emberly knew that wasn't the time to go into who Dallas was to her, or the drama that had occurred between her and Enya over him. She wasn't sure he'd understand why she wasn't over it yet, especially since they were now a couple. Even if Emberly told him about all of that, it still wouldn't totally explain her attitude.

It took a few moments for her to notice that most eyes were on her, especially the newly married couple's. Enya was looking pensive, and Dallas seemed as if he forgot she would even be there. Emberly couldn't help but remember that he had yet to apologize for standing her up twice and then getting with her sister, despite all of Enya's claims about how sorry he was for it. Whether Emberly was now with August or not, she couldn't help the burn in her chest over this whole scene.

"Excuse me," she finally muttered, hurrying from the room. She blindly scurried to the first spare bedroom she came to, closing the door behind her and easing down on the queen-sized bed. She tried to take a few deep breaths to calm down, but her head was spinning.

Then as if just remembering the bulk of the reason she was so upset, she yanked a worn, folded piece of paper from her back pocket, carefully unfolding it before perusing it closely, looking for any kind of loophole that would give her some relief. There *had* to be something. She didn't want to believe that her sister had just bested her yet again.

Suddenly the door burst open and Miriam stormed in, and Emberly scrambled to hide the paper behind her back, hoping she didn't tear it. She'd been carrying it around with her for months, though it would've been smarter to keep it in a folder or a file cabinet, or laminate it. But at least it was just a copy; the original was locked in her desk drawer at home.

Miriam's eyes narrowed, immediately knowing something was going on. "What are you doing, Emberly?"

"Hmm? Nothing."

"Why did you run in here like that? And what's that behind your back?"

"It's nothing for you to worry about, Auntie. And as for why I came in here, I just needed a minute."

"Right after Enya announced she and Dallas got married, huh? 'Cause you were just fine before that, over there laughing and joking with your new man."

Emberly shrugged, trying to keep her face even. "I can't help that it threw me for a loop. I wasn't expecting that to happen."

"Nobody was, but the rest of us are still happy for them. You're clearly not."

"That's not a requirement," Emberly couldn't help but retort. "Just because I have to accept their relationship doesn't mean I have to be over the moon about them deciding to run off and get hitched."

"Uh-huh." Miriam moved closer to where Emberly sat. "I'm gonna ask you again; what is that you're hiding?"

Not putting it past Miriam to physically try to take the paper from her, Emberly sighed and held it up in front of her before dropping her hand to the bed. "It's just this."

"And that is?"

"It's..." Emberly bit her lip and looked away.

"Girl, don't make me start counting."

"Fine. It's something I found in the attic over at the house a while back. It promises a trust fund to whichever one of us stays married the longest."

Miriam's frown eased slightly before she stood at full height and crossed her arms, pushing up her cleavage in her v-neck sweater. "So you found it, huh?"

"Yes," Emberly replied, only marginally surprised that her aunt knew about it already. "I thought it was a lost cause since Evelyn had been married to Travis, but then they got divorced. And it says that divorce basically disqualifies you and makes whatever years the marriage lasted irrelevant. Collection would be ten years after our parents' deaths, which is in a few months."

"Mmm-hmm. I know."

"So...I was hoping to find a husband so I could get the money," Emberly admitted. Saying the words out loud made her feel funny, though. "I felt like August could've been the one for me but that's all shot to hell now."

"So you don't actually like August, then?"

"No, I *do*! I'm honestly into him, Auntie, regardless of all this. But I'd be lying if I said this wasn't an ulterior motive for wanting to ramp things up between us."

"So that's why you've been acting like such an asshole to your brother and sisters, trying to keep them from pursuing who they wanted?" Miriam surmised, going over to join her on the bed. "And being totally dismissive and unsupportive?"

Emberly's face tightened. "You don't have to say it like that, Auntie."

"I'm calling it what it is. And let me guess; none of them know you found that document, huh?"

"No. I was up in the attic cleaning stuff out when I found it. No one had wanted to help with that part so..."

"So you figured they didn't deserve to know, even though it involves all of y'all? Emberly, are you really this childish?"

Suddenly defensive, Emberly scowled and turned away. "I had my reasons. But I don't expect you to understand any more than any of them would."

"And what does *that* mean?" Miriam gently grabbed her sulking niece's chin and turned it to face her.

Emberly opened her mouth to answer, but nothing came out. Shaking her head, she swiped at the tear that was now rolling down her cheek. "It doesn't matter. I'll be the one in the wrong, regardless. Nobody ever takes my side in this family. That was the case back in the day and it still is."

Miriam looked at her niece and some of her annoyance evaporated. She could see the hurt in Emberly's eyes and the disappointment that radiated from her like heat from an oven, and Miriam sensed there was more to it than just losing out on some money.

She brushed some locs from Emberly's shoulder and slid her arm around her. "Tell me what's going on with you, baby. I really want to understand what's behind all this."

"What's the point? At the end of it, you'll still get onto me for hiding this from them. Not to mention lecturing me for holding grudges and being petty without dealing with whatever has been upsetting me before now. So just go ahead and cuss me out and get it over with."

"You're clearly hurting over something. Do you not believe I care about that?"

"Even if you do-"

"*If* I do? Is that what we're doing now?"

Sighing, Emberly swiped at her tears again before turning away. She didn't have the energy to get into all that again. "Can we drop this, please?"

"All right," Miriam conceded, deciding to let it go for the time being. Clearly Emberly was dealing with some things that ran deeper than Miriam realized, and now wasn't the time for scolding, whether or not she deserved it. She lovingly rubbed Emberly's shoulder. "I won't get onto you and I'll leave it alone for now. But there *is* something you should know."

Emberly turned her slightly red eyes to her aunt. "What?"

"Did you read the whole document, baby? I mean, *really* read it?"

Frowning slightly, Emberly hesitantly replied, "Yes...more than a few times."

"Hand me the paper."

Slowly doing as she was told, Emberly dabbed at her eyes and waited. Miriam casually scanned the worn paper before pointing near the top of it.

"Have you never noticed this?" she asked, eying Emberly pointedly.

Leaning in, Emberly looked where Miriam's manicured nail was resting. It took a few seconds, but when it registered what she was seeing, her jaw dropped to her lap.

"Oh my god..." she whispered.

"Yep."

"How could I have missed that??" Emberly's hands flew to her cheeks in embarrassment.

"I'm kinda wondering that, myself."

"Does that really say The Law Office of...*Tricks and Meat*??"

"It surely does. Kinda hilarious, when you think about it. Check the signatures at the bottom."

Emberly dropped her eyes to the bottom of the paper and after reading what was scrawled there, she wished she could vanish into thin air. She'd never felt more stupid.

"Minnie Mouse and Smokey the Bear," she muttered, feeling herself shrink by the second. She didn't even want to look at her aunt.

"*I* made this," Miriam informed her, shaking the paper slightly. "It was just something I did for the hell of it. Your parents never knew anything about it. I know they were high on marriage and family and all that, but do you really think they'd put something like this in place that wouldn't benefit all of you?"

When Emberly thought about it like that, she realized her aunt was right. Her parents respected the institution of marriage too much to essentially turn it into a competition. The fact that Emberly had been carrying that document around for as long as she had and never even noticed those now glaring details was humiliating. Clearly, all she'd cared about was the part concerning the money she could possibly get.

Sensing Emberly's embarrassment, Miriam quietly folded the document and put it on the bed beside her, then laced her fingers over her knee. Music blared from the living room, the others apparently starting the karaoke. Then Evelyn started belting out a god-awful rendition of "I'm Every Woman."

"As tempting as it is to clown you right now, I'm not gonna do it," Miriam said. Emberly had both hands covering her face in embarrassment. "I'm not gonna kick you while you're down, 'cause I'm sure you're feeling pretty ridiculous."

"That's an understatement," Emberly muttered from behind her hands.

"I get it. And it's *so* tempting to tease you 'cause I simply cannot believe you missed all that…" Miriam couldn't resist a giggle, and Emberly peeked at her between her fingers. "But I'll try to control myself."

"Yeah. Thanks."

"I know you're not gonna want to hear it, but you need to come clean with them about this."

Immediately shaking her head as her hands dropped to her lap, Emberly retorted, "I can't."

"You can. And you will."

"Why?" Emberly was whining but she didn't care. "It's clearly moot now. I'm more than willing to live with my shame. They don't need to know about any of this. It's embarrassing enough as it is."

"They deserve to know why you've been treating them like you have," Miriam countered, all amusement now disappeared. She not-so-gently nudged Emberly's arm. "I get that you're feeling like shit right now but you're gonna have to suck it up and deal with it. How would you have explained it, anyway, when you suddenly got a stash of money and they didn't?"

Emberly hadn't even thought that far ahead. Though if she was honest with herself, she probably would have just made something up about where the money came from, if she'd told them about it at all. The realization didn't exactly make her feel proud of herself. "I don't know."

"Uh-huh. Like I said, put your big girl panties on and tell them the real deal. Not tonight, because we don't need to let this nonsense overshadow Enya's good news. Or Noah's, either, for that matter. But soon. I don't want to have to ask you about this again."

Knowing better than to protest, Emberly just meekly nodded, looking at her hands. "Yes, ma'am."

"Good." Miram stood then leaned down, grabbing the sides of her niece's face with both hands before planting a kiss to the top of her head and pinning her with an intense but tender glare. "I love you, baby. Regardless of what you feel, how you mess up, or anything else. You're like a daughter to me and I want nothing but the best for you, because you deserve it. Know that, you hear?"

Pursing her lips, Emberly nodded again. "Love you too, Auntie."

Miriam winked at her before turning for the door. "Don't stay in here too long. Get yourself together. You've left that man you brought out there by himself while you're in here in your feelings. I'm sure he's probably wondering what the hell is going on, too."

Emberly groaned, having temporarily forgotten that she'd have to explain all of this to August, too. "Great."

"I must say though, baby, you have some good taste, with that August. Buddy is hot."

A proud smile tugged at Emberly's mouth, despite her mood. "Yes, he is."

Miriam left the room and Emberly ran her hands down her face before picking up the document, unfolding it and reading the fake law firm name and signatures again. They might as well have been written in neon ink, with how glaring they were to her now. She couldn't believe she'd been so foolish.

Balling the paper in her hand, she finally took a deep breath and stood, knowing she needed to get back out there to August. She could only imagine what he was thinking, with her having brought him there to meet her family for the first time then left him alone while she fumed over her sister's marriage announcement. Not only would she have to figure out what to say to her siblings, she'd have to figure out what to say to him, too.

She eased into the guest bathroom to splash some water on her face before rejoining everyone in the living room. August was talking to Tariq and laughing at Evelyn trying to sing, but immediately excused himself and went over to Emberly when he saw her.

"You all right?" he asked, grabbing her hand.

"Yeah, I'm fine." She smiled weakly, appreciating his concern. She placed her other hand on his chest. "I'm sorry for disappearing like that."

"You gonna tell me what's going on?"

"Yeah. But later, if that's all right. I don't wanna disrupt things any more than I already have."

He eyed her for a moment before giving a conceding nod, then kissing her forehead. "That's cool. As long as you're good. Come on, let's get in on the fun."

Emberly managed to put the drama out of her mind for a while and enjoy the rest of her time there with everyone. Thankfully, no one commented on her mini tantrum, even though there was still a thin line of tension between her and Noah, and her and Enya and Dallas. She just tried to forget everything else and enjoy her evening.

After almost everyone had their turn on the mike to get laughed at and the food and booze was practically gone, everyone started to disperse, their respective paintings in hand. Emberly's nervousness started to resurface as she and August headed out to his car, knowing that she would have to explain herself soon. At first she wondered how she could spin everything, but decided that she just needed to be honest. The last thing she wanted to do was start their budding relationship on the wrong foot by hiding things.

"It's only a little after nine," August commented once they were in his car. "Is there somewhere else you'd like to go, or do you want to just go back to your place? 'Cause I'm sure you probably don't want to go to mine since my brother might be there."

Thinking of Gideon just reminded Emberly that there was yet another thing she needed to come clean to August about. Even though she and Gideon hadn't hooked up since she'd met August, she knew she still needed to let him know about the fact that they'd been intimate at all.

"It'd be nice to be alone with you after all that so, yeah, my place is good," she replied, rubbing a hand along her thigh. Her mind whirled as to how to word what she needed to say, or what she should even start with.

August didn't seem to be in a hurry to get any answers, though. He just took her hand in his as he drove, quietly listening to the comedy station on satellite radio. Thankful for the reprieve, however temporary, Emberly just followed his lead and enjoyed the ride, occasionally laughing at the jokes they heard and recalling some of the humorous events from their evening.

They were almost to her place when her phone chimed. Emberly pulled it from her bag and checked it, not thinking to hide the screen from August. Her body went cold when she saw it was Gideon. She didn't want to look suspicious by glancing at August, but could tell from her peripheral vision that he was still focusing on the road. She opted shoot Gideon a quick message to let him know she'd talk to him later, figuring if she acted casual, August wouldn't notice. As soon as she opened her text messages, though, Gideon chose that moment to send her a picture. And of course, August happened to glance over before Emberly could close it.

"What the hell??" he exclaimed, his shock causing him to swerve on the road. Emberly shrieked and he quickly jerked his Impala back into his lane. Thankfully there were no other cars on the road. "Is that a damn *dick pic* on your phone??"

"August, don't trip; it's not what you think-"

"How can it *not* be what I think?"

"I was gonna talk to you about this," Emberly insisted, turning to him with pleading eyes. "This...this doesn't mean anything, I swear. I haven't gotten with Gideon since I met you-"

"Wait, Gideon? As in *my brother*, Gideon??" August balked at her before making himself take a few deep breaths to calm down, turning his eyes back to the road. Emberly noticed that he leaned as far away from her as possible, and she tried not to take it personally. "So you're sleeping with my brother."

"Was. I *was* sleeping with your brother," Emberly corrected. She started to reach for his thigh but his warning glare stopped her. "It was never anything deep; we're cool but it was totally physical. I never wanted anything real with him like I do with you."

"And I'm supposed to be flattered? Why did you wait so long to tell me about this?"

"I was going to tell you tonight! You and I, we were just getting to know each other, and then you told everyone we were dating tonight and I was thrilled about that, but then I also knew I had to let you know about me and Gideon."

"You should've told me about that regardless."

"Maybe I should have. But...doesn't it count for anything that I stopped hooking up with him as soon as I met you? August, you've had *all* my attention since that first day, and that's the god's-honest truth. What we're building right now, that's what I want. Gideon and I are over."

"Does *he* know that? Gideon might have his flaws but I've never known him to pursue a woman that he knows is already spoken for. So the fact that his dick is in your phone right now must mean he has no idea about you and me."

"I..." Emberly felt tears pricking her eyes. "Okay, clearly I've handled this wrong. But I hope you believe me when I tell you that you're the one I want to be with. I was going to tell Gideon everything when I was sure this thing between me and you was going somewhere."

"Yeah, well, now you don't have to bother." August pulled up to Emberly's building, putting the car in Park but leaving the engine running. He rested his left arm on the door and rubbed his forehead, still not looking at her.

Her eyes widened. "What are you saying?"

"I'm saying that this can't work, Emberly. Look, I like you a lot. And I really did want to do this with you. But knowing you've been with my brother-"

"What does that matter, August??" She ran her hands down her face before dropping them into her lap with an anguished groan. "Are you seriously going to throw this away over something that happened before I even met you?"

Finally turning his eyes to her, he asked, "Would you be comfortable with it if I'd knowingly been with one of your sisters and didn't tell you until after we got together?"

She opened her mouth to say yes, but nothing came out. The truth was, she probably wouldn't have been any happier about it than August was.

"Exactly my point," August concluded with a shake of his head.

"August-"

"Emberly, just..." He held up a hand, looking weary and frustrated. "Just go. We don't have anything else to talk about. I'm done."

She couldn't believe it. It hadn't been a full evening and she'd already lost the first man she could actually see a future with. How could she have messed this up, too?

Looking over at him, Emberly wished there was something she could say that would make him change his mind, but figured there was nothing. The realization hit her square in the chest, and she knew she needed to get out of the car before she humiliated herself any more than she already had.

"I'm sorry," she whispered before pushing open the door and getting out of the car. She didn't see the pained expression on August's face as she shut the door and hurried into her building.

Chapter 16

IT WAS ALMOST TWO IN the morning and Emberly still couldn't sleep. She just sat in the middle of her queen-sized bed, her mother's old quilted blanket around her, with a plate of untouched apple walnut muffins next to her. A half-empty bottle of Ciroc was on her nightstand. Her mind was all over the place, thinking about the past few months.

Ever since she found that document in her parents' attic, she hadn't been herself. She'd let greed take over and make her forget everything her parents ever taught her about family and love and marriage. Scheming on her siblings to get a check wasn't something they would have wanted, and she knew it. In truth, she knew it when she was doing it, but she'd managed to rationalize her actions to herself, believing she deserved to have this since her siblings usually got everything else. Noah was the successful businessman who could snap his fingers and be in a relationship. Evelyn might have been divorced, but she'd had the longest relationship out of all of them. And everything always seemed to come easy for Enya. Not to mention her sisters being so close with each other and never seeming that interested in being as close to her.

The more she thought about it, the guiltier she felt. Emberly knew her parents would be ashamed if they saw how she'd been acting lately. Not only towards her siblings, but towards men. They'd become nothing but potential avenues towards getting what she wanted, even going so far as to look online for a potential husband she might be able to tolerate marrying just so she could get the money.

Then she met August, and everything changed. The money became secondary to getting closer to him simply because he made her heart beat in a way it never had. And now she didn't even have him. It felt cruel that her relationship with him was over practically as soon as it began, but she knew she only had herself to blame.

She slid her phone closer and scrolled to August's name, itching to text him. At least to tell him again how sorry she was. But she needed to give him some time to cool off. And she could hear her Aunt Miriam's voice in her head telling her not to beg; she'd already apologized. The rest was up to him.

Figuring there was no point in sitting up moping about it, Emberly made herself get up and take the muffins back to the kitchen before flopping back into bed and burying herself under the covers. She laid in silence for all of two minutes before sitting up and reaching for her remote, turning her television to an old episode of *Living Single* to distract her mind. It only marginally worked, but she'd take it. Eventually she managed to drift off to sleep.

The next morning, she got up, brushed her teeth, and grabbed her phone. Everything in her wanted to call August, but she called his brother instead.

"Hey, what's up?" he greeted after only a couple of rings. "This is a nice surprise."

"Hey, Gideon."

"What's going on with you? Haven't heard from you in a minute; thought you were still mad at me."

"Is that why you sent me that picture last night?"

"That was more just my way of letting you know I was thinking about you."

Emberly might have been charmed by that weeks earlier, but now, she was even more turned off. "You could've just said that with words, not your dick."

"What fun is that?'

Shaking her head, Emberly knew she needed to get on with the point of her call. "Look...I called because I wanted to let you know that we can't hook up anymore."

There was a pause, and she briefly thought he might've hung up on her. When he finally spoke, his voice was missing some of the levity from moments before. "Why?"

"Because I have feelings for someone else. And I might as well be all the way honest and tell you that it's your brother."

"Whoa, wait...you're hooking up with my brother now?"

"We're dating. Or at least, we were," she noted sullenly. "But we've never hooked up like you're probably thinking. We haven't gone there, but I absolutely want to be with him. So whatever it is you and I have going on has to stop. No more booty calls, no more dick pics, no phone sex, none of that."

"Damn, Emberly..." He blew out a long breath, and she could imagine him running a hand through his locs. "Just like that, huh?"

"Yeah, just like that. Let's be real, Gideon; you and I don't want the same things. You've already said you weren't interested in getting married any time soon, and I am. And I enjoyed our time but I'm trying to have something real now. And I want it with August."

"Well, I guess the thing about me and him liking the same women continues. It's no surprise he didn't mention anything about this to me. And I guess this explains why he moved out last night."

Emberly stopped her half-hearted bed making. "He what?"

"He moved out. As soon as he got home last night, he started packing his shit. I tried to get him to tell me what was up but he just said it was something he had to do. Let me guess; he was with you last night?"

"Yeah." Emberly wasn't about to mention that August had ended things with her. She was keeping hope alive that he would change his mind.

"He moved in with you?"

"No. I haven't seen him since he dropped me off. I had no idea he was going to move out of there."

"Hmm. Well. I can't say I'm happy to hear this but I guess I can't hate too much. So he's going along with this marrying-for-money situation you asked me about?"

Emberly momentarily squeezed her eyes shut, embarrassed that she'd suggested that. "No, I haven't even mentioned that to him. You said you couldn't do something like that and I can only imagine he'd be even more against it. That's off the table now, anyway. I want the real deal. I want love."

"I get it. And true enough, I'm *not* interested in a deep relationship right now and if that's what you want, it's probably best we leave well enough alone."

"Yeah. So...take care, Gideon."

"Yeah. You, too."

They ended the call and Emberly chewed her lip, thinking about what Gideon told her. She felt a surge of hope upon hearing that August had moved out. It had to mean something, didn't it? Maybe he wasn't as done with her as he thought, if he couldn't even remain in the same house with his brother after learning about him and Emberly. If he was *really* done, maybe he would've just stayed where he was.

She tried to hang onto that rationale as she went on about her day.

NOAH WAS GLAD TO BE out on his first real date with Camilla as an official couple. In the few days since Valentine's Day, they'd been spending as much time as possible together and he was already hooked.

"I think this is the first time I've ever been on a date to a museum where the woman actually enjoyed it," he commented amusingly as he and Camilla strolled out of the Black inventors exhibit hand-in-hand. "It's wild how much we have in common."

"Isn't it?" Camilla smiled up at him. "I've always loved museums. Most of my dates the last few years have consisted of takeout and Netflix in a guy's living room."

"Those weren't dates, babe. Just pretense for what they actually wanted, more often than not."

"Unfortunately you're right."

"Well, I intend to keep finding ways to make you happy." He squeezed her hand. "You deserve that."

She grinned up at him, easing closer as they walked to his car, her free hand clutching his forearm. "You're such a sweetheart. I'm definitely enjoying what we have so far. I've been kinda riding high since we got together."

"That's what I wanna hear. I'm certainly loving it, too." He deactivated the alarm on his car and opened the passenger's side door for her. "You hungry?"

"Very. Can we get sushi? I know you're not a huge fan of that..."

"I can tolerate it enough, if that's what you want."

"I'll stay over tonight, if that will further incentivize you."

"I didn't need any incentive but I'm damn sure not about to turn that down. I was planning on extending that invitation before the night was over with, anyway."

Camilla giggled as he rounded the car to the driver's side, her captivated gaze fixed on him the whole time. There were times since they got together that she still pinched herself; as much as she'd fantasized about this man, he was finally hers.

They headed off to the sushi restaurant, talking about different parts of the exhibit they'd just visited. As soon as he opened the door to the restaurant for her, a woman rushed over so fast she startled them both.

"Is that Noah Holliday??" she exclaimed, trying to throw her arms around him but he evaded her with a slight frown. She drew back, actually looking offended that he wouldn't hug her in front of his date.

"Babe, this is Raina," Noah said to Camilla, bringing their joined hands to his chest. "Raina, this is my woman, Camilla Towns. It's nice to see you but we need to get going."

"Wait, we can't even get caught up first?" Raina jumped in as Noah started to lead Camilla towards the hostess stand. "I haven't seen you in forever. I'm sure Carlotta here won't mind if-"

"Her name is Camilla," Noah stated, his voice strong. "And *I'd* mind. So like I said, bye."

He brushed past her, pulling Camilla along with him. Camilla tried to keep her face even as she passed by the persistent woman, who eyed them in shock for several moments before finally going on her way. Noah had already forgotten her but Camilla couldn't resist another glance over her shoulder as they were shown to a table. She couldn't help but notice how leggy and stylish and beautiful the woman was, and she immediately wondered just what kind of history she had with Noah.

Once they were seated and their drink orders were placed, Noah perused the menu. "What do you recommend, babe? Or I might just stick to California rolls and be done with it."

Camilla managed a half-hearted chuckle. "How 'bout if you just get the same thing I'm getting?"

"It's not eel, is it? I'm willing to be adventurous but not that much."

"It's not eel."

"All right, then." He put down his menu and waved the server over to get their orders. Once that was done, he took a sip of his water and reached for her hand. "Do you know that my stress has gone way down since we got together?"

She eyed their joined hands. "Really?"

"Yeah. It's wild that I've never felt this...*free* with anybody else. What we've got going on just feels natural, like it's meant to be. Does that sound corny?"

"No," she shook her head, giving him a small smile. His words had warmed her all over. "That's actually reassuring to hear because I've been feeling the same way. And even if it *is* corny, I don't care."

"That's good. Because it's real." He smiled at her as his thumb slid across her skin. "You're everything I could want."

Her smile tightened and she averted her eyes, reaching for her glass of water with her free hand. Noah's brow furrowed in concern as he leaned back in his seat, letting go of her hand.

"What's wrong, Camilla?"

"Hmm?" Water dribbled down her chin, his question surprising her. She dabbed it with her wrist, feeling ridiculous. "What do you mean?"

"Let's not do that. We might not have been together that long but I can definitely tell when something's on your mind. What's going on?"

"I..." Suddenly feeling silly for marring their nice evening, Camilla shook her head and waved her hands in front of her. "It's nothing. We don't have to get into it."

"Camilla..."

"It's silly."

"If you're concerned about it, it must not be that silly, at least to you. I don't want us to have the kind of relationship where we keep stuff from each other. If there's something bothering you, I wanna know about it."

Eying him for a moment, she finally sighed. "All right. I can't believe I'm admitting this, but...as happy as I am that we're together now, I can't help still feeling a little insecure."

He frowned. "Insecure? Why?"

"Noah. You're this gorgeous, successful entrepreneur who excels at practically everything you try to do, and I'm an assistant pastry chef who lives in a tiny studio apartment. I can only imagine that I'm quite a stretch from the women you usually date."

"Quite. Though I see that as a plus while you clearly don't."

"How can I? I mean, look at that woman from a few minutes ago."

"Who, Raina? What about her?"

"Was she your ex?"

"Yeah..."

"See, that's what I mean. She was *stunning*."

"So what? Clearly it takes more than that, otherwise she and I would still be together. The only woman I'm worried about is the one I'm looking at right now who, for the record, I find quite stunning. Do you think all I care about is looks?"

"No, Noah, it's not that, it's just...look, I realize how I sound right now but I just can't help but feel like you're *so* out of my league. And I guess I'm just worried that you'll eventually get bored with me and move on."

Noah eyed her. Insecurity in women was usually an almost automatic turn-off. He appreciated women that were sure of themselves and displayed a certain level of confidence. But he could also understand that at least part of this was probably thanks to his big-mouthed sister. There was no telling what Emberly had filled Camilla's head with when she was trying to convince her to steer clear of him.

Before he could speak, their server came back with their meals. Noah thanked her and turned his attention back to Camilla, not caring about the food.

"I'm gonna say this and you can choose to believe it or not," he stated, looking right into her eyes. "Camilla, I'm sincerely into you. I don't give a damn about your job or where you live or any of that unimportant shit; I'm into *you*. This isn't just a fling for me or something that I'm considering temporary. Of course we have no way of knowing what's gonna happen and I'm not trying to guarantee anything other than my honesty and faithfulness, but I haven't been this sure about anyone in years, if ever. And I'm all in. But if *you're* not sure-"

"I *am*," Camilla jumped in, putting down the chopsticks she'd been mindlessly playing with and leaning forward, her hands splayed against her chest. "Believe me, Noah, the last thing I'm trying to do is drive you away."

"Is it really that hard to believe that I could be as into you as you're into me?"

"I've just never been with anybody like you, Noah. And it's throwing me a little bit."

"I'm just a man, Camilla. I'm not a god. Don't put me on some pedestal I don't deserve to be on."

Camilla absolutely thought Noah deserved to be on a pedestal, but she knew that she'd have to get past being so in awe of the idea of him that she couldn't just enjoy being with him. She didn't want to get on his nerves so much with her insecurities that she ran him out the door.

"I need you to trust me, babe," Noah continued. "Trust what we have so far. I get that putting yourself out there in a new relationship can be scary. But I don't want you constantly doubting me or worrying about some other woman capturing my attention. So if you don't think you can get past these kinds of issues, let me know now."

He was giving her an out that she didn't want. She could almost feel the sincerity radiating off him from across the table. He was there, with her, because he wanted to be. Had butted heads with his own sister because he wanted her that badly. Camilla knew she needed to get out of her own head and enjoy having what she'd been wishing for since she met Noah.

Moving her cloth napkin from her lap and placing it next to her plate, Camilla stood and rounded the table, easing herself down onto Noah's lap. She took his face in her hands and laid a deep kiss on him, which he readily accepted. Such a public display of affection wasn't normally in Camilla's wheelhouse, but in that moment, she didn't care about who might've been watching them. No one else mattered but Noah.

"I want it all with you, Noah," she whispered against his lips. "I trust you. I trust *this*. I'm not going anywhere."

"Music to my ears," Noah smiled, tenderly rubbing her back. "I'm glad we're good, babe, 'cause I'm damn sure not going anywhere, either."

"We're more than good," she assured, smiling at him. Her fingertips grazed his face.

After another lingering kiss, she returned to her seat and they finished their meals, with Noah actually enjoying what Camilla had recommended so much that he ordered more for them to take with them.

"You still coming back to my house?" Noah asked her once they were in his car a while later.

"Yeah. We just need to go by my place so I can get some things, if that's okay."

"No problem."

"I have some news," Camilla announced once they were on the road.

Noah glanced at her. "What's that?"

"I got offered a head pastry chef position at that new restaurant across town, Black 47."

"For real?" Noah grinned, reaching over and grabbing her hand. "That's great, congratulations! I didn't even know you were going for that."

"I applied a while ago but figured it was a long shot; there were several people going for it. But my interview went really well, and they seemed really impressed with the ideas I had for the direction of the menu. And they gobbled up the éclairs I made."

"I'm not surprised at all. You're super talented. *I* certainly can't get enough of your stuff."

Camilla knew he was talking about baked goods, but that didn't stop her body from waking up and imagining he was referencing something more intimate. The thought of Noah enjoying her *stuff* was enough to have her thighs rubbing together all on their own.

"I appreciate that, sweetie," she managed to say with an even voice. "Now I just have to break it to Emberly. I didn't tell her I was going for the position because I wasn't sure I'd get it, but now that I have, I'll have to let her know. I hate to leave her hanging because I know this will put her in a bind."

"She'll manage," Noah grunted. He wished he could get over his frustration with Emberly but he hadn't been able to yet. Every time he thought about how selfish she acted, his irritation flared like a grease fire doused with water.

But, he knew he'd have to find some way to get past it. He and Camilla were together now. And he and Emberly had always been close; he didn't enjoy being at odds with her.

"I should go on and tell her so she can start trying to find someone else," Camilla noted, playing with Noah's fingers. She resisted the mild urge to inch his hand further up her thigh. "I'm sure she's gonna be upset."

"Probably, but she'll handle it. She couldn't have expected you to stay her assistant forever. You're too talented not to move on to something bigger eventually. Just be straight with her but yeah, now that you know you're moving on, tell her sooner rather than later."

"Yeah. I'll tell her tomorrow. With her being so popular, though, it shouldn't be too hard for her to find someone as eager to work with her as I was."

They got to Camilla's apartment and she tried to quell her nervousness as she unlocked her door. There was no reason to be worried about Noah's opinion of where she lived. He'd already said he didn't care about that but more importantly, Camilla liked her space. It was plenty for her at that point in her life, as small as it was.

"I'll just be a minute," she told him, flicking on the light. "Make yourself comfortable."

"Take your time."

She went about gathering her things while Noah took in her décor. The limited wall space was filled with art, both paintings and pencil drawings. The wall displaying most of it was painted a deep magenta color, while the rest of the space was a bright sunny yellow. A large white bookcase served as both storage and as a partition between her full-size bed and the rest of the apartment. A purple chenille loveseat faced a wall-mounted television, and a rolling trunk did triple duty as a coffee table, a dining table, and storage. Her L-shaped kitchen area featured white countertops and a pale pink retro-style refrigerator. A couple of hanging spider plants and a fiddle leaf tree in the corner gave the place even more of a homey vibe.

"Babe, if I ever need to move into a studio, I want you to decorate it," Noah commented. "This is awesome, what you've done in here."

"Thanks, sweetie!" Camilla grinned, joining where he stood near the couch, her duffel bag in hand. She was still getting used to using pet names for him but loved doing it. "It's small but I love it."

"I can see why. It's a hell of a lot better than my first couple of apartments."

"Yeah, my first one out of culinary school was even tinier than this. If I had one complaint, it would be that I wish I had more counter space for when I'm baking."

"Makes sense. Did you do all of this art?"

"I did. Over the years I've built up my own little collection. You like it?"

"Love it. And you're always raving about my paintings but yours are just as good, if not better."

"Stop, Noah."

"I'm for real. Where do you keep your easel?" he asked, looking around.

"Under my bed. It takes up too much space to leave it out when I'm not using it."

"Is it crazy to say that seeing all this makes me feel closer to you?" he asked, gently pulling her to him and sliding his arms around her waist. He leaned down for a brief kiss before sliding his lips along her jawline to her ear, earning a sharp intake of breath and whimper from her when his tongue touched her earlobe. His hands pressed her body to his. "And I want to get as close as I can to you, babe. You have no idea."

"That's what I want, too," she breathed, dropping the duffle bag and sliding her hands up his arms to his shoulders before circling her arms around his neck. She leaned her head over to give him better access, her eyes fluttering closed as he continued to nibble her ear, which had always been her weakness. Her fingers gripped his leather jacket. "More than I can tell you."

"I'm glad," he whispered, his lips grazing her ear and sending another shiver through her. His hand slid into her hair. "Tell me if I'm going too far..."

"No," she immediately shook her head, biting her lip at the feel of his other hand gripping her hip. "I want you to...Noah..."

"Yeah?" He claimed her lips, grunting deeply as his tongue immediately found hers. Their grips on each other got even tighter as they sighed and moaned into each other's mouths, getting lost in the moment. "Tell me what you want, baby."

"I want you to pick me up and take me to the bed." Her leg lifted and rubbed against his, his hand quickly grabbing her thigh. "I want to feel you on top of me."

"*Hell* yes...you sure?"

"I'm more than sure." She pushed his jacket from his shoulders before grabbing his shirt and beginning to inch backwards towards the bed, their kiss never breaking. "There's no such thing as too soon with you; I *want* you, Noah."

Needing no further assurance, Noah swooped her up in his arms and crossed the small apartment to her bed, laying her down with a hunger in his eyes that matched hers.

"Take your shirt off," she ordered, eying him as her fingers began unbuttoning her blouse.

Noah pushed past the mild surprise at her boldness and pulled his white Henley over his head. When he saw her black lace bra, and how her breasts filled it to capacity, everything on him hardened almost to the point of pain.

Her shirt landed on the floor next to his feet. She leaned back on the bed and held out her arms. "Come here."

With no hesitation, Noah crawled on top of her, their kiss picking up right where it had left off. Her legs immediately lifted around his waist, a slow grind beginning on cue as if choreographed. She gripped his strong biceps, internally marveling at the feel of them, not to mention how his back muscles flexed when she slid her hands across them.

Her grip went to the back of his neck as he began to slide down her body, licking and sucking her neck. She squirmed as his tongue met the valley of her breasts, her back arching before she could do anything about it.

"Touch me, Noah," she pleaded in an urgent whisper. "Please..."

This thumbs grazed her nipples through the lace, sending her arousal through the roof. He lowered the cups of her bra before covering one nipple with his mouth and palming the other breast with his hand, making Camilla's hips buck so hard she almost knocked him off of her. Every way he kissed and licked and touched her felt so amazingly good that she thought she might pass out from the pleasure.

They never made it back to Noah's place that night. Camilla didn't want Noah to stop what he was doing, and he was already hooked on her scent and the taste of her soft skin, and the sounds she made when he pleasured her. They spent their first night together in her full-size bed in her studio apartment, knowing that they each finally had what they'd been looking for.

Chapter 17

"DO YOU KNOW WHAT THIS is about?"

"No idea, E2," Noah replied with a shrug. He glanced over at Enya. "You?"

"Nope. I'm surprised she even reached out to me at all. You know she hasn't had a lot to say to me lately."

"You think it might have something to do with her and that guy August?" Evelyn asked. They were all congregated in Emberly's living room, waiting for her to return from the back. "The one we met on Valentine's Day? Maybe they're engaged or something."

"She could've posted that in the group chat," Noah muttered, sitting forward on the couch with his elbows resting on his knees as he scrolled through his phone. "Don't see why that would require her calling us all over here."

"Still mad at her, huh?"

Noah glanced at Evelyn, then sighed. "I know I need to get over it."

"Hey, it's not the easiest thing," Enya commented. "Really, it was Dallas that convinced me I needed to forgive her for slapping me. And anyway, life is just too short to keep holding grudges with family, especially over stuff I played a part in."

"Speaking of Dallas, how are the two of you doing?"

"Oh, we're still neck-deep in the honeymoon phase." Enya beamed, as she usually did lately whenever the subject of her new husband came up. "Sometimes it still trips me out that I'm actually married. But now I can't imagine *not* being with my boo Dallas."

"That's so sweet!" Evelyn grinned. "I'm so happy for you, sis."

"So am I," Noah added. "It's kinda fast but it happens like that sometimes. But you know what to do if he starts acting up."

"Kick his ass, then call you to come finish the job," Enya replied dutifully.

"That's my girl."

Emberly finally emerged from her bedroom, walking swiftly to the couch with her hands clamped in front of her waist.

"Sorry about that, y'all," she commented, taking a seat next to Evelyn. "That was a business call I had to take."

"It's all right. So what's going on?" Evelyn asked her.

"Well..." Emberly tapped her fists on her thighs, flitting her eyes between her siblings, "I wanted to get you over here so I could explain some things. Namely about how I've been acting these last few months."

"Okay..."

Taking a deep breath, Emberly continued. "One day when we were over at the house cleaning it and getting it ready for remodeling, I was in the attic and found something. And I never told y'all about it."

Noah frowned curiously. "Found what?"

"It was a document saying that whichever one of us was married the longest by a certain date would get a big sum of money."

Noah's frown deepened while Enya and Evelyn's jaws dropped practically to the floor.

"What??" they exclaimed in unison.

"I know, I should have said something about it as soon as I found it," Emberly quickly admitted, scooting forward a little in her seat. "And I'm sorry. But at the time, I felt justified in keeping it to myself."

"Wait a minute," Enya held up a hand, "Before you try to explain your shady behavior, tell us more about this document."

"And I was married for years, even before Mama and Daddy passed; how could I not have known about this, anyway?" Evelyn asked. "This doesn't make any sense."

"Now that I'm thinking with a clear head, I agree with you," Emberly replied. "I should've known something was off about it. But to answer your question, Evelyn, it said that if you got divorced, you were basically disqualified from getting the money. Like, the years you were married didn't count."

"This is just getting crazier..."

"So our parents actually had a legal document drawn up that would basically pit us against each other for money?" Noah clarified. "And you didn't see anything wrong with not telling us about it?"

Emberly hunched a shoulder. "At the time, no I didn't. Because I felt like I was always getting left out of things with y'all, so it was only fair that I left you out of this."

"What are you talking about?" Enya asked.

"Come on. You know how you and Evelyn have always been joined at the hip while I was left to entertain myself. It's been like that since we were kids. Even now, you two meet up for lunch or go shopping or hang out drinking wine and giggling together and don't even think to invite me. It's kinda hard not to take that personally."

Enya and Evelyn glanced at each other, their anger cooling off significantly. They knew there was validity in their sister's words.

"Not to mention, you two were always more popular and got more attention from the guys, even after I lost all that weight, which I admit I mainly did so I could look more like you," Emberly continued. "Thankfully, I realized how unhealthy that was and started embracing my curves. But still, I can admit I've always been jealous of you two. We're triplets but I've never felt that bond with y'all, as much as I wanted to. You might as well have been twins with me as just a cousin or something."

"Okay, but what about me?" Noah challenged, unmoved. "I've never left you out of anything. Hell, I was the one who had your back the *most* over the years. Not to mention, it was me who would spend time with you when the two of them were off doing their thing. And not because I had to, but because you were my little sister and I loved you, and hated seeing you upset."

Emberly's eyes fell to the floor. "I know..."

"So none of that counted for anything? You still felt *justified* in keeping it from me, too?"

"Noah, please understand that I wasn't thinking rationally," Emberly pleaded, looking at him with moist eyes. "Yes, you've always been there for me and I love you for that, but I've also always been jealous of you, too. Everything always comes so easy for you, from work to hobbies to relationships. I have to scrape and plead for every little thing I get. Hell, you had to lend me the money to start my business."

"But you worked and paid me back, with interest. That's something to be proud of, Emberly, not vengeful over."

"I know. I know you're right. But like I said, I'd talked myself into believing that I deserved to have that for myself, even though I had no prospects for getting married at all. That's why I've been...discouraging you all when it comes to your relationships. And why it hit extra hard, Enya, when you got with Dallas. I felt if I could at least get the money, that would be one thing I'd have that y'all didn't."

"Wow, Emberly," Enya marveled, shaking her head. "I mean, I get it, but...wow."

"I hate that you always felt like that with us," Evelyn stated, placing her hand on Emberly's arm. "I know that was never *my* intent. You've been feeling like this for all these years and never said anything?"

"Didn't think it would matter," Emberly mumbled with a shrug. "Figured this was just the way it was."

"Oh, Emberly..." Evelyn slid an arm around Emberly's shoulder and pulled her closer. "I wish you would've said something. We're family. There's no way we would've wanted you feeling like some kind of outcast."

"I should have," Emberly admitted. "The only one I really confided in about all this was Mama, not too long before she passed. She tried to get me to talk to y'all about it but I thought you might tell me I was just being a baby and brush it off."

"Of course we wouldn't have done that!"

"Emberly, girl, she's right," Enya added. "Now that I think about it, we *did* exclude you a lot. And I guess we still do. But just because Ev and I are closer doesn't mean we don't still love you. At the end of the day, we're still sisters. We - *I* – don't want you feeling like you don't matter, because you absolutely do."

"I appreciate you saying that," Emberly sniffled. She dabbed her eyes with the sleeve of her shirt, her head resting on Evelyn's shoulder. "But regardless of all that, I know I was still wrong, at the end of the day. Not even just with y'all but with the men I was dating. Yes, I wanted to get married before I found that document, but it became some kind of unhealthy mission once I did. It became more about that than anything."

"So that's why you got with August?" Evelyn asked, rubbing her shoulder.

"No, I sincerely liked August. More than anyone in a while, if not ever. But I managed to mess that up a whole other way."

"How?"

"That's a story for another day. But it has nothing to do with all this."

"So what happens now that I've married Dallas?" Enya asked.

"Turns out, nothing." Emberly sat up, the edge of her sleeve balled up in her palm. "The document turned out to be fake."

"Fake how?"

"After I showed my ass at Noah's on Valentine's Day after you and Dallas announced you'd eloped, Aunt Miriam checked me and then I admitted to having found the document. She then let me know that she's the one that made it up."

"What, as a joke?"

"Not really; just as something to do. She never expected anyone to find it; it was in a box of random papers. She'd forgotten all about even making it. And my dumb ass never even noticed the fake law firm and signatures she made up. Believe me, I felt incredibly stupid after she pointed that out."

"So you did all of this for nothing?" Noah finally spoke up, his dark eyes boring into her. His voice still held plenty of edge. "You schemed against us for nothing."

"Noah...I can't even tell you how ashamed of myself I am. I've been thinking about all of this these past few days and it...it's just embarrassing, how I've been acting. I'm so sorry, y'all. I really hope you can forgive me for all this."

"Of course," Evelyn spoke up immediately. "I've certainly done my share of stupid stuff. And you realized what you did wrong. Truth be told, you could've gone ahead and not told us about any of this, even after finding out the document wasn't real. I respect you for letting us know about it, and to our faces."

"Yeah, she's right," Enya added. "Yeah, what you did was jacked up, but at least it wasn't on some malicious motive. I can understand why you did it. And honestly, part of me still felt bad about you being so upset over Dallas, so we can just call it even and leave the past in the past."

"I'd like that," Emberly smiled, relieved. "And if you're truly that happy with Dallas, I'm happy for you. For real."

Enya smiled and reached over to grab her hand. "I appreciate that, sis."

Evelyn looked over at their brother, who was still fuming. "Noah?"

Noah didn't speak for several moments, his jaw still clenched in frustration. He turned his head away from his sisters, trying to get his thoughts together.

Finally, he spoke. "I'm glad you two can forgive and let this go, Evelyn and Enya, but I can't."

Emberly's smile fell. "What?"

Looking over at her, Noah replied, "Like I said, I've always had your damn back, Emberly. And to find out that you would do something like this is like a knife to the chest."

"Noah, come on," Enya pleaded. "She apologized."

"So?"

"So that should mean something," Evelyn retorted. "People do things outside of themselves when they're hurting, you know that. At least she recognized what she did and owned up to it."

"She only owned up to it because she had to; if Auntie hadn't let her know the document was a fake, she'd probably still be keeping it from us. Especially if it would've meant her not getting anything since Enya beat her to the altar."

"Noah, don't be like that..."

"Why shouldn't I?" He stood, jamming his phone into his pocket. "She tried to keep me from my woman. Had selfish reasons for keeping you from going after Travis, even though you needed to leave his punk ass alone, anyway. And she acted a whole fool over Enya getting with Dallas despite never even pinching the dude, let alone having any kind of relationship with him. All over some money. That's not something I can just let go because she says she's sorry."

"Noah!" Emberly exclaimed when he turned and headed for the door. She shot off the couch, hurrying over to him. "Are you really going to leave like this?"

"Yeah. I am." He glared at her. "Because I'm too pissed off to deal with you right now, Emberly. And I don't want that to make me say something out of pocket."

"There has to be something I can do to make this up to you." Tears rolled down Emberly's face as she grabbed his arm with both hands, her eyes begging for understanding. "You know I hate you being upset with me."

"You didn't give a damn about that when you were being deceitful. So you need to just leave me alone for the time being and let me process this how I need to process it." He reached for the doorknob, shrugging her hands off. "When I'm ready to talk, I'll let you know. Until then, don't call me."

"Noah..."

He yanked open the door and stormed out, slamming it behind him, leaving her standing there with her mouth hanging in shock. She couldn't believe that had just happened.

"He'll come around, sis," Evelyn assured as Emberly trudged back to the couch in daze. "Once he calms down, he'll be ready to hash all this out."

"Yeah, you know Noah doesn't hold grudges all that long," Enya chimed in. "The important thing is that you came clean and apologized. Just give him some time to cool off."

Emberly wanted to believe her sisters, but she saw the look in Noah's eyes before he walked out. She couldn't help but fear that she'd done some irreparable damage to their relationship.

A COUPLE OF DAYS LATER, Evelyn was visiting her sister and new brother-in-law. She'd tried to get Emberly to join her, but she was too bummed over Noah being mad at her and losing August. After Noah stormed out that day, Emberly had admitted to having a fling with the new tenant of their house and then falling for his brother, and her sisters were too empathetic to berate her for breaking their rule about not dating renters. It was clear that Emberly was hurting, and they just wanted to focus on being there for her more than anything else.

"How are you two getting adjusted to living together?" Evelyn asked once they were seated around the kitchen table. They started to dig in to their crab legs and shrimp. "I can only imagine it's a huge change for you, sis, since you've never lived with anyone before."

"Yeah, we're still getting used to it, honestly," Enya admitted, glancing at Dallas. "I moved into his house since it was bigger, then there was the issue of having to merge our stuff and deciding what we were gonna keep and what we had to give up. It got a little testy for a minute."

"True. We both can be a little stubborn," Dallas added, peeling his shrimp. "We had to let go of the idea we were losing control just because we had to concede on using my bed instead of hers or her couch instead of mine. But we worked through it, thankfully."

"Yeah, we were being silly, really. At the end of the day, that stuff wasn't important. Us being together is the main thing."

"I know how that is, though," Evelyn stated. "Travis and I kinda went through that."

"Speaking of Travis, how are you doing with all that?" Enya asked her, taking a sip of her white wine. "Do you feel like you're finally over him?"

"Oh yeah, I didn't tell you about what happened..."

"What?"

"I had a little...slip-up with Travis," Evelyn confessed, part of her wishing Dallas wasn't listening to this part. "Long story short, he came over one night, put the moves on me, I gave in, he left without a word afterwards, then I come to find out he's engaged to that woman we saw him with."

Enya gasped. "You lyin'!"

"Wish I was. But it doesn't matter now; Travis is out of my life for good."

"You sure? I have to admit I've never heard you say that about him before."

"I mean it. That part of my life is over. That whole incident just showed me it was really time for me to move on."

"Well, thank the Lord," Enya stated, playfully waving her seasoning-stained fingertips in the air. "I hate that he dogged you like that but if it gets him out of your life, it was worth it."

"Yeah."

"Are you gonna start seeing Caliph again? If not, I can set you up with somebody else. I know a few guys that you might hit it off with."

"Thanks, but I'm good." Evelyn cracked open a crab leg and gently slid the meat out before dipping it in melted garlic butter and popping it into her mouth. "As far as Caliph goes, we're cool and text occasionally and that's where I'm leaving it for now. I don't need to rush trying to be in a relationship. If it happens organically, great, but I need to learn to be by myself for the time being. I haven't had that in my adult life. Plus, I've got Savior to keep me company."

"Who?"

"I told you I got a dog."

"And you named him Savior?" Dallas asked, amused.

"He was already named," Evelyn clarified with a chuckle.

"Well, more power to you. There's no way I could be satisfied with a dog instead of a man," Enya muttered, sucking the seasoning from her fingertips.

The three of them continued their dinner, talking about Enya and Dallas's plans for their upcoming honeymoon and funny work stories from Evelyn. Once they were done eating and Dallas left them alone, the sisters hung out in the kitchen with their wine and store-bought pound cake.

"Can you believe Noah getting with Camilla, of all people?" Enya asked, twirling her bare foot in front of her. "I mean, don't get me wrong, she's great. But I *never* would have imagined Noah would be into her like he is. I mean, buddy is sprung."

"Yeah, but it's refreshing to see, given his history," Evelyn commented. She stuffed a hunk of cake into her mouth. Once she swallowed, she continued, "Yeah, Noah's had a lot of girlfriends but usually it's like he's just there; he's not really invested, you know? The way his eyes lit up when Camilla showed up to his place on Valentine's Day...I've *never* seen him get so excited."

"Oh wow. I bet he hated that he had a house full of people, with that kiss he laid on her. Auntie told me about it."

"Oh my gosh, yes. They actually had me blushing, watching that."

"Wanna place a bet on how long it'll last between them?"

Evelyn broke off another piece of cake and shook her head. "Nah. This one is different, I can tell. I don't think Camilla is going anywhere 'cause she seems equally as sprung over him. I wouldn't be surprised if they're next in line down the aisle."

"I suppose."

"I'm worried about Emberly, though. I don't think I've ever seen her so depressed."

"It's still wild to me that she actually thought our parents would ever draft anything like that; a cash prize for winning the marriage marathon." Enya refilled her wine glass and held the bottle out to Evelyn, who drained the last little bit of it right from the bottle. "To think she would've actually married someone just to get some money..."

"Like she said, she wasn't herself with all that. And if I'm honest about it, I can see her point about us excluding her."

"Yeah." Enya nodded, remorse making her sag against the counter. "She said something a little while back about how she felt I loved you more than her. In fact, she's made a few comments about how close you and I are, but it never clicked what she meant. Now I get it. I didn't even realize we left her out so much; I know a few times back in the day I did it on purpose 'cause she got on my nerves, telling on me all the time. But I didn't realize I'd *kept* doing it as we got older."

"Well, thankfully we can fix all that now." Evelyn glanced at her watch. "I'm wanna go by and check on her, though I know she said she didn't want any company. I just hope she doesn't do anything crazy."

"She'll be all right. We've got her back. Let her have some time to herself tonight and then we'll go over there and try to get her to snap out of it; maybe take her out somewhere. Get her good and drunk."

THEY HAD NO IDEA THAT Emberly was already getting to that stage on her own, especially after the call she'd just gotten. Camilla had given her notice, revealing that she'd gotten another job. It was completely out of the blue; Emberly had no idea that Camilla was even looking for anything else. She had to believe that this was at least partially due to Emberly discouraging her from seeing Noah, and the realization certainly didn't make her feel any better.

Noah still wasn't talking to her, and with each day that passed, Emberly questioned whether they'd ever get back to the close relationship they had. It almost embarrassed her that she didn't realize the damage her deception could've caused when everyone found out about it, which they undoubtedly would at some point. No, all she'd been thinking about at the time was what she wanted. And now she was losing people more important than whatever amount of money she'd been scheming to get.

If there was any consolation, it was that she and her sisters were mending fences. They'd sat up talking for hours after Noah left that day, getting a lot out on the table. They hadn't had quality time like that with just the three of them in years, and Emberly realized how much she missed it. They might not have been super close and Emberly knew she still had to work through her jealousy issues, but it reminded her how much she loved her sisters. And she appreciated their forgiveness, though she wouldn't have blamed them if they'd shunned her like Noah had.

And of course, she'd lost August. He still wasn't responding to her, though she'd managed to make herself give him a few days to cool off. Even though they hadn't been together long at all, she still missed him terribly. Enya suggested hooking her up with someone else to get over him, but Emberly didn't want anyone else. She still wanted August.

As huge of a task as it was, she had to try to suck it up and focus on her business, especially now that Camilla was leaving. She'd have to find someone to replace her, which exhausted her to even think about. But she had no choice, because there was no way she could do everything that needed to be done with one less person on her staff. She actually grew to appreciate having something else to focus on besides all of her own drama.

After a particularly long day, she headed home, picking up a pizza on the way. All she wanted was to get off of her feet and find something funny to binge-watch so she could turn her mind off. The sooner she got into bed, the sooner she'd be another day towards hopefully her brother forgiving her, and her accepting that things were over between her and August.

So when her phone rang and she saw his name on the screen, she sincerely wondered if she was asleep already. She spent so much time rubbing her eyes and pinching herself that she almost let the call go to voicemail.

"Hello??" she practically shrieked after finally snatching it up. Telling herself to calm down, she cleared her throat and took a deep breath. "I mean...good evening."

"Hey, Emberly." August's voice was like music to her ears. He didn't sound angry, which gave her premature hope. "Is now a good time?"

"I guess that depends on if you're calling to talk or to drive the stake further. If it's the second one, let's just say I've gotten the message and call it day, huh?"

"That's not why I'm calling. I'd like for us to talk, if that's okay. Can I come by?"

"Uh, sure, yeah." She anxiously smoothed a hand over her locs, looking down at her clothes and wondering if she should change into a cocktail dress. "Yeah, come on over. I just got home a little while ago."

"Okay. I'll be by in about twenty minutes."

"All right."

As soon as she hung up the phone, she couldn't resist rushing to take a super-quick shower and, throwing on some caramel-scented body butter before putting on a fitted tank and some shorts. Whether she was going to like whatever it was he had to say or not, she was going to look and smell delicious while he said it.

August arrived when he said he would, looking unfairly good in a fitted sweater and slacks and smelling even better. Emberly yearned to hug him, but she forced her hands to stay at her sides.

"Hey," she greeted him, gripping the doorknob so hard it almost hurt.

"Thanks for letting me come see you," August commented. His eyes roamed her freshly-moisturized face.

"No problem. Um, come on in."

August stepped inside, and Emberly tried to ignore the instant tingles covering her body at being so close to him again. He turned to her once she had the door closed. "I'm sure you're wondering what this is about."

"To put it mildly."

"Can we?" he asked, nodding towards the couch.

"Of course."

They sat on the couch, not quite on opposite ends but still not close. Emberly tucked her feet underneath her and looked at him, bracing herself.

"I was prepared for us to never speak again," August began, and Emberly felt herself tense up. "But then Gideon talked some sense into me."

Surprised, Emberly sat up a little straighter. "What?"

"Once I found out about the two of you, I moved out of the house. I couldn't even look at my brother after that. This wasn't like any of the other times that we'd liked the same woman; those were just crushes, but I really felt something for you. And it didn't sit well with me knowing that – for lack of a better way to say it – my brother had you first."

Wincing slightly, Emberly briefly closed her eyes. She wondered where he was going with this. "Okay...but I told you that what I had going on with Gideon wasn't anything like what you and I had."

"I know. He told me the same thing. Along with a bunch of other stuff about what a dumb ass I was being."

"He really said that?"

"Yes. He thought it was idiotic of me to throw us away just because the two of you had a fling. A fling that you stopped as soon as you met me."

"I knew what I wanted," Emberly stated in a low voice, playing with the drawstring on her shorts. "As soon as we met, that was it for me. There was no need to keep wasting time with a man who didn't want what I wanted."

"Yeah, Gideon isn't trying to have anything serious. I think he was in his feelings a little bit that you chose me over him but at the end of the day, he said he just wanted you to be happy."

"*You* make me happy, August," Emberly dared to say, looking at him. "And I miss you."

"I miss you, too." He reached for her hand, and she slid it over to him, their fingers linking. "I shouldn't have flipped out on you like I did."

"Well...I should have told you about my history with Gideon as soon as we started showing an interest in each other like that."

"We both could have handled things better." He moved a little closer to her on the couch, and Emberly's lips twitched with a tiny smile. "And the more I thought about it, the more I realized I'm not ready to throw us away before we've even had a real chance. I'd like for us to start over, if that's what you still want."

Allowing her smile to break free, her hand gripped his. "It absolutely is."

He smiled, relieved. "I'm so glad to hear that. I thought you might make me sweat for a while."

"I'd rather not waste any more time. Are you gonna come closer now?"

They grinned at each other as he braced his knee on the couch cushion and caged her between his arms, one hand on the back of the couch and one on the arm. Emberly pulled her bottom lip between her teeth as he lowered his face to hers, her hand gripping the front of his shirt. She welcomed his lips, savoring the taste and feel of him for a moment before her mouth eased open wider, letting him in further.

"Is this close enough?" he asked against her lips.

"No."

"I agree."

Their kiss intensified as he lowered his body onto hers, pushing her onto her back. She welcomed his weight, holding him as close and as tightly as she could. Part of her wanted to pinch herself again to make sure this was really happening. She couldn't believe she actually had her August back, and she wasn't going to do anything to mess this up again.

"I swear I didn't come over here to seduce you," he insisted between kisses, lifting her leg higher around his waist.

"You hear me complaining?"

"I want to court you, Emberly. It's important to me that we-*shit*..." His eyes slid closed as she began slowly sucking his neck, moaning as she did so. Briefly biting his lip, he released his own moan and managed to continue. "It's important to me that we make this last and I..."

"You what?" She grabbed his chin and captured his lips again. "Tell me."

But August was done talking. He just kissed her passionately, his hand engulfing the side of her face, emotion overtaking him. He was grateful to be back with the woman he hadn't been able to get out of his head or heart.

They got lost in each other, choosing to let their actions speak louder than their words and discuss their future later. And for the moment, that was good enough.

Thanks so much for reading! I recall taking a long brainstorming walk as I worked out the details of this story (talking out loud to myself, as I do); I'd wanted to do something featuring triplets but kept starting and stopping as I was writing this. But that walk got me together; I rushed into the house to get it all down before I forgot. LOL

However you felt about this story, please consider leaving a review. And if you want to show *extra* love, share that you read it on social media! ☺

You can find me on Instagram, Threads, and TikTok at @authorjessicaterry and on Twitter/X at @itsJessicaTerry. And don't forget to subscribe to my email list at jessicaterry.com.

# Also by Jessica Terry

Some Like 'em Thick
It's All Right...Now
Not By a Long Shot
Get Right
Decisions and Consequences
Take One For the Team
When You Share Too Much
Backtalk
Emasculated
Restless
The Beginning of Again
Always and Nevers
She is Me
Split By the Bell
The Karma Call
Forehead Kiss
All Because of Ava
Love Intolerant
Mr. Time Waster
The Stubborn Kind
From Meltdown to Mistletoe
Mrs. Soul Crusher
I Want Us

Trade Rumors
Sugar Daddy Sweet Tooth
More Than What It Is
Hooked on Valentine's
Forced
**The Introvert Series**
An Introvert's Christmas
Wooing the Introvert
The Introvert Roast
I, Take Thee Introvert
The Introvert Series Compilation (paperback only)

# Discussion Questions

## (Mild spoilers ahead so I hope you've read the book first)

1. As you were reading, did you get the sense that Emberly was the outcast of her siblings?
2. The Hollidays had some rather unusual holiday traditions. Did you think they were silly or could you see some merit in them?
3. Did Enya break the sister code by seeing Dallas? Did you think she was in the wrong at all?
4. Evelyn pined over her ex-husband for most of the book. Could you understand her giving into him like she did after all the effort she'd put into moving on, given all of their history? Or did you think she was weak?
5. Emberly had some deep-seeded issues with her siblings. Was that enough justification for the secret she kept from them?
6. What did you think of Aunt Miriam?
7. Do you see Noah and Camilla lasting? Were they a good match?
8. Who do you think Emberly had more chemistry with: Gideon or August?

9. Dallas never did formally apologize to Emberly for ghosting her a second time, though he admitted he was wrong. Did his actions towards her make you root against him and Enya at all?

10. Did Noah overreact when Emberly confessed what she'd been keeping from them, or was his anger justified?

11. Which sibling's relationship would you want to read more about, if any: Noah's, Emberly's, or Enya's? Would you want to see Evelyn finally find the right one for her?

# Bonus story:

# More Holliday Drama

# Friday

"They're late."

"Babe..."

"I *knew* this was gonna happen! How could they-"

"Come here." August took his bride-to-be Emberly's face in his hands and gave her a lingering kiss. She whimpered, some of her tension easing as she sagged against him, her hands sliding up to his chest. When the kiss tapered off, he bit his lip and rested his forehead to hers, their eyes locking. "Regardless of who's here and who isn't, I don't want you stressing. This is our wedding weekend. It's about *us*. Nobody else. Remember that, all right?"

"I know," she replied, her voice still softened by her fiancé's kisses. She caressed his face. "You're right; I'm finally about to marry the man of my dreams after two amazing years together. It would just be *nice* if my family was here when they were supposed to be to see me do that."

"They will be, babe. Evelyn is here. You know Noah is never late for anything-"

"That was before Camilla got pregnant. His pregnant wife has taken precedence over everything, including his punctuality."

"Still, he'll be here. You know he wouldn't miss your wedding. Aunt Miriam and Tariq will be arriving within the hour-"

"If they're not humping on the side of the road somewhere," Emberly muttered, earning a laugh from her fiancé.

"Okay, I acknowledge that's a very real possibility, " August conceded, rubbing her arms, "But regardless, they're not far away. And Enya and Dallas are just a little delayed but I'm sure they'll show up before everything kicks off. My family is here. And keep in mind, we're early."

"I wanted to beat the traffic." Emberly took a deep refreshing breath and smiled at her handsome man. "I'll try to chill out."

It was a beautiful Friday afternoon in Sugar Lake, a serene city a few hours north of their hometown of Terston, Georgia that was popular for relaxation, special occasions, or romantic getaways. It was perfect weather in the perfect spot to kick off a wedding weekend. Emberly was counting down to going from Ms. Holliday to Mrs. Wheeler, and she just wanted her family to leave their usual drama back in Terston so that everything could go off without a hitch.

Evelyn, Emberly's younger sister by three minutes, bounded through the front sliding doors of the Amiria Hotel where everything was taking place. She stopped on a dime to do a dramatic twirl and nearly collided with a bellhop and his luggage cart.

"Sorry!"

Emberly shook her head as August chuckled. "You need a hat to toss in the air, Mary Tyler Moore?"

"Oh, hush up, Emberly. I didn't see him there." She squealed and threw her arms around her sister, doing little jumps in a circle and not caring that Emberly wasn't joining in her excited calisthenics. "It's your wedding weekend! Aren't you excited??"

"I absolutely am but you might have me beat." Emberly brushed some of her long locs from her shoulder, mentally reminding herself when her hired loctitian was supposed to arrive to finagle her super-long hair into an updo so she wouldn't have to deal with it for her honeymoon. Eying her giddy sister, she asked, "Are you on something?"

"Of course not! I'm just excited for you, sis! So much good has been coming to you; your pastry business was already killing it and now you've got your brick and mortar open, selling all those fancy apple desserts to the masses. You had a segment on that morning show a few months ago. And now you're marrying this amazing man, here," Evelyn shuffled over and hugged August around his waist, shaking him playfully and earning another chuckle from him. "I'm just thrilled that you're finally getting everything you want!"

"Riiight," Emberly replied. "And that's *all* that's behind this extreme giddiness?"

"Can't I just be happy for my darling sister?" At Emberly's arched brow, Evelyn huffed a playful sigh and adjusted her dark-framed glasses. "Okay, so I admit I'm also feeling very free nowadays. I'm over all my baggage and I just wanna let loose; I'm officially ready to put myself back out there. Come find me, future boo! Woohoo!"

August cracked up at this while Emberly tried and failed to suppress giggling at her silly sister who had her arms up in the air as she did some awkward hip swivel. Evelyn was good at a lot of things but dancing was not one of them.

"Yeah, okay," Emberly replied, the smile still on her lips as she went over and lowered Evelyn's arms before giving them a pat. "And I'm happy for you for finally moving on from that trifling ex-husband and all, but if you could save your boo-finding mission for another weekend, I'd appreciate it. Don't forget what you're here for. This weekend is supposed to be about me."

"Us," August corrected.

"Right, us." Emberly shot him an apologetic glance over her shoulder before turning back to her sister. "I'm just saying...I don't want you so focused on getting your groove back that you're not keeping up with your maid of honor duties."

"Don't worry about a thing, Em," Evelyn encouraged, her smile widening as they headed inside the hotel. "I want to have some fun but I'm well aware of what we're here for. And as happy as I am for you and August, the last thing I'd *ever* try to do would be to steal your thunder."

Just then, one of the elevators dinged and August's twin brother Gideon stepped off. He stopped and glanced around the spacious lobby, his muscular body, dark skin, trimmed beard and locs that hung past his shoulders drawing the eye of several of the lingering patrons.

"Speaking of thunder..." Evelyn muttered, drawing a look from Emberly.

"Over here, man," August called out to his brother.

Spotting them, Gideon smiled and sauntered over. He slapped hands and shared a hug with his brother before giving Emberly a strong but polite hug. "Can't believe you're gonna be my sister in a couple of days."

"Funny how things work out, huh?" Emberly quipped with a smile before stepping back underneath August's arm. "Kinda sounds like something out of one of the books my sister here likes to read."

August's smile remained in place though he still didn't love the reminder that Emberly and Gideon were former lovers. Despite the fact that it was before he and Emberly met, there were times he still winced at the fact that his brother had been with her first.

"Speaking of said sister," Emberly continued, looking back and forth between Evelyn and Gideon, "When's the last time you two saw each other?"

"A few months ago, I guess," Evelyn replied. She ran an anxious hand through her freshly-pressed dark brown hair. "I think it was at Auntie's costume party. You were Dracula or something, right?"

"Maximillian from *Vampire in Brooklyn*. Close enough, though." Gideon stepped forward, hand extended. "But it's crazy that our siblings have been together all this time and we've never been formally introduced. Gideon Wheeler. Though I'm sure you already know that."

"Yeah, well. Formality isn't always wanted or needed." Evelyn placed her hand in his. "Evelyn Holliday."

"I thought you were divorced?"

"I am. Had hyphenated but dropped that bastard's last name. Didn't want any more ties to him whatsoever. So if you see me chugging the champagne extra hard, that's why. I'm celebrating."

"As if your sister getting married isn't sufficient enough reason to celebrate," Emberly muttered.

"Well hell, say less," Gideon replied, grinning at Evelyn. His eyes hadn't left her face since she was brought to his attention. "I was actually about to go find the bar right now, if you wanna join."

"Absolutely!"

"Y'all, it's barely noon," August reminded amusingly.

"Which means it's barely five o'clock somewhere." Gideon offered his arm to Evelyn, who took it with a widening grin of her own. "We'll see y'all later at the party."

They headed off to the hotel bar, and Emberly didn't even try to hide her frown as she watched them.

"OH MY GOD, *finally*," Enya, the third Holliday triplet, droned when the car pulled into the parking space. She shot a venomous look over at her husband Dallas in the driver's seat. "I thought we'd never get here."

He shook his head, not bothering to return her glare. "Can you not be so dramatic for once?"

"We would've been here an hour ago if you hadn't insisted on waiting until the last minute to get gas."

"*Or* if you hadn't kept changing your mind about what to pack. We're here for a weekend and you brought damn near a full set of luggage."

"Don't try to blame this on me. If Emberly starts bitching about us being late, it's on you."

Rolling his eyes, Dallas opened his door. "How convenient to put it on me since you know she doesn't like me, anyway."

"Not my fault."

It had been a long four hour ride from Terston, with them either sniping at or ignoring each other. Things hadn't been very harmonious in the Cutler household for the past several months. It started with a disagreement about a belated wedding gift and snowballed into fights over everything from money to household chores to whose side of the family to spend which holiday with. Every day was filled with either cold shoulders or heated barbs, and neither wanted to be the one to put away their gloves first.

Enya defiantly checked her makeup in the visor mirror before her arms sagged, then fell into her lap. She sighed and got out of the car, stepping over to where Dallas was yanking their luggage out of the trunk. "Look. It's my sister's wedding weekend. Nobody needs to know about our bullshit so, for these next couple days, can we just call a truce?"

He shrugged, not looking at her. "Fine by me."

"We'll have to act like we're not fighting. Like we're happy."

"Those are two different things. One easier than the other."

"It's not like I'm over the moon about this either. But we're here for Emberly and she'll never forgive me if we cause some drama. Especially since I know she never totally got over what you did to her, despite her saying she did."

"You act like you didn't play a part in that, Enya. Yeah, I ghosted her-"

"*Twice.* Then blocked her without explaining yourself. And you never really apologized like you kept saying you would."

He glared at her. "You didn't have a problem seeing me after I did all that, did you? You're the one that took your sweet time telling her about us and wanted to sneak around behind her back so she wouldn't find out, so don't try to act like some kind of saint now."

"Whatever. Let's just...try to summon a little of what we had back then." Her eyes softened, glazing over. "When we loved each other."

He pursed his lips, unable to break their stare. "We still love each other, Enya. I think you know that isn't the issue. But you're right; this isn't the time or place to deal with our mess. I'll chill out if you will."

"Agreed."

MEANWHILE, NOAH WAS carefully driving along the highway. His wife Camilla looked over at him before placing a gentle hand on his arm.

"Noah, sweetie, will you please go a little faster? We're late."

"No can do. I've got precious cargo in here."

"The wedding cake can survive you going above the posted speed limit."

"I was talking about *you*, Camilla. You don't need me to be driving like a speed demon in your condition."

"Noah, I love you, but I really need you to chill out. I'm only four months."

"But you're carrying twins."

"And they're totally fine. So am I." She squeezed his arm. "I love you for being so concerned but you can't be this overly cautious throughout my entire pregnancy. You'll drive me crazy. And we were supposed to be at the hotel an hour ago. Emberly is probably losing it."

"I called and let August know. He understands."

"You called him because you knew she'd bite your head off for being late. Noah, this is your little sister's wedding weekend. She's marrying a wonderful man in August. Please don't be so overly consumed with every little move I make that you can't be there for her. She needs you."

Noah sighed as he sat back in the driver's seat, his right hand gripping the wheel. He knew his wife had a point. They'd been married a little over a year when they discovered Camilla was pregnant, and Noah had been in hovering husband mode ever since. He was thrilled but he was also terrified about being a first-time dad, and to twins, no less. He knew he went a little overboard at times but it was only because he couldn't imagine anything happening to his wife or his unborn babies.

But he also wanted to be present for his sister. He and Emberly had come a long way back to their close relationship after months of estrangement, and he was glad that was all behind them. He'd been there when August popped the question to Emberly at the family Christmas party, and he looked forward to walking her down the aisle.

"You're right," he conceded, reaching over to grab her hand. He kissed it before resting their joined hands on his thigh. "I know I've been doing the most. I'll ease up *some.*

But I still need you to promise to try not to do too much. You already offered to make her that overly extravagant and strenuous wedding gift."

"Oh my god; I made her wedding cake, Noah. I didn't rebuild her kitchen," Camilla said amusingly. "Emberly gave me my start in my pastry career; I wanted to do that for her. And it was neither overly extravagant nor strenuous."

"It took forever. You spent all that time on your feet-"

"Noah."

"Fine."

"Believe me, I just want to get to Sugar Lake, rest, celebrate with Emberly and August, and make love to my gorgeous husband as much as I can. And not necessarily in that order."

He looked over at her flirtatious smirk and grinned. It still amazed him how much he loved this woman and how it only intensified the longer they were together. "Guess I'd better step in it, then."

SEVERAL HOURS LATER, after everyone had arrived, checked in, and had a chance to rest, it was time for Emberly and August's welcome party.

There was plenty of music, dancing, and laughter around the hotel ballroom Several members of Emberly and August's families had taken turns getting on the mic to wish them well, offer marital advice, or crack a few loving jokes.

Despite the occasion, Emberly wasn't exactly floating on air. It irked her that two of her three siblings had been so inconsiderate as to show up late. And her Aunt Miriam, while on time, had been so preoccupied role playing Groupie and Professional Athlete with her husband Tariq that Emberly had barely seen her since their arrival.

"Can you fix your face and try to look like you're having a good time, please?" August asked as he joined where she stood near the bar. He handed her a glass of Prosecco and she immediately downed half of it. "You've been in a mood all day, babe."

"I'm sorry, but it's not like I can help it."

"Why can't you? You're so hung up on the fact that a couple people were late instead of being thankful that they made it safely and are here now. They didn't miss anything. I wish you'd just let it go."

"Our families were supposed to have lunch together, remember? They missed that."

"Still not a big deal. I enjoyed myself just fine with the people that were there."

"It's not *just* that they were late, August," she insisted, turning to him. "Auntie seems to just be using this as another one of her and Tariq's sex getaways. Noah can't seem to leave Camilla's side. There's clearly something going on with Enya and Dallas, considering how they're trying to stay as far away from each other as possible and both look like they'd rather be anywhere else but here. And Evelyn has been in and out, and she hasn't exactly been quick to answer my calls or texts when she goes scarce. I think she might be trying to enjoy her newly-proclaimed 'freedom' with Gideon."

August eyed her. "Why does *that* bother you?"

"If it were any other time, I wouldn't care."

"Are you sure about that? Or is it that you don't want your sister having your leftovers?"

Emberly's mouth fell open. "August!"

"I'm just saying, babe. She's your sister and he's your former lover. If you're feeling some kind of way about them possibly hooking up-"

"I'm not." Emberly placed a hand to his cheek, stepping directly in front of him. "Baby, you are the only man I love, want, and need. I've told you Gideon and I were never anything serious. This isn't about jealousy or being territorial. Please tell me you're not worried about me still wanting your brother."

"If I thought that for even a second, Emberly, we wouldn't have gotten to this point. I just don't love hearing you include it on the list of things that are bugging you."

"I explained why, though. Come on, I don't want this to be an issue. Look...I know I've been a little too consumed with what my family is doing instead of enjoying the moment with you. And I apologize." She leaned in and placed a lingering kiss to his lips, feeling relieved when he immediately returned it as he pulled her closer by the waist. When they parted, she wiped her lip gloss from his lips with her thumb. "I'm over the moon about becoming your wife and I don't want to do anything to make you doubt that, even for a second."

He gazed into her brown eyes that reminded him of sweet tea; it was one of the first things that attracted him to her. "Know that I'm trying to be empathetic because I know how much your family means to you. But this is a time that's only gonna happen for us once and I don't want either of us so distracted that we can't enjoy and appreciate it for what it is."

"You're right."

They were sharing another kiss when Aunt Miriam strutted up to them carrying a glass of champagne. Emberly almost didn't recognize her at first.

"Umm, Auntie…I'm almost afraid to ask, but what's with the getup? This isn't a costume party."

"Girl, I know," Miriam insisted with a dismissive flick of her wrist before running her fingers through her long sandy brown wig. She was dressed in a black patent leather tube dress that left little to the imagination and sky-high stilettos. "Can't a woman switch it up every now and then?"

"Auntie."

"What?"

"Please tell me you and Tariq aren't role playing again."

"So what if we are?"

"Y'all have to do that now? Can't you save your…escapades for a time *other* than your niece's wedding?"

"Your wedding isn't until Sunday. It's Friday. I'm totally here for you and August but that doesn't mean I can't have some fun with my husband, too."

Emberly huffed as she shot a *see what I mean?* look at August. "That's not the point, Auntie. You and Tariq can unleash on each other all you want within the confines of your hotel room but during our festivities, is it too much to ask to have your full attention? Do I not deserve that?"

Before Miriam could respond, a Black man in his sixties sidled up to August and slapped him on the shoulder before shaking it enthusiastically. "Found ya, nephew! I finally made it; damn flight was delayed."

Grinning, August turned and shared a hearty back-slapping hug with the man. "Don't worry about it, Unc; I'm just glad you made it safely." He turned to the ladies, the smile still on his face. "Ladies, this is my uncle Leroy, in from Memphis. Unc, this is my gorgeous future wife Emberly Holliday and her aunt, Miriam Holliday-Smart."

"Nice to meet y'all," Leroy greeted, though his eyes were fixated solely on Miriam. They openly took in her revealing outfit, shining with appreciation. "Damn sure nice to meet *you*. Can I get you a drink, pretty lady?"

Miriam lifted her glass. "Got one."

"Well what else can I do for ya, then? 'Cause for your fine ass, I'll make it happen."

Rolling her eyes, Miriam huffed, "Honey, my husband is six-two, fine as hell, and twenty years younger, and even *he* needs to stay hydrated to keep up with me. Don't embarrass yourself."

She turned and strutted away, and Leroy licked his lips appreciatively as he watched. "Umph!"

"Behave yourself, Unc," August warned. "She's a married woman."

"That doesn't have to mean anything."

Emberly blinked. "Well, it does. Auntie doesn't step out on her man. And Tariq doesn't play about her so if I were you-"

"If you don't learn anything else about me, baby girl, know that I am relentless when I see something I want,"

Leroy interrupted, his hungry gaze still locked on Miriam who was now across the room talking flirtatiously to Tariq, who Emberly noticed was dressed as a low-budget police officer, minus the hat. She closed her eyes momentarily as she shook her head, realizing what roles he and her aunt must have been executing. "And I want some 'a *that*."

He moved over to the bar before either of them could respond, and Emberly looked up at August incredulously. He shrugged.

"That's my uncle," he said, the only explanation he could offer. "He's gonna do what he does."

"Is he gonna be chasing after my aunt the entire weekend?"

"Possibly."

"You can't stop him??"

"There's no detracting him when he's this locked in on something. Best we can do is hope there's another woman that catches his attention. But don't sweat that, babe; Aunt Miriam can handle herself. She's clearly not thinking about him, anyway."

He nodded towards the other side of the room and Emberly looked over in time to see Tariq escorting Miriam towards the door, his hand grasping both of her wrists behind her back.

"Oh my god..."

"At least they didn't bring actual handcuffs. 'Cause I'm willing to bet they have some."

She cut her eyes at him. "That's not funny."

"You'll think it is one day. And anyway, we're not letting what others do bother us, remember?" He grabbed her hand. "Come on, my beautiful bride-to-be, let's dance."

Evelyn swayed over to them, nursing a glass of wine and grinning. "Need anything, Em?"

Emberly started to ask what she was so happy about, but stopped herself. At least she wasn't looking miserable like her other sister was. "I'm good."

"Awesome! Let me know if you do." Evelyn danced away from them, taking a long sip of her merlot as she moved her body to the Rhianna song blasting from the speakers. She bumped into a hard body and whirled around, her smile widening when she saw it was Gideon.

"My bad," he said, biting his bottom lip as he eyed her up and down.

Evelyn felt her body warm and resisted the urge to rub the back of her neck. "No biggie. I wasn't exactly watching where I was going."

"You don't hear me complaining."

Now she was warm and tingly, feeling the blush spread across her chest and up her neck. She wondered if it was as visible on her light brown skin as it felt. She cleared her throat and took another fortifying sip. "Enjoying yourself?"

"That depends."

"On what?"

"On if you'll agree to dance with me."

Her face was on fire. "I might embarrass you. Gracefulness isn't my strong suit. In fact, if you care about the shoes you're wearing we should probably just stick to talking, since I'll surely step on them more than once."

He chuckled as he reached for her waist and pulled her closer, turning her so her back was to his chest. "I'll risk it."

His deep voice in her ear made Evelyn shudder. Her free hand floated down to cover his on her waist as she leaned back against him, every part of her body singing at the contact. It wasn't lost on her how sexy Gideon was. Ever since they'd gotten drinks at the bar earlier, she'd developed a little crush on him that she fancied herself to think wasn't one-sided, given the way he openly flirted and seemed to keep finding his way back to her. He had even asked for her number before they parted ways to get ready for the party, admitting he found her attractive and wanted to stay in touch. Evelyn had hoped she wasn't too eager when she reciprocated his sentiments. Enya probably would've suggested she play coy but seeing as how Evelyn had only been in one serious relationship that had spanned from her teenage years to her thirties, being crafty with men was a skill she'd never had to develop.

The music and chatter around them seemed muted as Evelyn sank against Gideon, letting his hands guide her hips as they moved to the music. They weren't exactly grinding their bodies together but it still felt plenty suggestive to Evelyn, and she bit her lip as she let herself enjoy the delicious feeling of being in another man's arms. She hadn't wanted to be bothered in the time since her ex-husband Travis asked for a divorce, as it had taken time and months of therapy to mourn the end of her long relationship with her high school sweetheart.

Gideon's hold on her tightened slightly as he leaned down to murmur in her ear, "You haven't stepped on my feet yet."

She grinned. "Guess you're a good guide."

"I'm good at a few things," he assured, his lips brushing her ear. Evelyn sucked in a breath, feeling her nipples tighten and her stomach clench underneath her dress. "And I have a feeling you are, too."

She turned in his arms, looking up into his smoldering eyes. The heated gaze he was giving her was jarring, but in a good way. She looked at him just as brazenly as she responded, "We could both find out."

His crooked smile sent a rush to her middle that she hadn't felt in too long. "I like the way you think. Your room or mine?"

"I can't be gone too long; I need to be available for Emberly. I'm sure there's a bathroom or storage closet that locks around here, isn't there?"

"I *damn* sure like the way you think. Let's go." Taking her hand, he turned and led her towards one of the side doors of the room, with Evelyn stashing her half-empty glass on the first table they passed. Emberly eyed them over August's shoulder, seething.

UNFORTUNATELY, SHE wasn't the only Holliday sibling that was trying to keep her frustration in check. Enya sat at a table in the back of the ballroom, mindlessly taking in its features and décor as she sipped her third vodka sour. Her eyes strayed to her husband, who was talking to August and

Gideon's parents near the DJ booth. She shook her head. Despite their truce, they hadn't had much to say to each other since their arrival, as all their energy seemed to be saved for when they had to put on airs for everyone. Enya was determined not to mar her sister's festivities with her issues, though she was having a hard time forcing festiveness. The last thing she felt like doing was smiling or partying, and she knew it probably showed. She wondered how long it would be before she could escape to her hotel room to drink and mope in peace.

Camilla came over and took a seat next to her. "Are you okay, Enya?"

Immediately plastering on her practiced smile, Enya nodded. "Totally fine."

"Really?"

Enya looked at her. "What are you getting at?"

"I'm not trying to pry, but I couldn't help but notice that you and Dallas seem to be keeping a wide berth. And the looks you give each other haven't exactly been full of warmth."

Pursing her lips, Enya looked down at her glass. She hated that she and Dallas were so transparent. "We're dealing with some stuff but it's nothing to worry about."

"What's nothing to worry about?" Noah asked, appearing behind Camilla. He started massaging her shoulders as he looked down at her, concerned. "Is something wrong with you or the babies? You ready to head back to the room?"

Camilla shook her head with a subtle roll of her eyes. "No, sweetie. It's nothing like that."

"Then what were y'all talking about?"

"Don't worry about it, Noah," Enya chided. "Can you chill out? I've never seen you so anxious."

"You don't know the half of it," Camilla muttered. "This is nothing compared to what I deal with everyday."

"I'm just taking care of my wife and babies, like I'm supposed to," Noah defended, pulling a chair close to Camilla's and dropping onto it. He rubbed his wife's baby bump. "Nothing's going to happen to them on my watch."

Camilla sighed as she placed a hand over her husband's, giving him a tight smile. Enya eyed them. She could tell Camilla was irked by Noah's hovering but trying not to show it. She could only imagine how he was in private. Even though Noah was usually the main enforcer of adherence to their family holiday traditions, it'd been like pulling teeth to get him to do anything since Camilla got pregnant unless she was right by his side. Enya knew such paranoia would drive her nuts and she guessed Camilla didn't love it, either.

Figuring she'd change the subject, she asked them, "Are you gonna find out the sex of the twins?"

"Yes," they both replied immediately. Noah continued, "I want to know what's coming so we can best prepare for it. Discovering we were having twins was enough of a surprise."

"I honestly wasn't all that surprised by it," Camilla admitted. "You have triplets for sisters."

"True enough. I've been reading some blogs and watching videos from parents of multiples to try to see what I'm in for. It's gonna be a lot but I can't wait."

"That's beautiful," Enya commented with a smile. "You're gonna be a great dad, Noah. And I pray all y'all's strength if you end up having two girls."

"Shut up. I keep waiting for the day when you and Dallas make your own pregnancy announcement, since you said you couldn't wait to have his babies after you two eloped."

"Yeah, well," Enya cleared her throat, trying to keep her expression even. "It hasn't really been the right time for me and Dallas to bring babies into the equation."

"You're right about that." Dallas walked up to the table, hands in his pockets as he gave a pointed look to his wife. Enya just cut her eyes at him.

Noah glanced back and forth between them. "Is something going on with you two?" Camilla lightly nudged him.

"No, we're fine," Enya quickly responded before Dallas could. She forced another smile before waving at their surroundings. "Wow, this is a great party, huh? I can't believe Emberly is finally getting married."

Her deflection attempt was blatant, but thankfully no one called her on it. Camilla and Noah shared a look and Dallas shook his head.

"Yeah, August is a great guy," Camilla commented pleasantly. "They're so crazy about each other, too."

"Hope it lasts," Enya couldn't resist muttering, picking up her vodka sour and taking a long gulp.

"E3..."

"I didn't mean anything by that, Noah, so don't start. These vodka sours are just going to my head, is all."

"Stop chugging them, then," Dallas muttered.

Before Enya could retort, Emberly approached the table. "Y'all are supposed to be enjoying yourselves, not huddled up over here."

"We're just taking a break, E1," Noah informed. "And Camilla doesn't need to be on her feet too long, anyway."

"My feet are fine, Noah," Camilla insisted. "I only came over here to talk to Enya; it wasn't because I'm tired."

"You probably are and just don't realize it, though, so we should probably go on up to the room."

"Noah!"

"Where's Evelyn?" Enya asked, glancing around.

Emberly didn't want to mention seeing her sneak away with Gideon earlier. She knew that would likely monopolize everyone's attention. "I don't know."

"Did Aunt Miriam leave?"

"You know how she and Tariq do. Their role playing apparently took precedence over being here for me."

"Don't let it bother you. The important thing is that she'll be front and center for the wedding, next to the seats reserved in Mom and Dad's memory," Noah commented. "I'll be walking you down the aisle. Ev and Enya will be standing right beside you. We're all here for you and August."

"And I'm sure you'll make a beautiful bride, Emberly," Dallas added politely.

Emberly briefly cut her eyes at him. "Thanks. Anyway, let me know if Evelyn finds her way back in here; I need to talk to her about something. Enya, don't forget about our spa appointment in the morning."

"Believe me, I won't. I could use some de-stressing." Enya shot a brief glance up at her husband, who just rolled his eyes and looked away.

Any other time, Emberly might have been concerned about what was clearly going on with them. But given the fact that she didn't want to get consumed with whatever her sister's marital issues were during this particular weekend, she refrained. It wasn't that she didn't care; she just wanted to enjoy a rare time when things were supposed to be all about her. Her sisters always got all the attention back in the day and that continued as adults, with Enya's stylishness and charisma effortlessly drawing men to her and Evelyn's easygoing nature making everyone feel like they had a friend in her. Emberly had always been (or felt like) the outcast, but this weekend, she was finally getting the spotlight and she had no intentions of sharing it with her siblings.

Emberly left to re-join August, needing some of his positive energy. He smiled as she approached, and she felt some of her mild tension ease.

"You good, babe?" he asked, wrapping an arm around her waist before kissing her lips.

"Yeah, I'm fine. I'm glad things are starting to wind down, though, 'cause this long day is starting to catch up with me. I can't wait to get up to the room and lay up under you."

"You and me both. Hey, how long is your spa stuff going to last tomorrow? Mom wanted to take you out to lunch or do some shopping before the rehearsal, if there's time."

"I'm not sure, actually; Evelyn set everything up." Emberly glanced towards the door she'd seen Evelyn and

Gideon slip out of earlier. "But of course, she's nowhere to be found so we can ask her."

"I'm sure she probably just went to the bathroom or something. It's fine; just shoot her a text or ask her tomorrow and let me know."

Emberly wished she could be as easygoing about Evelyn's absence as August but she felt herself getting agitated again. Evelyn was supposed to be readily available for whatever she needed but she was too busy having her little tryst with Gideon to be on her maid of honor duties. They'd been gone for over thirty minutes.

When Emberly eyed the door for several more moments with no signs of her sister, she sucked her teeth.

"Can we get outta here?" she abruptly asked August, a hint of testiness in her voice. "I'm kinda over this."

He frowned slightly. "What do you mean, you're over it?"

She shook her head, kicking herself for her word choice. "I just meant I'm tired and ready to be alone with you, that's all. Evelyn will make sure everything is handled in here, once she finally makes her way back from wherever she's disappeared to."

His frown cleared, to Emberly's relief. "Fine by me. I'm ready to get off my feet, anyway. It seems Gideon has gone scarce, too. But as my best man, I know he'll help Evelyn out with whatever she needs getting everything handled in here tonight."

*Yeah, I bet he will*, Emberly thought to herself. Not wanting another loving lecture from her fiancé, though, she just smiled and grabbed his hand, waving goodnight to people as she led him out of the ballroom. As they got onto the elevator, she told herself to try to relax; with a good night's sleep, everyone would be ready to focus on what they were all there for the next day.

# Saturday

The serene atmosphere of the spa was usually an ideal place to let go of any stressors or worries, even if temporarily, but it was only partially working for Emberly and her bridal party.

Emberly was itching to grill (and berate) Evelyn for going scarce at her party the night before. She was trying her best to put it out of her mind and enjoy her hot stone massage, but it still irked her.

Evelyn was itching to gush to her sisters and sister-in-law about her rendezvous with Gideon. They had ducked into a storage closet and ravaged each other, losing all track of time. Whenever Evelyn would start to say they should go back to the party, he would lay another one of his spine-melting kisses on her or slide his hands to another long-neglected part of her body and any thoughts of stopping went up in smoke. She'd never been dicked down so good and part of her still couldn't believe she'd done such a thing; she hardly knew Gideon. But she didn't regret one second of it and her body tingled at the thought of a repeat, which he'd already said he wanted with her. It kept a naughty smile tugging at her lips.

But she didn't want to upset Emberly. She already sensed her sister wasn't too happy with her; when she and Gideon had finally gotten back to the ballroom the night before, Noah had informed her that Emberly wasn't thrilled about both her and Aunt Miriam disappearing. Emberly and August had already left, and when Evelyn sent a text to check on her, her message was left on 'read.' Evelyn reminded herself to be more present for her sister, especially since Emberly had already asked her not to use this weekend to get her groove back.

Enya was tense and slightly hung over, and she didn't think there was a massage or spa treatment that could fix it. She and Dallas had gone up to their room separately the previous night, and barely said two words to each other once they were there. They spent the night on opposite sides of the bed, and before Enya left to join the ladies at the spa that morning, they got into a silly argument about whose (identical) room key was whose. As much as she needed one, Enya really wasn't in the mood for a spa day, but it beat forced civility with her husband.

Camilla was just glad to have a break from Noah's hovering. She loved that he cared about her so much, but he was getting on her nerves with wanting to know every move she made. She couldn't even get up and go to the restroom without him insisting to wait for her outside the door. He'd even called down to the spa to get the name of her massage therapist, demanding their credentials and questioning their experience with prenatal massage. It was so embarrassing. She didn't know what she needed to do to get him to relax but she didn't want to put up with that for another five months.

Aunt Miriam was present in body only, as she had refused to stash her phone and was checking it every two minutes. Emberly figured her aunt and Tariq were probably sexting like it was an Olympic event, and gave up attempts to engage her aunt in any conversation.

By the time they'd all been pampered sufficiently, Emberly didn't feel as relaxed as expected. What she'd hoped would be a time to connect and have some girl talk with her loved ones had ended up being a practically mute three hours as everyone basked in their own thoughts. There was no talk of the wedding the next day or the honeymoon to follow. There was no teasing the bride about her lack of desire for a stripper-laden bachelorette party. No friendly grilling about how Emberly felt about finally getting to live with August, their future plans, none of that. Everyone was too caught up in their own stuff to worry about any of that and the reality caused a fire inside of Emberly that she could only hope didn't end up exploding.

ENYA RETURNED TO HER room after the spa, feigning a headache when her sisters invited her to join them for lunch. She knew she should've just sucked it up for Emberly; she could tell her sister wasn't happy about the invitation being declined. But Enya just needed some time to herself to recalibrate. The state of her marriage had her emotions all over the place.

She and Dallas had met, fallen in love, and eloped all within a couple of months. And they were blissfully happy for the first year or so. But now they could hardly stand to be in the same room together and Enya still couldn't pinpoint exactly why. Things were great until they weren't. How in the world had things gotten to this point?

She was glad to see an empty hotel room when she made it upstairs. Dallas must have still been out with the guys, doing whatever they were doing. Enya resisted the urge to raid the minibar and plopped onto the king-sized bed, staring up at the ceiling as she blew out a long, emotionally-tired breath. Somehow she was going to have to get it together before the wedding rehearsal and the subsequent dinner that night.

Her quiet solitude only lasted about a half hour before she heard the beep of the door lock disengaging. Groaning, she rubbed her eyes, wondering if this was going to be a time she and her husband ignored each other or traded hurtful barbs. She mentally reminded herself to be pleasant.

"Oh," Dallas said once he noticed her. Enya couldn't deny his voice still affected her. "I thought you'd still be with the girls."

"Well, I'm not," she snapped automatically, then winced. So much for being pleasant.

Scoffing, Dallas rolled his eyes. "Whatever, Enya. I'll just go 'cause I'm not trying to argue with you right now."

"No, Dallas, please," Enya called out, jumping off the bed and facing him. She ran her hands down the back of her neck. "I'm sorry. I hate that being snippy is our go-to now."

He eyed her for a moment and she felt a surge of hope when he finally nodded. "Yeah. Me too."

"How did we let this happen? What's going on with us?"

Hunching his shoulders, Dallas's eyes fell. "I wish I knew."

"So, now what? 'Cause I'm sure you'd agree that we can't keep going like this."

"No, we can't. Part of me still can't even believe this is our life right now."

She gazed at him, trying to summon the warmth she always felt around him. "Do you hate me, Dallas?"

"No," he immediately replied. He crossed the room to stand in front of her. His eyes bored into hers, trying to dredge up some cozy feelings of his own. "Regardless of what we're going through, I could never hate you, Enya. Do you hate *me*?"

"Of course not." She grabbed his hands and stepped closer, her eyes pleading. "Dallas, baby...all this animosity and turmoil between us these past few months has been tearing me up inside. I miss how we used to be. Do you realize this is the most physical contact we've had in weeks? And don't even get me started on how long it's been since we've kissed or made love."

Briefly closing his eyes at the realization, he cupped her face in his hand. "I guess time flies when we're both being stubborn." His thumb stroked her bottom lip, and his breath hitched at her whimper. "Can I kiss you?"

Her hands fisting his shirt, she pulled him closer, her chest heaving slightly. "Please do."

Their lips came together in a tandem of aggressive moans, their hands wasting no time grabbing and exploring each other. Enya felt like she was going to explode, being in Dallas's arms like this again, and she couldn't get close enough. She jumped into his arms and her heart surged when he gripped her tightly, seeming to need this as much as she did.

Before too long, their clothes were tossed to the floor and Dallas was sexing his wife with a vigor that hadn't existed since they were newlyweds. Enya wrapped her legs around his waist as she eagerly took everything he gave her, then begged for more.

"Yes, Dallas," she panted. "Harder. Fuck me harder."

"You sure?" Dallas grunted, obliging. His brow was furrowed in a concentrated frown. "That's what you want?"

"Hell yes."

Months of restraint had them unleashing furiously on each other, neither trying to be discreet with their screams and taunts of pleasure. Enya pushed Dallas onto his back, quickly resuming their intense and slightly erratic sexing as she braced her hands on his chest.

"Tell me you missed this," she ordered, eyes locked on his.

"Fuck yeah I missed it." He slapped her ass, his hips thrusting to meet hers. "And you've been wanting this dick, haven't you?"

"Every day." She bounced on him harder. "Every. Fucking. Day."

"Take it, then. It's still yours."

They continued their frenzied lovemaking, their long abstinence fueling them so much that neither wanted to be the one to tap out first. It was a couple hours later when they finally collapsed next to each other, sweaty limbs blindly reaching for contact as they immediately fell into a sated sleep.

Enya woke up with a jolt a while later, briefly disoriented. Remembering where she was, she immediately glanced around her, starting to panic when she noticed the slightly darkened sky through the hotel windows.

"Oh my god, what time is it??" she screeched, searching the rumpled bedsheets for her phone.

"Relax. The rehearsal isn't for an hour and a half."

Enya slumped in relief before her eyes bugged again, then squeezed shut. "Emberly had said something about wanting to go wine-tasting this afternoon. I'm sure I missed it. She's gonna be pissed!"

Dallas gave a light shrug from his seat in one of the cushioned chairs near the window where he was sipping a cup of coffee. He'd put his pants back on but nothing else. "Nothing you can do about it now. I'd have woken you up if I'd known about that."

"Ugh" Enya groaned. "I know I'm probably already on thin ice for making myself scarce today. I'm sure she or Evelyn have probably tried to call. Have you seen my phone?"

"On the desk."

She started to ask him to toss it to her when she took note of how he looked sitting there shirtless. He'd always been so sexy to her. She felt her arousal begin to box out her remorse over not being there for Emberly, her slightly-aching body yearning for more delicious make-up sex.

"Why don't you come back to bed?" she suggested, biting her lip as her lustful gaze raked over him.

His eyes swung to her before returning to the muted women's basketball game on the television. "We really don't have time, Enya."

"That's what quickies are for. Or you can join me in the shower. Have you taken one yet?"

"No. Look, Enya," he set his coffee cup on the desk beside him and leaned forward, resting his elbows on his knees as he rubbed his hands together thoughtfully, "I loved being with you earlier. But let's not pretend everything is fixed between us."

She reared, frowning. "I didn't say it was."

"I'm just saying, before you go thinking we're good-"

"How does me suggesting we take a shower together indicate that? I'm not an idiot."

"I didn't say you were."

"You're clearly not trying to waste any time letting me know this, so, what, we're back to you giving me the stiff-arm? I'm your wife, not some one night stand that you need to give the brush-off speech to but that's what this feels like."

"Enya, can we not argue about this? I'm simply reminding you that we still have some issues and us having sex doesn't make them go away."

"I'm well aware of that, Dallas. But I'd *hoped* it would at least be a first step towards us mending things between us. I mean, isn't that what you want?"

He hesitated, and Enya felt every inch of her skin burn. She scrambled out of bed, holding the bedsheet around her naked body.

"So what was this, huh?" she demanded, sweeping her arm towards the bed. "Did you use me just to get your rocks off?"

"Don't you dare try to accuse me of that." Dallas shot out of the chair. "I would *not* do that to you. But...look, I'm just wondering if whatever is wrong between us is something that's only going to get worse. Hell, neither of us can even say what the real problem is. An argument about a damn wedding gift shouldn't lead to all this."

"So you just wanna give up on our marriage without even trying? Is that what you're saying?"

He released a long breath as he gazed at her, his eyes softening with the love he still had for her. The biggest part of him wanted to go to her and take her in his arms, but somehow he couldn't get his feet to move. When he saw her eyes start to glisten with tears, his chest tightened, knowing he'd hurt her yet again.

Enya's face started to crumble but she quickly blinked back her tears, shaking her head vigorously. She refused to break down. Even though her heart was breaking at the notion of her husband apparently thinking their marriage wasn't worth saving, she needed to somehow suppress that and put on her game face for Emberly.

"Enya...babe, I didn't mean-"

"I'll take my shower first," she interjected, gathering the bedsheet so it didn't drag on the ground as she turned away from him. "We should start getting ready so we can head downstairs for the rehearsal. That is, if us going together isn't too taxing for you. But know this, Dallas; I was raised to believe that marriage is a lifelong commitment that may not always be easy, but it's worth putting in the work for. Outside of extreme circumstances, divorce is just a cop-out. I'm willing to stop being stubborn and do what's necessary to fix us. Are you?"

She hurried into the bathroom, shutting the door behind her. Dallas sank back into the chair, his head in his hands.

EMBERLY LOOKED AROUND the room at her loved ones that were gathered together for her and August's rehearsal dinner. The wedding rehearsal earlier had thankfully gone off without any hitches, despite the still-present tension between some of her loved ones. Emberly had promised August she'd put whatever happened earlier out of her mind and enjoy the evening, and she was trying her best to keep that promise.

"Where's that fine-ass aunt of yours?" Uncle Leroy asked Emberly, his eyes scanning the room. "She's hiding from me."

Emberly had to remind herself to be respectful; this was her fiancé's uncle, after all. "She must've stepped out. *With her husband.*"

"You don't have to keep reminding me she has one of those."

"Clearly I do. Even if she was the kind of woman to step out on her man, she's made it abundantly clear she's not interested in *you*. So, respectfully, back off."

He waved a dismissive hand. "Whatever. I'll get to her. I know she wore that skintight red dress for my eyes, too."

*No, she wore it 'cause she and Tariq are some selfish freaks*, Emberly thought to herself as Leroy strutted away. Miriam's red dress was clearly a Jessica Rabbit getup, complete with the abundance of cleavage and thigh-high slit. Miriam was even sporting a dark red wig that fell in sultry waves over one smoky eye. Emberly had taken one look at her when she arrived and stalked off in the other direction, seething at the clear fact that her aunt had ignored her request to chill with the role playing with Tariq and just be there for her.

She tried to just focus on her wonderful man August, who was still taking everything in stride. Emberly wished she could be as easygoing as him, but then again, it wasn't his family that was causing issues. Outside of Gideon distracting Evelyn from her maid of honor duties, August's family had been low-key and fully focused on the occasion. Emberly hated that she couldn't say the same for her family.

"Hey everyone. It's speech time," Evelyn announced to the room as she stood, lightly tapping her glass with her fork. "Feel free to keep stuffing your faces 'cause I'm not the best at public speaking."

Everyone laughed except Emberly, who couldn't help but notice Evelyn's slightly unkempt appearance. This wasn't like her customary slightly haphazard-yet-still-put-together look; her hair looked hastily finger-combed back into place, her shirt was un-tucked and slightly wrinkled at the bottom where it was previously tucked in during the rehearsal, and she was missing an earring. Clearly she and Gideon had indulged in another one of their trysts sometime between the rehearsal and the dinner. Emberly couldn't believe it. Not only was her sister still creeping around with Gideon, she didn't even have the decency to fix herself back up afterwards.

"For those that don't know, I'm Evelyn, the bride's sister," Evelyn introduced with a hand to her chest. She grinned and turned to the head table where Emberly and August sat. "I can't begin to express how happy I am for you two. I could see the spark between you when Emberly first brought August to our Valentine's Day party a couple years ago, and it's still as bright as ever. August, I already consider you a part of the family but it becomes official tomorrow, and I can't wait. I want you two to be happy, communicate, trust each other, make a bunch of babies, and just be happy together. You can get through anything if you're both willing to put in the work."

Across the room, Enya and Dallas ventured looks at each other.

"I wish you two all the happiness in the world," Evelyn concluded her speech, blowing a kiss to the betrothed couple before passing the microphone to Gideon. Emberly didn't miss the heated gaze they shared.

"I'm Gideon, August's twin brother. In case that wasn't obvious." More chuckles. Gideon winked at Evelyn before turning towards Emberly and August, and Emberly forced a smile. "I'm not really one for speeches, either, though I *am* tempted to share an embarrassing story about the groom, here. But I'll keep it classy and just say how thrilled I am for y'all. My brother has never been happier than since he got with you, Emberly. You're it for him. If I'm honest, I'm a little jealous; hopefully I'll be blessed with a relationship as solid as yours one day."

His eyes flitted back towards Evelyn, who beamed. Emberly shifted in her seat.

"I wish y'all nothing but the best," Gideon continued, and Emberly forced her smile back onto her face yet again. He lifted his glass. "To the future Mr. and Mrs. Wheeler."

Everyone lifted their glasses around the room, toasting the bride and groom. Emberly looked at August, who was already gazing at her with a euphoric and unbothered grin. She felt her agitation vanish slightly. Despite whatever frustration she might've felt towards her family, her love for August and desire to be his wife certainly hadn't budged. She reminded herself, yet again, to just focus on him.

Everyone continued to eat and mingle, eventually getting up from their seats and milling around the room after dessert. Lots of pictures were taken, both personal and professional. Chatter and laughter filled the room and Emberly was finally feeling at ease, enjoying the moment. She held onto August's arm as they joked around with his parents, enjoying their tales of their early marriage days.

All of a sudden, a scream and breaking glass punctured the room. Everyone whipped around to see what the commotion was, and Emberly was floored when she realized it was Camilla, who was absolutely fuming as she faced off with Noah. Emberly didn't think her mild-mannered former assistant was capable of getting so pissed.

"I told you to back *off*, Noah!" Camilla screeched, her brown skin reddened from anger. "Now you're trying to tell me what I can and can't eat??"

"Babe, you've gotta calm down, all right?" Noah pleaded. "I was just suggesting that you ease up on the cake, that's all. All that sugar can't be good for the bab-"

"Are you my freaking doctor now, too?? You are *always* in my face trying to tell me what to do, what to wear, where to go, trying to monitor my every damn move and I'm sick of it!"

"Camilla!"

"I have asked you repeatedly to chill out but you *stay* on my back!" Camilla fanned her heated face with both hands and Noah instantly took a step towards her, concerned, but she pushed him in the chest. "Do *not* come near me right now!"

"Camilla, babe, can we please just go up to the room?" Noah pleaded. Hurt at her words and worry for her condition were battling for position within him. "It's freaking me out that you're so worked up like this."

"Well deal with it, 'cause it's your fault!"

"How the hell am I wrong for trying to look after my wife? Would you rather I not give a damn?"

"I am *not* having this discussion with you again. Just leave me alone!" With that, Camilla turned and stormed out.

"Camilla!" Noah started to follow her, but Miriam grabbed his arm.

"Let her go, baby," she advised. "Just give her a minute."

"I don't want to leave things like this, Auntie. What if something happens to her or the babies and I'm not there?"

"Enya's going to see about her. She'll be all right, but you have to stop hounding her about every little thing. Being pregnant didn't turn her into glass. She just wants to enjoy this experience with you but you're driving her nuts."

Noah finally noticed his aunt's getup and shook his head. "It's kinda hard to take you seriously when you're dressed like an old school cartoon character."

"Way to go, Noah," Emberly droned, appearing next to them. "Thanks for causing a scene at my rehearsal dinner. That's lovely."

"I didn't cause anything. Camilla is the one who flew off the handle at me. And I'm about tired of everybody acting like I'm some kind of villain for worrying about my wife."

"You're in your feelings right now 'cause you're more than smart enough to understand what everyone's been trying to tell you."

"Whatever." Noah frowned when he saw Enya heading towards them. "What are you doing back in here? I thought you were checking on Camilla. She doesn't need to be by herself right now."

"Actually, Noah, that's exactly what she needs," Enya countered. "And I did check on her but she wants to be by herself, which is something she hasn't gotten to do since you insist on being in her face twenty-four-seven. But she assured me she'd let me know if she needed anything."

"She'd let *you* know. I'm her husband but she'd rather call you, huh?" Noah scoffed. "Yeah, all right. But if she thinks I'm gonna keep my distance for long, she's got another thing coming. I don't care how mad she gets."

"Noah. That's not how it's supposed to work and you know it."

"I don't think you're the one that needs to be trying to give marital advice when you and your husband have been acting like you barely know each other since we got here."

Enya's jaw dropped and Emberly shook her head, telling herself to keep her mouth shut.

"Noah, that wasn't necessary," Aunt Miriam chided.

"Is it less necessary than you and Tariq acting like this is some kind of hedonistic retreat? You seem to be more focused on playing out your little freak fantasies than what you're supposed to be here for."

"Yeah I saw Tariq running naked down the hall last night," Evelyn chimed in, having joined the discussion. "I'm still trying to purge that image. I can only hope you two were playing some bold game of Truth or Dare."

"And how would you know about *that*?" Miriam challenged, folding her arms. "That was after three in the morning. Somebody must have been coming from their own little hedonistic activities."

Her face immediately flushing, Evelyn stammered, "I, uh..."

"Yeah, I hope you don't think nobody's noticed how you keep disappearing for long stretches of time then coming back glowing and rumpled," Noah commented to his flustered sister. "If you're gonna creep, E2, you need to be a little less obvious about it. Kinda defeats the point."

"Shut up, Noah!"

"Girl, who are you sneaking around with??" Enya asked, grabbing Evelyn's arm.

Casting a nervous glance at a silently fuming Emberly, Evelyn quickly said, "Now isn't the time to get into it. Not that I'm confirming sneaking around with anybody."

"You never were a good liar. Don't think I can't get it out of you."

"You're clearly too distracted by whatever's going on with you and your man 'cause you are *way* off your game," Miriam noted to Enya. "Usually you'd have been the first to notice. She's clearly been fucking around with Gideon."

"What?!?"

"Auntie!" Evelyn screeched, her face reddening even more at being called out.

"What?"

"I can't *believe* you just-"

"Enough!" Emberly finally exploded. She glared at her stunned loved ones. "I am so *sick* of y'all! Do you not realize that you all have been so consumed with your own crap since we got here that you've barely been able to enjoy and celebrate what we're here for? Is it too much to ask of my *family* to put aside their bullshit for three damn days and focus on me? But nooo...it's all about your pregnant wives or your marriage issues or getting dickmatized or taking every apparent opportunity to get your freak-on with your husband, as if you don't do enough of that!" she added with a glare at her aunt. "It's *always* about y'all and I guess I should've known better than thinking this weekend would be any different. At this point, I don't even care if y'all come to the wedding. You don't seem to really wanna be here, anyway!" She glared at all of their shocked faces before noticing that they had an audience. Most of the conversation around the room had stopped as everyone was riveted on the drama between the Hollidays, and Emberly hated that this was now likely going to be what everyone talked about for the rest of the night.

Unable to stand the sight of them another second, Emberly hurried out of the room. August, who'd been looking on in concern ever since he heard his fiancée's outburst, immediately followed her. By the time he entered their hotel suite behind her, Emberly was in tears.

"Babe," he took her into his arms, holding her tightly. "Please don't cry."

"It all just got to be too much," Emberly whimpered, her face buried against his neck. "I tried to put all their mess out of my mind, baby; I really did. But it just burns me that they don't seem to care how their actions are upsetting me."

"I don't think it's that they don't care, babe." He smoothed a hand along the back of her head. "Life is just life-ing for them and unfortunately it's not always easy to hit the pause button on that, despite the occasion. But you know they love you, right?"

"I wish they loved me enough to put me first." Emberly sniffled, leaning back to wipe her eyes. "For once."

"Emberly...babe, I know the reasons for you feeling this way stem from childhood, and I hate that you're basically feeling neglected by your family right now. What can I do to help you feel better?"

She looked up at him. "I'm so sorry. This isn't how things are supposed to be. I know my frustration with them has been affecting you, too. Maybe we should've just eloped and been done with it."

"Is that what you want?" He peered down at her. "Do you want to just call the minister up here and have him marry us right now, and then we can go ahead and leave for our honeymoon?"

Emberly hesitated. As mildly intriguing as the thought was, she knew it wasn't what August wanted. "You don't want to get married in our hotel room, August."

"We can find a nice spot outside in the garden or something, then. We don't have to tell anyone."

"You want your family there; I know you do. *They've* actually been here for us this weekend. And your mama would never forgive me if she didn't get to see her son tie the knot."

"I'm more worried about *you*," August insisted, taking her face in his hands. "They'd just have to deal with it. And I'd marry you anywhere, babe; in a hotel room, in a garden, or on the side of the road. As long as you end up as my wife, it doesn't matter where it happens."

"Oh, August..." She wanted to melt. It amazed her that she'd been blessed with such an amazing man, and her frustrations towards her family started to float away like dandelion seeds in the wind. She pulled him to her for a kiss, their tongues immediately finding each other. Everything else was forgotten as the heat increased between them, causing their kisses to become sloppier, their moans of desire more urgent, their hands more aggressive.

Emberly was fumbling with his belt buckle when August suddenly stepped back, clamping a hand to the back of his neck. She looked at him, panting and confused.

"What's wrong?"

"We should probably chill out."

"Why?"

"We've been abstaining since we set the wedding date. Remember saying you didn't want to sleep together until after we were married?"

She huffed in disbelief that he'd think of that at a time like this. "Well, clearly, I'm not worried about that. I've changed my mind."

"Yeah, and how many times have you said that since instituting that abstinence stuff only for you to change it back at the last second? There's been more than one occasion where you *swore* you wanted it and we've been naked with me about to slide inside of you and you pumped the brakes, saying you wanted our wedding night to be special, as if that should have anything to do with it."

The testiness in his voice was clear, and Emberly frowned. "If you had a problem with this, August, why haven't you said anything?"

"Because as silly as it is, it seemed important to you."

"Silly??"

"Emberly, we've already slept together. *Many* times. Us not doing it for a few months hasn't done anything but leave us both sexually frustrated; it's not going to suddenly make the wedding night sex *magical* or whatever other bullshit it was you said."

"Oh, so now it's bullshit??"

"Yeah, Emberly, it's bullshit. But I've respected your wishes on that just like I've respected your feelings about everything that's happened so far here this weekend. And you're not gonna use me to mindlessly fuck away your frustrations, nor am I trying to hear any fussing from you tomorrow about how we should've waited. That'll just piss me off."

"Oh, you mean more than you are now?" Emberly's head was swimming; how had they gone from making out to this? "What are we doing, August?"

He eyed her for a moment before sighing wearily and rubbing his hands down his face. "I've been trying to hold it together for you because I saw how emotional you were about everything with your family. But I'm tired, Emberly. This has no bearing on how I feel about you nor does it mean I don't want to marry you; I absolutely do. But you've been on edge since we got here; even last night when we left the party, you kept going on and on about everything and nothing I said or did for you seemed to make any difference. I just...I need some peace tonight. All right? Can you grant me that?"

Tears burned Emberly's eyes at his words. It hadn't occurred to her that he'd been carrying around so much frustration of his own for so long. Here she was accusing her family of being selfish towards her when she hadn't been much better towards her man. The realization made her chest ache.

"Of course," she acquiesced, her voice softened with humility. "Whatever you need."

Pursing his lips, August nodded his thanks before going into the bathroom and closing the door. Emberly just moved over to the bed and sank onto it, hanging her head.

# Sunday

**"** *Fuck...*"

August hissed between his teeth before looking down at Emberly, who had woken him up the next morning with some vigorous fellatio. One hand gripped the bedsheet while the other grabbed her hair through her bonnet, any thoughts of stopping her evaporating with every bob of her head on his dick.

Emberly pleasured her fiancé until he released down her throat, his roars of pleasure like music to her ears. She crawled her naked body up on top of his, laying a deep kiss on his lips before pulling back to look him in the eyes.

"I'm sorry, baby," she said, her voice as serious as her intent. "The stuff you said last night...I had no idea."

"I should've been more up front," August admitted, sliding his hands up and down her back. "I can't expect you to read my mind."

"Regardless, I've been acting like it's all about me and it's not. You're in this relationship too, and your feelings are just as valid as mine. Please forgive me."

He smiled, squeezing her. "Of course I forgive you, babe. We're in this."

"Good. Now," her eyes slanted as her legs spread, straddling him, "Now please get inside of me."

"Emberly-"

"This isn't about distraction and you damn sure don't have to worry about me changing my mind at the last second. I swear on my parents' graves that's not gonna happen." She began grinding on him, earning a tortured moan as August's eyes slid closed, his head mashing into the pillow as he bit his lip.

"What about tonight?"

"Oh, we're gonna get it in then, too. We can make love as man and wife. Now, though," she sat up and reached between them, grabbing his dick and slowly sliding onto it, "I want one last fuck with my fiancé."

"Oh yeah?" August's eyes darkened before he suddenly flipped Emberly onto her back, earning a surprised squeal. "That's exactly what you're about to get, then."

August gave Emberly what she asked for, stroking hard and fast like she liked it. They took up every inch of the bed as they repeatedly changed positions, clinging to each other and getting so caught up in the throes of their passion that they almost forgot where they were or the fact that their room wasn't exactly soundproof. Emberly was especially loud as August pounded her from the back, his hands gripping her thick hips and their skin slapping together in time with August's grunts.

"Don't stop, baby, *please*," Emberly pleaded, her hands gripping the sheets as she threw it back at him.

"Didn't plan on it." He pushed her back down further, deepening her arch and upping the volume of her screams. "You gonna keep this from me again?"

"No!"

"You sure?"

"Yes! Yes!"

He pulled out and flipped her over, quickly re-entering her as he captured her chin in his hand. "Look me in my eyes and tell me that."

"I promise I won't keep this from you, baby. Oh my *god*," she breathed when he rolled her nipple between his fingers, "I swear!"

"That's what I wanna hear."

They kissed hungrily and sloppily as they continued sexing each other to exhaustion. Emberly held onto August as they tried to catch their breath, not wanting him to move from on top of her. She held his face in her hands.

"Promise you'll never leave me," she whispered.

His eyes roamed lovingly over her flushed, sweaty face before leaning down and pressing his forehead to hers. "I promise, babe. This is for life; whatever comes up, we're gonna deal with it together. Just like my parents do, just like your parents did. I'm never letting you go."

She blinked back tears as she pulled him down for another kiss, the emotion warming her as well as giving her a jolt of energy. She wrapped her legs around his back and they were revving up to go another round when there was a sudden and hard knock on the door.

"What the hell…"

"Emberly!"

"Is that Enya?" August asked.

"Sounds like it," Emberly frowned. "Though I don't know why she'd be banging on our door so early."

"Emberly, are you up??" Evelyn's voice called out.

"Good grief..."

"It must be something important," August surmised.

"Hmph. They *would* decide to wanna pay me some attention when I'm getting my wedding day freak-on. It just figures."

August chuckled as he planted one more kiss to her lips before pushing himself off of her. "Go ahead and see what's up. I'll get in the shower so I can go get my hair cut and everything else I need to do before I marry your sexy ass later on."

Grinning, Emberly enjoyed the view of his naked body as he gathered his things and headed to the bathroom. She finally rolled out of bed and threw on the plush bathrobe provided by the hotel, stalking over to the door and throwing it open.

"Finally!" Enya exclaimed, throwing up her hands in relief.

"What the hell are you two doing here??" Emberly hissed. "August and I were *busy*."

"Oh...*oh*!" Evelyn exclaimed, getting the drift. "We're sorry about that but we had to be sure to talk to you before everything kicked off today."

"Talk to me about what?"

"Can we come in?"

"August is in the shower."

"Come to my room, then. This is really important, Em."

Emberly was tempted to make a snarky comment about Gideon being in Evelyn's room, but refrained. She wasn't going to allow anything to ruin her mood today. "Fine. Let me throw something on real quick."

She quickly got dressed in some leggings and a tshirt, then let August know where she was going before grabbing her room key and following her sisters to Evelyn's room. Once inside and seated, Evelyn wasted no time getting to the point of the impromptu conversation.

"We owe you an apology," she announced, looking at Emberly with earnest. "You were right; we've all been way too distracted with our own stuff instead of being present for you this weekend."

"Yeah, I thought Dallas and I were keeping our tension under wraps but now I know we haven't done a good job of that," Enya chimed in. "I've let our issues get in the way of me really being here for you like I should be."

Emberly hesitated before asking, "What's going on with you two?"

"No," Enya shook her head emphatically. "We're not getting into it now. This is your wedding day and I'm not bogging you down with my shit. Dallas and I...we'll be fine eventually. Today is about you and August. And I'm sorry for even not arriving here in the right frame of mind."

"Me, too," Evelyn added. "I admit that I got so ga-ga over fooling around with Gideon that I didn't always use my best judgment. There should never have been a time that I wasn't there when you needed me, or that my mind was more on him than on you. I sincerely apologize for that."

Emberly looked at the sincere looks on her sisters' faces. She hadn't expected them to apologize; those hadn't been in abundance towards her over the years. But it touched her that they'd made a point to atone for their actions in person.

"I accept your apologies," she let them know.

Enya blinked in surprise, and Emberly couldn't help but chuckle. "Just like that?"

"Yeah, I thought you were gonna make us sweat for a while," Evelyn stated.

"Nah." Emberly fiddled with her engagement ring, smiling at the reminder that she would be getting married in mere hours. "Once upon a time I would have, but I'm just trying to have a positive and amazing wedding day. All I care about is marrying August; I don't have time to fixate on anything else."

"Are you gonna let us be there to see it?" Evelyn asked, almost shyly. "It was like a kick in the gut when you said you didn't want us at the wedding."

"Yeah, sis, I was stuck for a while after you stormed out last night," Enya admitted. "That's when it really hit home how selfish all of us had been. Especially Noah; we had to stop him from coming up here after you."

Just then, Evelyn's phone rang with a Facetime call from their brother. In the next few seconds, Noah's handsome face was on the screen, looking serious.

"E1, can I talk to you?" he asked.

Emberly smiled. "Yeah."

"I apologize for not being locked in on what this weekend is about. There's no excuse. You're my little sister and I love the hell outta you, and you absolutely deserve the spotlight. Please give me another chance and let me walk you down the aisle today. I want and need to do that for you, especially since Dad can't be here."

The sisters blinked back tears, each wishing their parents Jessup and Wilona Holliday were there for the occasion.

They'd passed about twelve years earlier, and Emberly still missed them so much it ached sometimes.

"Of course," Emberly said, patting her face and trying to get her emotions in check. Her smile widened when she saw how Noah grinned in relief. "I can't imagine not having you there. You've always been my favorite person, you know that."

"Stop trying to make me cry, E1. I've made a fool out of myself enough this weekend."

The sisters giggled. "How's Camilla?" Enya asked.

"She's fine. Sitting right here watching me eat my crow while she scarfs down my pancakes."

Everyone laughed. Emberly looked at her siblings, finally feeling the closeness towards them that she'd been seeking since they arrived at Sugar Lake.

"Thank y'all for making a point to talk to me this morning," she said, the smile still on her lips. "It really means a lot. I considered letting my wedding just be me, August, and the minister but as hurt and pissed off as I was, it wouldn't have felt right not to have our families there. And I know August feels the same way. So in answer to your question, Evelyn, y'all will absolutely be there to see it."

"Great!" Evelyn grinned, momentarily forgetting she was holding the phone and clapping her hands. She scrambled to catch it before it fell to the ground, and Enya shook her head while Emberly chuckled.

"Let's get in gear so we can start getting you ready for your big day," Enya ordered, beaming at Emberly.

"Yeah, the hair and nails people will be coming in a couple hours," Evelyn noted, glancing at the time. "Have you eaten yet, Em?"

"Not yet."

"We can have breakfast together or I can run down and get you something. Whichever you want."

"Yeah, I'm sure you need some replenishing after all that wonderful morning sex with August," Enya teased.

"And with that, I'm gonna sign off and order me some more pancakes," Noah grunted, making the sisters laugh again. "I'll see you downstairs later, E1. Love you."

"Love you, too," Emberly called out before he hung up.

"Come on, girl. Let's get you fed and beautified," Enya said, standing and grabbing Emberly's hand. "August isn't gonna know what hit him when he sees you come down that aisle."

Emberly basked in her sisters making a fuss over her the rest of the morning. There'd never been a time when she'd been the center of attention like this, and the emotion threatened to bring the tears more than once.

The glam team arrived and all assembled in Evelyn's room to take care of the hair, nails, and makeup for the ladies. Emberly hadn't wanted a huge wedding party and just opted to have her sisters and Camilla stand with her as she got married. Her sister-in-law was looking a lot happier now after her showdown with Noah the previous night; they'd clearly hashed things out.

Aunt Miriam breezed into the room, and Emberly was mildly surprised that she was sans any kind of costume and just donning some tight jeans and a baby tee. "Well, you look...regular."

Miriam's eyes narrowed slightly. "I'll take that, since I know what you mean. Because we all know I am anything *but* regular."

The sisters muttered their agreement.

"Look, baby," Miriam said, putting a hand to Emberly's face as the loctitian worked on her hair, "You were right about everything you said. I was being selfish and I hope you can forgive me for that."

Smiling, Emberly lightly grabbed her aunt's wrist, slightly leaning into her hand. "Thank you for saying that, Auntie. You're absolutely forgiven."

"Good." She leaned down and kissed her niece's forehead before going over to sit next to Enya on the bed. "And just so you know, you might or might not see August's uncle Leroy later."

The sisters looked at her curiously. "Why not?"

"He's in the hospital."

"Oh no...did he have a heart attack or something?" Evelyn asked.

"Girl, no. Tariq jacked him up after seeing him try to grab my ass this morning."

"What??!" everyone shrieked.

"Yep. He pushed up on me one too many times and my husband handled that. Two black eyes and probably broke his nose. Would've been worse if Gideon hadn't pulled Tariq off of him. I tell you, there is no bigger turn-on than seeing your man beat somebody's ass over you."

Everyone laughed, including the glam team. Emberly didn't feel the least bit sorry for Leroy. She'd tried to warn him more than once.

"I'll tell you one thing, baby," Miriam said to Emberly as she plucked a grape from the fruit tray on the bed, "You damn sure won't be able to say you had a boring wedding weekend."

Emberly shook her head but she couldn't help but smile. "You're right about that, Auntie."

Finally, it was wedding time.

Emberly was practically vibrating with excitement and anticipation as she and the ladies made their way down to the ballroom where the wedding was being held. Her sisters gave her hugs and makeup-protecting air kisses before scurrying into place, and Noah grinned when he saw Emberly approach in her mermaid-style wedding dress.

"You look gorgeous, E1," he admired, placing a gentle kiss on her cheek.

She beamed up at him, taking his offered arm. "Thank you, Noah."

"You're showing a lot of cleavage, though."

"Shut up, Noah."

The music started and the doors opened, and they waited for their cue to take their measured trek down the aisle. Emberly barely took note of the job the decorators did of transforming the ballroom in her peach, red, and cream wedding colors. All she saw was August, standing at the end of the aisle looking more handsome and sexy than she'd ever seen him. His fresh haircut, his smooth dark skin, his strong stature in his cream linen suit all had her wanting to run to him and jump into his arms.

Noah gave August a firm handshake before handing Emberly off to him. Emberly immediately passed her bouquet back to Evelyn, needing to have her hands in his. They stared at each other, both smiling and eager.

"We are gathered here today to join Emberly Holliday and August Wheeler in holy matrimony..."

The ceremony proceeded with prayers, a brief poem and song from one of August's cousins, and a note of encouragement from the minister. They were halfway through the vows when the doors suddenly burst open.

"Stop! Don't marry him!"

Everyone gasped as murmurs erupted around the room. Emberly and August's heads whipped towards the intruder, the wedding band halfway on Emberly's finger.

"Travis??" Evelyn screeched, almost dropping both of the bouquets she held. Her eyes bugged at her ex-husband jogging down the long aisle. "What the hell are you doing??"

"I'm stopping you from...oh," Travis sobered as he got closer and realized who the bride was. His light brown skin flushed. "I thought *you* were the one getting married, Evelyn..."

"Even if I was, what are you doing here? You're married to Perla!"

"We're separated. She got fed up when she realized I wasn't truly over you. Look, Emberly, I'm sorry for the disruption," Travis stated, looking remorsefully at the bride and groom. "I clearly got my wires crossed about which sister was getting married. But, Evelyn, hopefully we can talk about this later because I *do* want you back."

"Too bad. She's spoken for," Gideon barked from his place beside August. His face had hardened upon realizing who this man was, and he itched to be the one to escort him out and away from the woman he was crushing on.

Evelyn grinned and shared a muted squeal with Enya, loving that Gideon was apparently as into her as she was into him. Travis whirled around, his eyes widening at Gideon's imposing figure.

"You..." He turned back to Evelyn. "You're with him?"

"Yep," Evelyn beamed.

"Get him outta here," August barked, fed up with the side show.

"Somebody please toss him out on his ass," Emberly added.

"Say less." Gideon lunged for Travis, but he ducked and sprinted back up the aisle and out the door, wanting no parts of the hulking best man. Everyone laughed at the scene. Enya's eyes found Dallas's in the second row and her heart raced when he winked at her and smiled. She grinned back at him and mouthed 'I love you.' He nodded, returning the gesture.

Once everyone calmed down, the ceremony resumed. That whole scene was forgotten as Emberly and August were pronounced man and wife a few moments later, and he swept her into his arms for a long, emotion-filled kiss. Everyone cheered, hooting and whistling at their display of affection. It got even louder when they finally came up for air and joined hands, turning to everyone with the biggest grins on their faces and tears of joy in their eyes.

"We got married!" Emberly happily screamed, causing another uproar of cheers.

She proceeded up the aisle with her new husband, happier than she'd ever been. Once they were through the doors, August pulled her to a side hallway and swept her into his arms, swinging her in a circle and causing her to laugh and squeal gleefully.

"I can't believe you're finally my wife," he muttered once he returned her feet to the ground. He touched his forehead to hers. "I love you so much, Emberly. Thank you for making me the happiest man alive."

"No, thank *you*, baby," Emberly retorted, happy tears streaming down her cheeks as she caressed his face in her hands. "I thought I could only dream of a man like you. You...you're everything I've ever prayed for. I love you so much it freaks me out, and I promise to be the best wife I can possibly be, 'cause you deserve that."

"We deserve each other." He pulled her closer, taking another kiss. "And *I* deserve to get to peel this wedding dress off you."

"Down, boy. We still have to get through pictures and the reception-"

"All that can wait. I want you *now*." He grabbed the back of her neck and laid a tongue-filled kiss on her. They could hear everyone emerging from the ballroom and he knew the wedding planner would be looking for them shortly, if she wasn't already. He backed Emberly against the wall, their kiss intensifying. Emberly hated that she was in such a form-fitting dress because she was ready to open her legs to him right there in the hallway.

"Let's go," she panted, her lustful gaze now matching his. "We'll just get back whenever we get back."

August grabbed her hand and they ran towards the back elevator, just the two of them.

Did you love *Holliday Drama*? Then you should read *Forced*[1] by Jessica Terry!

Cousins Mya, Destiny, and Callie Woods are hardly BFFs, but a deathbed promise requires them to stay close. Never mind that they don't always like each other.

Destiny is a spoiled wannabe influencer who has a wonderful man, but greed might just make her lose him.

Mya is focused on building her fashion brand, because burying herself in work is easier than watching her cousin prepare to marry the man she foolishly dumped years ago.

---

1. https://books2read.com/u/490wK0

2. https://books2read.com/u/490wK0

Photographer Callie is still getting used to her new body as she tries to navigate the dating scene, the battle between settling and being alone...and the forced-upon role of mediator between her constantly-feuding cousins.

When an unexpected tragedy hits, will it bring them closer together or make them realize that life is too short to force relationships, even if it's family?

**Content warning:** This book contains scenes with or mentioning drugged seduction, a fake miscarriage, a panic attack, and a character death.

Read more at https://www.jessicaterry.com/.

## About the Author

Jessica Terry caught the writing bug at a young age and loves little more than holing up at home in Douglasville, GA, cranking out contemporary novels. And eating. www.jessicaterry.com

Read more at https://www.jessicaterry.com/.